# WHEN
## I lost my
# WAY

by
## jennifer rodewald

*When I Lost My Way*
Copyright © 2020 Jennifer Rodewald.

ISBN: (Paperback) 978-1-7347421-1-4

Any references to historical events, real people, or real places are used fictitiously. Names, characters, and places are products of the author's imagination, and any similarities to real events are purely accidental.

Scriptures taken from the Holy Bible, New International Version®, NIV®. Copyright © 1973, 1978, 1984, 2011 by Biblica, Inc.™ Used by permission of Zondervan. All rights reserved worldwide. www.zondervan.com The "NIV" and "New International Version" are trademarks registered in the United States Patent and Trademark Office by Biblica, Inc.®

Front cover image Prixel Creative, Lightstock.com. Design by Jennifer Rodewald.

First printing edition 2020.

Rooted Publishing
McCook, NE 69001

Email: jen@authorjenrodewald.com

https://authorjenrodewald.com/

Now to him who is able to do immeasurably more than all we ask or imagine, according to his power that is at work within us, to him be glory in the church and in Christ Jesus throughout all generations, for ever and ever! Amen.

Ephesians 3:20

Jennifer Rodewald

# *Chapter One*

*WHY DID I TAKE THAT LEFT TURN?*

Sophie sighed, looking down at the nearly black muck that had claimed her car as its newest victim. It had seemed like a good idea. The truth was, she'd taken a drive because it had been one of those days. One of those stuck-in-the-mud—figuratively, at the beginning—days. She'd thought back in August, nearly six weeks past, her life was good. Now there seemed to be a whole lot of blah coupled with a familiar uncertainty—and growing loneliness, something she'd been too familiar with all her life. After her relocation, she'd hoped that both had stayed behind. When, that early afternoon, it became apparent that the emotional companions had found her new life, taking a drive out in the country to clear her head, search her heart, and pray had seemed like an entirely harmless, perhaps exceptionally smart thing to do.

*Don't look now, but your city-girl ignorance is showing.*

Yeah, that. Exactly. She should have known better, even with having not grown up country. Rain on a dirt road equaled mud, and yesterday the skies over Big Prairie had opened up and wept. That left-hand turn off the highway two miles back had dumped her onto a county road that was a thin layer of gravel over nothing but dirt.

At first she'd thought *eh, a few puddles. Road's bound to dry up past the pocked entrance.* Seemed reasonable—after all, this particular country road saw a lot of traffic. In fact, more cars turned down this way than many of the paved roads in town, thanks to that big sign off the entrance that read *River's Edge Vineyard.* Surely, given the growing popularity of the successful vineyard Sophie had yet to visit, the only county road leading to the tourist attraction had been put on a special maintenance regimen. Though most of the picking had been done, the tourist season wasn't finished.

So she'd continued, confident the road would firm up.

Sophie tested the frosting-textured ground with the toe of her Converse. The gravel-laced soup sank beneath the slight pressure of her foot. Decidedly, that whole hope about the roads firming up had been a fatal miscalculation. She jerked her foot back, shook it above the squishy ground in a failed attempt to remove the muck that had come up with her shoe, and gingerly laid her now-soiled foot back on the floorboard of her car.

"Now what?" Slumping against the back of the driver's seat, she gripped the steering wheel, tipped her chin up, and shut her eyes. "Lord, now I'm *actually* stuck. Like in the mud. In the middle of nowhere."

She'd thought it had been bad enough *feeling* stuck. Again. This...this was definitely worse.

*Call Craig.*

That was the logical solution. The most obvious thing to do. Craig, being the exceptionally nice man that he was, would certainly brave the gooey roads to come to her rescue. That, however, would muddy her mind up more. The paradox was not lost on her. Having a great guy come rescue you from being stuck in the mud should help clarify her thoughts about said gentleman, not further cloud the whole situation. But cloudy that whole deal was, and not just because of her personal always-stay-in-the-friend-zone track record.

There was Brenna to consider. Whether Sophie's best friend would deny that Sophie should add her into the matter or not, a strong thread of things-not-settled ran between Brenna and Craig. Strong enough, in fact, that Sophie felt certain she'd be a fool not to think long and hard about whether she wanted to step into that situation.

She'd been doing exactly that—thinking long and hard. And not loving the conclusion. One more not-the-right-fit in her growing file of nice men she'd dated.

Or was that the pain of a lingering wound putting fear into her heart? *It was so long ago, and not everyone thinks the way he did...*

"What's wrong with me, exactly?" Sophie directed her query to the moonroof of her sporty Jeep Renegade. Well, more specifically to the King who reigned over not only this muddy mess she'd inserted herself in but the figurative one that involved her heart, her future, and her hope.

She pulled in a long draw of air, then sighed again. "I know. I'm being dramatic. It was a couple of dates. And morning coffee. And me thinking maybe he was the reason you'd shut other doors. The reason I've been too timid to try again..."

It had been a long time past—and really, that wound not only should have healed up nicely, but it shouldn't have hurt so deeply in the first place.

*Sometimes people are blind, princess. I mean, they see color just fine, but much past that? Not so well, baby. Don't let that crush you. Don't let them tell you who you are.*

He father's words from that tearful evening had stayed with her all these years. Thank God for Daddy. But...

*Daddy, I still remember it...*

Squeezing her eyelids closed, Sophie indulged in a moment of self-pity. After all, she was stuck on a country road, car lashed tightly in the greedy clutches of mud, and all by herself. It was her party. She could cry if she wanted to.

But not for long. It was late afternoon, and though Sophie had stopped trembling at the unbelievably dark nights she'd fearfully discovered in her newly acquired country life, she still hadn't acclimated to the cry of the coyotes who liked to populate that thick blackness. She'd no desire to be stuck in her car, somewhere between the vineyard and town, all on her own after sundown.

*So again. Now what?*

She sat up, slipped her phone from the dash holder, and tapped the Home button. She knew lots of people in town.

Brenna and Grant topped the list of those who'd be willing to help. However, neither option felt comfortable when she considered them.

Craig then. *Don't want to.*

He'd come. Without a doubt. Wouldn't even tease her about doing such a dumb thing, getting stuck in the mud. He might ask why she felt the need to go out for a country drive though.

Might be the right opportunity to have an open talk with her fellow-music-teacher-turned-close-friend, without the distraction of their students, his foster boys, or his steady, blue-eyed gaze smiling down on her—because he'd have to drive them out of this mess.

Movement out in the field or pasture—whichever it was— blurred in the periphery of her vision. The back of her mind still fingered that fear of coyotes, and her heart lurched. Jerking her gaze to the right, toward the shadowy movement, she squinted to make out the form near the opposite fence line.

A deer. A harmless deer, raising her head to inspect the lady stuck in the mud. Sheesh, she needed to tame her imagination— and running fears. And also, she needed to get out of this predicament.

"Ugh. Call Craig." She rolled her eyes at herself, then pressed his name under her contacts list. Done. Phone was ringing.

It would be just as well. The time it'd take for Craig to get her safely back to town could be time she could use to be honest with him. It'd be uncomfortable, but...

The ringing clicked to voicemail.

Sophie held in a groan and employed her Sophie's-always-cheerful voice. "Hey, Craig. It's me, Sophie. Listen, I know this will be such an inconvenience, and the whole thing was really stupid—seriously, I don't know what I was thinking, and you can totally give me a hard time about it later." *Stop babbling like an idiot!* She cleared her throat. "Sorry. I'll get to the point. I'm in a bit of a crisis. As in, I'm stuck. In the mud. Is there any way you could come rescue me? Please?"

Tugging the phone from her ear like it burned, she smashed her thumb against the End icon. That was perfect. *This way he'll be the one to end this sort-of dating thing.* Good heavens, she had a propensity for being stupid. As the monologue she'd left on Craig's voicemail replayed in her head, a wave of embarrassment washed hot through her limbs. She tapped her forehead with her phone and growled.

Impulse took over, which was something she really needed to work on. Case in point—she was stuck in the mud because of an impulse. She *would* work on it. Later. At that moment, she yielded to the compulsion, hit Craig's name, and sent another call.

Voicemail again. *Whew!* Because, what was she going to say? *Hey. Me again. I just wanted to say that I'm not actually crazy. I think the last message I left might leave you with the impression that I'm a nut. I'm not. Not really. I don't think. But I am still stuck...*

Perhaps there was a reason she had an unquenchable instinct to keep all relationships in the friend zone. She clearly wasn't capable of acting like a grown up. Not on a consistent basis. Good thing Craig didn't answer that second call. And *thank You, Jesus* that she had enough sense—even if it was at the last second—*not* to leave another babbling, crazy-hinting message.

She was still stuck though. And alone.

*Text him.*

Yes. That was much safer. She could edit any ridiculousness out of the final copy before she hit Send. She tapped his name again, this time hitting the Text icon rather than the Call button.

*Hi. I left you a message that maybe you should not listen to. I have reasons. Anyway. I'm stuck in the mud. It was a bad decision of mine that I am repentant of even as I type. Care to play superhero?*

Sophie reread what she'd written. Too...much?

Possibly. He'd go and listen to that message for sure. Either way he would hear her babbling foolishness. Thus, she didn't need him to read more of it. With a rapid tapping of her index finger, she deleted ~~I left you a message that maybe you should not listen to. I have reasons. Anyway.~~ There. That left three reasonable, grown-up, not-babbling sentences. Four, if you counted the word *Hi.* Some people didn't. Maybe there should be a comma there instead of a period?

Good grief, she was overthinking everything! With an irritated stab, Sophie sent the text off into the cyber world. Craig should get it in a millisecond. *Help is on the way.* She smiled at the thought. Maybe it was a grimace. Sitting up straight, she checked the rearview mirror. Yep, a smile. Her mom often said Sophie could make people believe she hadn't a care on earth, because she could smile her way through anything.

*Never know if she's trembling in her UGGs or ready to break down into a wail. My girl smiles through all of it.*

Words Mom had spoken to Sophie's daddy—who was technically her stepdad—when Sophie had been thirteen. They'd recently started dating—her mom and Derrick—and Mom had been guarded about it. Didn't even let Sophie meet the man, or him meet her, until Mom had felt there would be a real reason to make the introduction. Sophie had been curious, though a touch resentful, about the man who had captured so much of her mom's attention, and she'd been shocked to find out it was the new associate pastor at their church.

Seemed like a lifetime ago. Derrick was Dad now—actually, he was *Daddy*—and Sophie adored him almost as much as Mom did. But she remembered that description Mom had first given him. Wondered if it had been a thing of pride, or a warning to the new man in their world, when Mom had said them.

Her gaze wandered toward the field outside while she meandered down that bit of personal history. When she came back to the present, she found the deer still stood in that corner, grazing on whatever was left to be had on the autumn ground. Apparently her presence no longer made the animal curious, and the two of them, Sophie and the deer, were to coexist.

A lovely thought. But hopefully they wouldn't have to coexist for long.

As if in agreement—or maybe insulted—the deer startled. Head came up, ears and eyes darted left and then right, and then she froze, attention pinned in Sophie's direction. Sophie had the most ridiculous urge to wave, as if a friendly gesture would lull the animal back into the peaceful coexistence they'd been sharing. Before she could, the deer pivoted and fled in one fluid motion, clearing the four-strand fence with no more effort than it would have taken Sophie to flop onto a couch.

Sophie sat forward again, watching while the animal bounded toward the afternoon skyline, losing sight of it when it dipped into a small roll of land. Slouching back, she felt abandoned, though she knew that was also silly.

Why hadn't Craig texted or called her back?
*Smile. It'll help.*

She didn't know where she'd learned that. Maybe she'd made it up all on her own? They were her words to live by, for better or worse.

The reason for the deer's flight found its way into her rearview mirror. On a chance glance into the reflection, she saw a red truck slip-slide toward her on the greasy road.

"Ah." Sophie kept a wary eye on the nearing vehicle, keenly aware of how unmanageable she'd found the mud. "So there is another fool in Big Prairie. Guess I can't claim solo hold on that."

The back of the truck fishtailing in a more controlled version of chaos than she'd managed with her Renegade, the other driver edged beside her.

"Please don't slide into me," she muttered. "This cute car isn't paid for."

A man wearing a cowboy hat held the steering wheel in the other vehicle, and as he maneuvered around Sophie's car, he leaned forward, gave her a good long look, and then waved—the country-boy kind of wave common to the Big Prairie locals: two fingers up while the palm stayed anchored on the steering wheel. If she was in North Omaha, she'd have assumed the cowboy was giving her the bird.

Good thing she knew better. Not so good, however, that Mr. Friendly Cowboy didn't seem to understand her situation, as he kept crawling on down the slick road.

"You're not gonna stop?" she asked his tailgate when his truck cleared her car. "Not very Big Prairie-ish of you, mister."

As she scowled, those brake lights lit up red, the back wheels slid left, and the driver corrected the skid with obvious experience. Then as if she'd been heard, the truck settled into a stop, mud oozing up around his tires when they ceased their movement. *Yikes. Please don't let him sink in too deep. Then I'll be responsible for both of us being stuck.*

The driver's-side door popped open, and a pair of long, jean-clad legs stretched out toward the ground. The man followed— hat still in place—glanced her direction, and then reached into the cab to snag a brown work coat. His back turned to her as he slipped the sleeves on, giving her a backside view of his lean, tall form, work-formed shoulders, and cowboy-cut jeans.

"Not a view you get much back home." She bit her lip, taming that girly grin that, had anyone else been in the vehicle with her, would have made her blush. There definitely were benefits to this country life.

Sophie gave her mirror another quick glance, checking to ensure her glossy ringlets hadn't gone the way of frizz and her black mascara had stayed where she'd brushed it earlier that day. *Yeah. And smile too. That should totally make up for the fact that you're stuck in the mud, and this good-looking cowboy won't notice you're a fool.*

Though the thought was sarcastic, she did brush up her always-on-hand smile as the man turned and picked his way over the black slime toward her car. She rolled down her window as he came within a few feet.

"Hey there." She tipped her chin up to look at him. "Thanks for not hitting me."

"Interesting place to park."

"Isn't it? I thought it would be a nice spot for a nap."

The corner of his mouth flickered. Maybe a miniscule grin? "Ah. I see. Here I thought you'd gotten yourself stuck."

Sophie made a *who me?* face.

"Very well then. Carry on with the napping." He bumped the hood of her car with the side of his fist.

"Whoa there, cowboy. That was not the truth." She reached a hand out of the car and smacked the door as if that should make him stop his slow retreat. "I am definitely stuck, and I can't get ahold of the person I thought could come help me."

"I see." His top lip curled a smidge—not as a leer, but in amusement. "So you're in need of assistance?"

"I'm in need of not being stuck here. I'm not fond of coyotes."

"They're mostly harmless."

"Perhaps. But they creep me out."

"Not from around here, are you?"

Sophie chuckled. "Clearly not. But I'm curious. What gave me away?"

He made a slow inspection of her car, the mud slurping up her tires, the road they'd traveled from the highway, and then finally her.

*Green eyes.*

That was what she thought when his survey stopped on her. Not *Help, please.* Or *What's your name?* Or perhaps more important than any of those options, *Can I trust you?* No. The first words scrolling through her quickly muddling brain were *green eyes.* And they were quickly followed with a deliciously buzzing sensation that started in her shoulders, sank through her chest, and then exploded in her belly, sending a charge of heated electricity through her body.

Sophie blinked, then looked toward her dash. Neither did much of anything to clear her head or stop the warmth creeping into her face. How juvenile was she that when she simply needed help out of a dumb situation she'd landed herself in, all she could think of in that moment was how mesmerizing those green eyes were?

*No. Not all. He's tall, and a little gorgeous in that hat too.*

Good heavens, she was a ninny.

"It was your shoes."

When she jolted her attention back to him, she found he had braced a palm on the roof of her car and leaned toward her.

"What?" What on earth was he talking about with her shoes? And sheesh, her heart was misbehaving.

"You're wearing white Converse tennis shoes while driving on a muddy road."

She lifted her left foot as if she needed to confirm his observation. "My shoes?" Lips parted, she looked back up at him.

He smiled. A whole, gorgeous, make-her-mind numb smile. "That's how I knew you're not from around here."

*Stop gawking.* Sophie blinked again, still searching for meaning in what he was saying. Or logic in her own brain. Had she ever been this entirely ridiculous in her life? Not once— certainly she'd remember.

Well, probably. At that moment she could barely remember her own name.

His smile dwindled to a remnant of pleasant memories. "Have I insulted you?"

"Huh?"

"I was teasing. About your shoes. Although, they are a puzzling choice, to be honest. Surely they'll wash though. Right?"

"Why?"

"Because they're about to get really muddy. Unless you prefer I carry you? I could. It would be no big deal. Just figured you'd not be comfortable with it, since I don't even know your name."

"Carry me where?"

A low chuckle rumbled from his chest, and he pointed toward his red truck. "I can't pull your car out of here. The road's still too soft. But I won't leave you alone with the coyotes, if you'd rather not stay."

Mud. Coyotes. Alone. Stay...

*Snap out of this!* Sophie shifted back to her default smile—and yes, it helped. "Right. I'd rather not stay here. Can you get me back to town?"

He shifted his jaw, doubt scrawling on his face. "Not sure how I can turn around, and the vineyard's not far after the next turn off. Would you be willing to hang out there for a couple of hours? This should firm up by sundown, I'd guess, and then we can get your girly Jeep out."

"Oh. Sure. That makes sense. Do you think the owner would mind?"

"Of the vineyard?"

"Yes. I've heard the lodge is lovely. Do you think they'd let me stay for a while?"

He chuckled again, the amusement making his green eyes deepen and that smile resurface. "Let me check." Looking skyward, he tapped his chin, and then his gaze landed back on her. "He says it'd be fine."

"You?"

The hand that had been anchored on her car slipped, and then he held it toward her. "I'm Lance Carson."

"You own the vineyard?"

"I do."

"But you're like..."

"Twenty-six."

"Oh."

"Too old or too young?"

*Too perfect.* Oh my goodness, was she really that shallow? Stick a good-looking cowboy in her face, slip some success in his pocket, and she was mush? *Sophie Shultz, put on your self-respect.* Her mom would give her an earful and lock her in her room for being so ridiculously mushy minded. "I'm sorry." Sophie straightened her shoulders, lifted her chin. "I'm acting like an idiot. I'm not normally this...well, whatever."

"I believe you. But I didn't think you were an idiot."

"Oh, okay. That's good."

"I would like to know your name though."

She wanted to drop her face into her hands and hide. Instead, she smiled. Again. "Sophie Shultz."

He pushed the hand he'd offered—and had been ignored—back toward her. "It's nice to meet you, Sophie Shultz."

# Chapter Two

SHE HADN'T MADE IT FOUR STEPS.

Lance glanced at the woman's feet as he shifted the truck into four low and put it into gear. Three steps and she'd been ankle deep in mud, her clean white Cons a casted memory beneath the slick loam that sucked her in deeper with every move. What on earth had this fox been thinking?

*Don't call her a fox. She'll take it wrong.*

Right. Sophie. Or, better, Ms. Shultz. She was a teacher—the band director the district had hired three years back. And if he was going to be honest—which he hadn't been entirely—he'd known that before she said her name. Sophie stood out in this little town. Not because she hadn't grown up there, nor because she drove a bright-orange Renegade, but because...

Well. Because she was beautiful. Stunning, actually. Like no other woman in town. Sophie Shultz stood out, and he'd wanted to make her acquaintance for quite a while. Especially when he'd heard others talk about her. Sophie Shultz, if the talk could be believed, was far more than a unique beauty. She was kind. Cheerful. Helpful.

*Gorgeous.*

No, he hadn't heard that last one around town, specifically. That was all his own thinking, and having the summation of her looks repeat in his mind made this serendipitous encounter uncomfortable.

He was not Lane. Hadn't ever mastered the art of charm as his younger brother had, and had a fairly pathetic résumé when it came to women to prove it. Particularly women he found attractive.

Attractive? No. *Gorgeous!*

Lance focused on keeping the truck in the center of the road, steering into the slides, and working to stay out of the ditch. The running thoughts in his head weren't helpful, so he muffled them with the task at hand. There'd be time later to think back on the lovely woman sitting in his truck right then. Or to wonder at his own unexpected boldness when he'd swept her up in his arms before that fourth attempt at a step could gain opportunity to suck her deeper into the road.

Plenty of time later to replay those fantastic moments between sweeping her up and depositing her onto the seat of the truck, during which she'd laughed, wrapped her long arms around his shoulders, and leaned into him like she thought the whole situation might be perfect.

*An interlude all of twenty seconds long, knucklehead. And she most certainly did not think anything about any of it was perfect.*

"Seems like with your vineyard being the popular place it is, this road would be paved." There was a question in Sophie's statement.

Lance shook his head. "Welcome to rural living. Taxes are limited by low population, and the money generally goes toward schools and roads in town. Not to worry though. The roads generally dry out fairly quickly. Between the sun, the wind, and the clay subsoil, my pickup will be kicking up dust by the morning."

"Oh." Her response was a breathy acknowledgement, followed by a lengthy pause. "You're thinking I'm an ignorant fool, aren't you?"

He glanced at her, finding her posture straight, but shoulders relaxed, and a pleasant bow on her mouth, despite her question.

"Not at all." He willed away the heat that threatened to crawl up his neck. Heaven knew he wasn't about to confess what he *had* been thinking.

"It's okay. You'd be right." She hummed—a sound of amusement. "I don't know what I was thinking, driving out on a country road after all that rain. Such a city girl, I guess."

"I'd heard that."

"You have?" Her voice dropped an octave.

Oh great. Cover blown. He cleared his throat and hunched his shoulders, as if he needed more strength to guide the pickup along the road. "Well." Might as well come clean. "Yes. I'd heard you were from Omaha or Lincoln or something. Truth is, I knew who you were before you said."

A pause rippled between them. Full of energy and snap. He glanced at her, nervous about which direction that energy ran. She met his look with a raised brow that seemed an unlikely mix of sass and sweet. There was a joyful pain in his chest—a jolt-like pleasure that made little sense and should likely not have made him grin. He looked back to the road, feebly pretending that the silent, two-second interaction hadn't happened.

"Omaha. Just outside of it, actually." Her presence leaned toward him, bringing with it a hint of something sweet and light to further swirl his already muddied senses. "And where did you hear that?"

He shrugged, still willfully suppressing a blush. Talking to women hadn't been something he'd really practiced in his lifetime. Truth be told, he wasn't much of a talker at all. "Around."

"Around where?"

"Town?"

"That sounds like a question, sir." Sass lilted her voice in the most fascinating way. "Not an answer."

"Around town." Lance focused on taking the turn that would have them on his winding driveway leading to the lodge.

"Hmm." Sophie relaxed into the seat. "So they talk about me?"

"*They* talk about everyone. Welcome to small-town life."

"What else do *they* say?" Her voice changed again, the tone now much more sincere. Maybe vulnerable?

He adjusted the hat on his head. If he wasn't mistaken, this astounding beauty beside him, rumored to be confident, ever smiling, and kind, possessed a hidden ribbon of uncertainty.

Common ground.

"Are you laughing at me, sir?"

"I am not." He tugged on the rim of his hat, as if tipping it to her. "Only a bit of a grin."

"A suppressed laugh?"

"No."

"Okay then, sir." Her cheeky tone returned. "Why do you grin?"

"What is with the *sir*?"

"I'm fond of *Masterpiece Theater*." She leaned toward him again, this time placing her long fingers on the console between them. "About that grin..."

"If I knew what *Masterpiece* was, I'm sure that would make everything clear. Since I am not..."

Her fingers drummed on the plastic between them. "Your ignorance should be overcome."

The first of two bends loomed ahead, and Lance let that irresistible—though likely innocent—invitation hang unanswered until he navigated (more correctly, slid with marginal control) past the curve. Once safely on the straight, which lay under the covering of brightly yellowed trees as if the entrance to something enchanted, he dared eye contact with her again.

Brows lifted, she met his gaze. *Maybe not so innocent.* Definitely irresistible.

"Perhaps you'll educate me." The words shocked him as they escaped his lips. Bold. Yes, Lance Carson was bold in many things in life. This vineyard, beyond the next curve, and the lodge that he'd built beside it stood as testimony to it: he was not a timid man. Not in the pursuit of dreams. Not in work. Not in business.

But with people? More specifically, women? With those attractive mysteries he'd never spent much time understanding, he had always been the opposite of bold. Which had been fine. He had other things to pursue and important reasons to ensure he was successful in them.

Women made him nervous. As a general rule, he didn't particularly like being nervous. *This* woman made him jittery. And apparently—paradoxically—bold. For some undefined reason he didn't mind the jitters. Perhaps he even liked the flood of energy currently racing through his veins. Boldness on a hefty dose of caffeine, thanks to Sophie Schultz.

He instantly liked her all the more for it.

Sophie laughed. The sound reminded him of a song his mother had loved. "Sweet Caroline"… It'd been years since he'd thought of that song—he'd spent more time over the last decade listening to his dad's choice in music. Yet at the sound of her amusement, Neil Diamond's lyrics sang through his mind as if he'd written them himself, bringing with them a longing for the music, the memories, and that almost forgotten sense of being anchored by something more valuable, not to mention stable, than goals and success.

"The grin, sir?"

"I'm sorry?" He nearly shook his head to return to the cab of the truck, away from boyhood memories and a life that had come unraveled.

Sophie's tone changed yet again, losing the light banter. "What happened to the grin?"

"Oh." He smiled in full. Surely she wouldn't know that the expression was now false. "The muddy road." With one quick brush of his hand, he motioned to the final bend before they'd reach the lodge. "We're too close now to land in the ditch."

"If we're that close, we could walk."

"I would not want that on my record."

"You have a record?"

With her? He sure hoped to start one. How was that for bold?

As they rounded the final elbow, the parking area he'd cleared nearly six years back opened, allowing a clear view of the lodge he'd built only a year after the parking lot. Beside him, Sophie sucked in a breath, provoking an honest smile.

"Wow." The word sounded breathy as her hand warmed his bicep. "Lance Carson, *they* were not lying."

He chuckled. "They who? And what were *they* not lying about?"

"You're a visionary." Her long fingers curled around his arm. "And this is breathtaking. I'd never have imagined such a thing hiding back here."

Her touch fluttered away, leaving him with a strange mix of disappointment and hope. One part of his mind whispering it back, and the other settling into a delighted surety that this was only the beginning. A presumptuous thought, but accompanied with a strong sense of rightness he'd experienced before. Only then, the confidence had been about grapevines.

In his limited experience, vines were much easier to understand than women. Perhaps that feeling of certainty was pompous and massively misplaced. Then again, he hadn't tried much with the latter.

The truck rolled onto the more stable stand of river rock he had brought in before the construction of the lodge. A slushy sound of mushy rocks grinding under the weight of his tires vanished as he put the vehicle in park and cut the engine.

Mutt, his black lab/corgi/and who-knew-what-else dog came running around from the garage with his warning bark at full volume.

"Don't worry about her. She's noisy but harmless."

Sophie laughed. "She's cute. What's her name?"

"Mutt."

"Mutt? That's not nice."

The dog stopped beside Lance's side of the truck, tail wagging and panting a happy hello, throwing in a greeting yelp every five breaths or so. "She doesn't seem to mind."

Keys in hand, Lance turned back to look at Sophie. She bent forward, head tilted, gawking at the backside of the lodge and then at the span of fields that yawned to the lower left of the log building. He was content to take in the curve of her shoulders, the outline of her jaw, and the profile of her wonder while she drank in the site of his creation.

"I really am shocked. I'd heard this was something out of a dream, but..."

"You have *not* heard that," he said.

Her head came around, wide eyes settled on him. "I absolutely have."

Something of an ache sank into his chest. As much as he'd felt ridiculed for pursuing this unorthodox agriculture project in the middle of corn and soybean country, there had been much support from town. Even so, he hadn't realized the people of Big Prairie had said such things about his emerging success. Hearing it reported from someone who had no skin in the game sliced into a place he needed to keep firm. The local opinions of his projects couldn't matter this much to him. He couldn't afford to allow it, because at some point the favor would shift. That point, more likely than not, was in the very near future.

It couldn't matter what the folks of Big Prairie thought.

"How about you take a look from the inside." He popped open his door but snagged her hand—which sat available on that console—before he slid out of the cab. "Wait right there, and I'll get you."

"I'm able to walk."

"It's muddy."

"So am I." Her lips scrunched into a smirk.

Lance didn't answer. The fact that she did exactly as he'd asked was not lost on him.

*Only the beginning.*

Indeed. With that thought came enough confidence to sweep away the nagging sensation of... Well, of trouble. He'd been wrestling with that enough over the past several months of negotiations. Sophie might prove to be the perfect antidote.

Thank God for that.

***

A thread of guilt wove through her gut at the conversation she'd had over the phone. Craig had finally answered her call, and without even knowing all the details, he'd been ready to come to her rescue.

She was relieved that he wasn't going to.

*You're in good hands—he's a good guy.* Craig's assessment of her situation after she'd mentioned Lance's appearance. Sophie's heart lugged in her chest, hot and fast. Lance Carson—a man Craig had full trust in, apparently—was definitely a good guy. Seemed so, anyway. Country eye candy, and nice on top of that. But the real reason her pulse surged with the heavy sensation of guilt? She'd been a flirt. Class-one, high-dose f-l-i-r-t.

Who even was she?

She'd been sort-of dating Craig—who was also good looking as all get out. *They grow 'em handsome out here in Big Prairie.* Thoughts she ought to shake loose from her mind, because *Girl! What a way to find trouble!* Being all boy crazy and ridiculous. She was an intelligent woman. Successful in her chosen profession. Respected in this cute little town.

What was more, she wasn't a flirt! Since her early teen years, she'd learned the difference between flirting and being nice, thanks to her persistent and somewhat overbearing mom (bless her for it though), and Sophie had resolved to be *nice*. Not a flirt.

Oh, but she'd flirted with Lance Carson. As easy as a casino dealer in Vegas, she'd laid on the charm like she'd been practicing the art of it her entire life. (Ahem. She hadn't.) All the while, there was this undefined thing with her and Craig.

*Craig's not in it.*

This was her self-defense, a line that had sprung up against her jabbing conscience starting all the way back to that moment when Lance had swept her off her feet—literally—and she'd delighted in being in his arms a little too much. There was more than a salt's worth of truth in that justification. Craig and Brenna, no matter what either of them said, were not done with whatever they'd tried to bury in their past. Sophie didn't want in the middle of that, and she had to fight to restrain an emerging resentment that she'd landed there. Entirely innocently, she might add.

Still. She and Craig were in limbo in that weird place dating often led to. Which was actually not really dating but would be called *hanging out* or *talking*. Who the heck could understand all these things, anyway? Whatever was between her and Craig was...nothing and something, and the lack of definition made Sophie dizzy. Not to mention frustrated. Mostly because, standing in the River's Edge Lodge, overlooking rows of neatly pruned and twined vines, her feet cozy in a pair of Lance's wool boot socks, and feeling almost giddy with delight as she waited for the man to return from the kitchen at the back with a promised carafe of hot cocoa, she felt guilty.

Sophie hated guilt. Lived her life with a very concerted effort to avoid the smothering emotion entirely. Which meant she pursued the squeaky-clean sort of life.

Maybe she should call Craig back. Clarify and end all undefined attachments right then and there.

Great idea. That should definitely help everything. Especially since Craig already sounded a tad miserable.

*I owe you.* Actually, he sounded more than miserable. He sounded defeated. Which left her with guilt.

So that meant what exactly? She was stuck at the lodge until Lance determined the roads had firmed up enough to go back to town. And the flirting thing? That had almost seemed out of her control.

*Maintaining yourself is up to you, Sophie. If you expect someone else to do it, you are bound for disappointment—and worse, you will be the one to pay for the failure.*

Another lesson from her mom. Thing was, Sophie knew Mom spoke from a place of experience, and she wanted better for her daughter.

The sound of a door shutting firmly clunked from the back, drawing Sophie's attention from the large trapezoid window. It was a shame she'd stood there for who knows how long with a spectacular view of Lance's vineyard and a ribbon of autumn-blazed trees that lined the river banks, all glowing in the hazy golden hues of the late-afternoon sun, and she'd failed to appreciate the beauty it deserved.

*Lord, I've done it.*

What exactly, she wasn't sure. But something. In a span of an afternoon, she'd found herself in a mess. The kind that, in contrast to the predicament of her vehicle, was not likely to dry up and disappear. Easily washed away with a high-powered hose and forgotten with a simple *no harm done.*

"Were you able to make your call?" Lance walked to one of several tables scattered in the gaping space of his lodge, his steps muted against the wood floor by his heavy socks.

"I was." Sophie turned from the vineyard view.

That cowboy hat still in place, Lance set down a tray loaded with a carafe, two mugs, a plate of something that looked chocolatey and delicious, a board of sliced cheese and whole strawberries, and several small bottles she suspected were wine samples. He seemed fully occupied with arranging the loot, and when he was satisfied with the spread, he stepped to the chair nearest her. Only then did he lift his gaze, allowing his face to peek from beneath the wide brim of the hat.

*Green eyes.*

Her breath caught. Yes, for sure. She'd done something. Or maybe he had. Either way, she and Craig would be having a talk. Hopefully, it would end with *no harm done.*

And this...

Lance swept a hand to the chair he'd pulled out, a silent, enticing, irresistible invitation.

# Chapter Three

THERE WERE SOME IN TOWN WHO WOULD CALL HIM
SELFISH.

Lance knew, to a large degree, those who would say so would be
right. Though he had his reasons for doing the things he did,
there was always the underpinning smudge of self-serving
ambition. Sometimes, more than a smudge.

Staring into the rich dark eyes looking back at him from the
other side of the table, Lance found himself battling against a
rising tidal wave of selfishness. For more than three hours, Sophie
had mesmerized him. They'd picked at the spread he'd put
together from the back kitchen, delicious scraps left behind by his
chef, who only days before had left for his home in the city
because the storm that had been predicted earlier in the week
pretty much had guaranteed an empty house.

Sophie had tasted two of his favorite wines bearing the River's
Edge label and had been appropriately impressed with his product.
Maybe as flattery. He chose not to believe that. They'd exchanged
the whats and wheres of life—covering the basics. She'd grown up
in Omaha—in a community outside of Omaha actually, where
there had been wealth, impressive schools, and a bit more
sheltered living than some of the areas closer to downtown.

"It's kind of what they used to call a white-flight suburb."
Sophie paused there, her wineglass tipped loosely in her raised

hand, her eyes holding with some kind of intentional, meaningful look on him. Then one dark brow raised. "Ironic, right?"

He felt the weight of her implied test. Wondered what, exactly, she expected him to say. "Ironic..." He held that mild challenge of hers and leaned against his forearm on the table. "Because of your skin?"

Amusement played in her expression. "Are we afraid to say it?"

"We? No." He felt his brow crumple. Maybe he wasn't passing this test. "What are we afraid to say, exactly?"

"To name my skin. Or my heritage?"

"African American?"

Those long, slender arms folded as she leaned back, though she still kept the glass lifted, as if she'd intended to take another taste of the sweet dessert wine. After a drifting silence, during which he felt cast off into a sea, she breathed a small chuckle. "So you had noticed."

"Hmm." He sat back as well, mirroring her posture. His mind went blank. Nothing to say.

"My mom is white and was single until I was thirteen."

"Should that matter?"

"I don't know. Does it?"

"Perhaps. If it's part of your story."

The amusement that had kept her mouth curved upward faded. "It is."

A sense of dangling wrapped around him, uncomfortable and growing more so as the ease of their earlier conversation swept away. Desperate for something to do, Lance reached for his nearly empty wineglass, swirled the pale-yellow liquid, and then drank what remained. "I noticed you a long while back, Sophie."

She laughed. It was not a sharp sound, but not delightful either. Not like the first laugh he'd heard from her, reminding him of "Sweet Caroline." "I do stick out in this town, don't I?"

What could he say to that? Simply the truth. "Yes."

Her look hung on him, as if whatever he'd say next would determine her entire estimation of his character forever.

"I thought you were beautiful, and I wanted to know your name."

At that her smile bloomed full, and then she truly laughed. The delightful kind. "How long ago was that?"

"I'm not sure. Two, three years? How long have you been in Big Prairie?"

She leaned forward, slipping her elbows onto the table. "You don't know? Not sure I can trust that."

He motioned to the building in which they sat, and then stood, moving toward the window. "This overgrown SAE project occupies the majority of my time. And to turn the tables, you've been in this community how long, and you've never been here? How is that?"

"Touché." She was at his side, and together they meandered closer to the glass. "I have been here about three years, and the River's Edge Vineyard is one of the first things I had heard about when I came. So I guess this visit is well overdue."

"Glad the roads could remedy that." Lance cast a look down his shoulder, finding her attention fixed on the rows he'd spent the years of his youth planting, tending, harvesting. "And that I could finally meet you."

Her chin slid toward him, eyes then held on his. A heartbeat. Then two—maybe five. He couldn't say. He stood captivated, locked in something breathless and addictive. If he slid closer, would she step away? Should he lean, would she skitter?

What on earth was wrong with him? He'd only just met this woman. He wasn't a believer in insta—*insta what*? Ridiculous thoughts not worth chasing.

There was attraction though. He wouldn't deny that. And he'd be willing to wager a few valuable acres of his family's property that she felt it too. She had flirted. Held his gaze. Challenged him to the point of awkwardness, presumably to see how he'd handle it. If he were Lane, and this woman had given him only half as much encouragement, he'd have well explored that pretty mouth within the first hour of this unintentional visit.

He was not Lane. Clearly. A fringe of resentment drew Lance away from the intoxicating sensation that had washed over him under Sophie's long look. Drawing away from her gaze, he moved closer to the window and looked over the property that had passed into his name.

So much responsibility. The greatness of it, he was certain no one truly understood.

No, Lance was not his younger brother. Not in personality. Not in character. And he did not possess the freedom to go and do whatever came into his head.

"Is the road passable, do you think?" Sophie's soft-spoken question drifted from near his arm.

He glanced back, finding her examining her hands rather than watching the blazing display of the sunset over the golden treetops.

Ah yes. There was that thing about him being selfish. He should have offered to take her back to town an hour ago. With the onset of the wind and the clear evening, the road would have been passable for a four-wheel drive vehicle and an experienced driver. He had both. He could have taken her home, told her he'd pull her Renegade out of the ditch the next day after church, and she would have had the remainder of her Saturday evening to do with whatever she'd planned.

"It is, I'm sure." He hoped he didn't sound distracted. Or, heaven help him, disappointed. Maybe she'd had a date set for the night? Talk around town had her and Erikson spending time together. Lance worked to ignore the way that thought made his muscles tense. "I'm sorry I've kept you prisoner so long. I hope I haven't ruined any plans." Not really. He didn't hope that at all, actually. Particularly if those plans included Big Prairie's most famous football star.

Sophie shook her head. "I got myself stuck—that wasn't your fault. And I wasn't doing anything this evening—that I know of."

What did that mean?

"I'm going to make a call real quick, and then we could go?" She strode back toward the table where she'd left her phone, glancing at him after she picked up the cell.

His gut twisted. Maybe she hadn't been flirting all along. Or perhaps he hadn't passed whatever that test was she'd pressed on him earlier. Shouldn't matter, not to the point of pain in his stomach. Still he looked at the stacked logs that made the opposite wall, rather than her, when he nodded. "Sure. I'll start the pickup."

Her teeth scraped the edge of her bottom lip, and then she nodded before turning away, her attention zeroed in on her phone. Back toward him, head tucked. He got it. It was a private conversation. *Probably with Erikson.*

Man, that really shouldn't annoy him. Wow though. It seriously did. With long strides, he took himself out of the main lodge room, through the back kitchen, and into the mudroom that faced his family's tiny home. Beside the door, he stooped to grip the tops of his boots, jamming each foot in with more force than necessary. Once his pant legs were settled into place, he straightened and ran a hand over his head.

His hat. Dang, but he'd left that in the lodge. Lance didn't go anywhere without his hat. *Cowboy with a vineyard.* That was what Lane called him, usually with contempt staining his younger brother's voice.

Looking back at his feet, he rolled one booted foot to the side, and then the other, giving him a peek at the condition of the bottoms. Both soles were slathered generously with dried mud. If he went back for his hat, he'd leave a trail of dirt clots from there to the main room, and as he was his own custodian, he'd rather not sweep up his own messy trail on a Saturday. Spent every other evening doing that activity—he preferred not to on the weekend.

Well then, he'd do as he'd said. Start the pickup. Then he'd come back, remove the boots, and fetch his hat. *Or you could live without it.* He snorted at the idea as he opened the door and stepped into the chilly wind, which felt unnatural as it toyed with his exposed hair. He paced around his high-clearance vehicle, kicking at clumps of half-dried mud near the tires, and then started the truck. On his way back into the lodge, a plop of loosened mud dropped from a wheel well and smacked the river-rock drive, drawing his glance. Only another mud clot, and good riddance. He didn't pause his stride, knowing without looking that he was near the door. But then the quiet squeak of the springs on the storm door had him whipping his face forward. Right into—

"Ouch!" He jerked backward, but not quick enough. Pain exploded in his nose as he plowed straight into the hard plastic edge of the door.

"Oh my goodness!" The door ripped away, slamming back into place, and then Sophie was in his line of blurring sight, one palm cupping his face. "Lance, I'm so sorry. I didn't see you." Her thumb brushed over his cheekbone, and she sucked in a breath. "Is it broken?"

Lance squeezed his eyes shut, fighting the sting in them and hoping to clear the fuzziness that had accompanied the pain. Searching for something steady to grip, he reached toward the building. Instead, he found her hip. He froze. Waited for her to jump away.

With one hand still holding his face, her other found his shoulder as if to steady him, though it seemed her wrist lay against his muscle there, not her palm. He blinked, finding the blurry vision passed, and looked down at her hand.

She lifted it, his hat in her grip. "You left this," she said, sounding hesitant. Maybe sheepish. Slowly, she pulled her other palm from his face.

"Yes. I was going to get it." He hadn't moved, her hip warm against his palm. *Unhand the woman. For all you know, she's dating Craig.* Lance did not obey his conscience. Rather, he slid half a step closer. That crisp, sweet scent curled upward toward him, reminding him of carefree summer days and enticing him to lean in and inhale deeper.

Sophie's expression seemed caught. Frightened? He couldn't read it for certain. But then she lifted her arms and settled his hat onto his head. With her lips tight, she molded a smile that certainly wasn't the same as the easy, natural grin he'd witnessed several times during their afternoon together.

Lance slipped his hand away, backpedaled two steps, and cleared his throat. "Thank you." He tugged on the rim of the hat she'd replaced.

"For breaking your nose?"

"It's not broken."

"You've already got a welt forming. I can just hear you explaining it to your mother. 'This woman came crashing out of the lodge and smashed my face with the door.'"

He glanced to the ground near his boot, then scratched his neck. Perhaps if his mother were around, they'd have such a conversation. As it was, he hadn't spoken to her since he was fifteen. Feeling once again vulnerable with the woman—and not particularly enjoying it anymore—Lance brought his chin up. "No explanation required." He stepped to the side and motioned toward the running pickup. "Back to town, then?"

Her scrutiny felt invasive. And then those no-longer-white Converse paced to his pickup.

Pain throbbed in his nose, making his eye twitch. But that wasn't really what he felt most. He felt like he'd stepped off a roller coaster—one he couldn't remember deciding to ride. That didn't settle well with him. Not one bit. He liked things he could take charge of. Predict. Control. So how on earth, in the span of a few hours, had he ended up on some kind of emotional ride?

*Blame it on the mud and move on.*

Seemed like the best plan he'd had all day.

***

The silence between them was stiff. If Sophie hated anything, it was a stiff silence. *Smile, it'll help* came to her mind like a dry cork to the surface of water. Always did, and she always obeyed. She brushed her mouth up while looking out her window at the fields passing by. Once they'd left the tree-littered banks of the river, the wide-open prairie had yawned, giving easy understanding to the town's name. Big Prairie indeed.

Certain that her practiced expression of relaxed and easygoing was in place, she turned to Lance. He gripped the wheel with both hands, his shoulders more tense than they had been when the roads had been significantly worse. Those last few minutes at the lodge—the moments after she'd plowed the door into his face—had shifted the energy between them. She couldn't understand it. More, she hated the tension now pushing between them. Had much preferred the electrical pulse that had been wrapping around them throughout the afternoon.

Ah, there was that thread of guilt again. She almost wondered where it had vanished. Nowhere, apparently. It was ready and waiting, right there beneath the surface of her attraction to Lance. That did not help the current stiffness, so she suffocated the thought before it could grow.

"You said some letters back there. About the vineyard." Random chatter was usually her go-to when it came to drowning discomfort. "What did they stand for?"

"Letters?"

"Yes. *S* something. You said it was an overgrown project of some sort."

"Oh yes. SAE."

"I don't know what that is."

His posture sagged into the seat, and one hand slipped from the wheel. Sophie's ease-the-stiffness plan was working. "SAE is an FFA thing. It stands for *supervised agricultural experience*."

"And FFA..."

That drew a mild chuckle. "You are the city girl, aren't you? Still, you grew up in Nebraska. This is surprising."

"Amend my ignorance."

The corner of his mouth poked upward, and he eyed her with a spark of that interest she'd been binging on all afternoon. "Seems we both need to inform each other. I seem to remember asking you to educate me on something earlier."

"You did."

"And you didn't."

"I didn't?"

"Educate me."

"Ah. Well, that would require a television and several hours to binge-watch a series."

Another pulsing glance. She might be addicted.

*You are not that girl, Sophie! Nice, but not a flirt.* The entire afternoon spent with Lance Carson was completely undoing that image of her character, which should have bothered her more than it did in that moment. "For the time being, how about you explain these letters to this poor city kid?"

"*FFA* stands for *Future Farmers of America*. It's an organization for high schoolers."

"Well, there you go. That would explain my ignorance. No one in my school farmed."

"It's bigger than that." He shifted in his seat, settling comfortably into a topic he clearly was passionate about. "The name was established in the 1920s. But what the organization does, what it's about, isn't simply farming—which by the way, isn't at all simple. FFA is about agriculture and everything ag encompasses. Science. Business. Entrepreneurship. Engineering and technology. There are so many disciplines and opportunities."

"You loved it then?" She didn't need to ask.

"I did. And my SAE, that supervised ag experience, is now my growing business. It started with researching grapes. Could I grow them here, and if so, what kind? I toured a few vineyards in the state, and several outside of Nebraska as well. I researched what to do with the products a vineyard could produce. Then what a business like that would require. The permits, the processes, the marketing. All the nuts and bolts that go beyond growing vines."

"Wow. Sounds like a lot."

"Yeah. Kind of a beast, if you want to know the truth."

"And this project you started in high school, it led to River's Edge Vineyard?"

"It *is* the vineyard."

Sophie sat back, absorbing that. Imagine a high school project exploding into something that big. That successful. It was a little shocking. "So you didn't go to college?"

"I did. An ag tech school. And I took business classes—you know, like management and accounting and marketing and such—online if they weren't available at the school."

"All the while you were working on the vineyard?"

"Yes. With my dad's help back then."

"And now?"

She didn't mean for the question to be intrusive. By his extended silence, and the clenching of his jaw though, it was.

"He's gone." Lance cleared his throat, lifting his hand to regrip the wheel as the truck approached the stop sign where they would turn onto the highway that would take them back into town. The vehicle slowed and then stopped, and Lance looked at her. "My parents both died. My mom when I was fifteen. She'd been sick a long time. My dad shortly after I finished tech school. He left the ranch to me."

"Oh, I'm so sorry, Lance."

He flinched, and his mouth tightened. Then he nodded. "Thanks."

And that was all. Sophie had no idea what to say or do.

What she wanted to do was to take his hand. Maybe pull him into a hug. She wondered what he'd do with that. For some reason, she wondered if anyone ever had.

Something in her whispered a sad *no* to that question, and as he looked away, attention again fixed on the road, she had the convincing impression that Lance Carson, though very successful in his life and endeavors, was alone in the world.

She couldn't smile at that. It wouldn't help anyway.

# *Chapter Four*

HE'D WEASELED HER NUMBER FROM HER.

*It was necessary.* Though the justification was technically true, Lance knew a sharp edge of a bigger, overriding fact.

He'd wanted it. That was all. Wanted to be able to text her, call her, anytime he chose. For any reason, not only to let her know that he'd freed her Renegade from the clutches of a messy road and would gladly meet her at the stop sign so she could retrieve it.

Actually, scratch that plan anyway. He'd get it back to the lodge. Pull his power washer out of the garage hidden on the other side of his small home and return that mud-slathered car to its shiny tangerine color. Then maybe he could invite her out for lunch after church—which would give him a reason to show up in town at the small brick building bearing a cross on its front. Heaven knew he'd become pretty good at finding excuses *not* to go. And better, if Sophie came out to the vineyard after services, he'd have the added excuse to *not* stick around to visit. Make it to church, not have to face Miss Jane, and have a spell-binding date all in one day?

Sounded too good for reality.

*Because it is, knucklehead. Factor in Craig Erikson.*

Ah that. There were moments, many in fact, when Lance wished he hadn't isolated himself so much from the people and doings of Big Prairie. This, for example, would have been one of those times it would have been useful to have an in-the-know connection he could call to ask for the scoop on the two district music teachers. Were they really a thing? Or was that a presumption because of the convenient fit of age, employment, and shared religious status?

Lance pulled into the drive behind the lodge as the last fingers of daylight curled westward, transitioning the day into night. The pickup stopped, he turned off the engine, and he sighed, gripping the steering wheel.

"I like her way too much." He slouched backward, glanced up to meet his own inspection in the rearview mirror, and tipped his hat backward. "Stupid. What real reason do you have to like her this much?"

She was beautiful. *Beauty is vain. Fleeting. Useless.*

She smiled often. *Charm is deceitful.*

She made him feel like a freshly opened bottle of champagne. *Emotions are treacherous.*

So then, what significant, valid reason did he have to invest this take-over-his-mind level of interest?

*I just like her.* He squeezed his eyes shut, palmed the top of his hat, and tossed it onto the dashboard. Once again, he looked up to meet the man in the mirror, noting the red welt running between his eyebrows had faded. "Knucklehead."

The man in the mirror shook his head, and then a ghost of a grin moved onto his face, as if daring a rebellion. Lance's attention left the mirror and landed on the cell phone resting in the console at his side.

He had her number.

*Game on, Erikson. May the best man win.*

Since they were no longer in high school, and this had nothing whatsoever to do with football, Lance felt a rise of confidence mingle with the unrelenting—though stupid it may be—

emotion of *liking* the woman in question. He had a fair shot. Every bit as Craig-the-superstar Erikson.

Lance moved his gaze beyond the cab of the truck, taking in the shadowy landscape of his home and business. He'd done this. Built this.

Maybe he had more than a fair shot.

***

Sophie stepped out of the steam swirling in her shower and wrapped a towel around her warm, dripping frame. Tiptoeing from one bathroom rug—the one stationed in front of the glass door—to the other, which lay in front of the sink, she used a corner of the towel to wipe her face. The mirror sported a fog blocking the view of herself. With a circular motion, she cleared the view with three fingers.

Hair pulled up into her "unicorn top," she scrunched at the thick mass of tight curls and then fingered her dark eyebrows in place. She thought for a fleeting moment about having her hair straightened—the mass of curls seemed to poof around her face as soon as she set the bundle free. Her coiled lion's mane.

*It's stunning, my Sophie Joyanne. Do you know what I'd give to have your hair?*

Mom's standard answer to any occasion when Sophie had resented the natural state of her head. At one point, in grade ten, Mom consented to her having the entirety of it chemically straightened. The memory of the time it took made Sophie brush away the idea as she stood there in the vanishing steam. Not worth it.

She fingered her mane into some kind of order and tipped her chin. What had Lance thought of her?

He'd said he'd thought her beautiful the first time he'd noticed her, and wanted to know her name.

Three years ago though? What on earth? Still, he'd seemed sincere. Everything about him seemed sincere, even when he did dare to flirt. Lance hadn't come across like...like a player would. Sophie rolled her eyes. Like she would actually know anything about that. She'd been a band nerd and one of two non-white students in her class of over one hundred. Seemed to her that combination of band nerd and minority slimmed down her exposure to the player types significantly.

Or she simply hadn't been a flirty girl herself. Sometimes like attracted like—or in this case *didn't*. Who knew for sure, and she wasn't going to waste her energy trying to figure it out. Not when there were too many other really great things going for her in life.

Things like Craig Erikson.

Her rib cage seemed to contract, smashing her vitals with a painful crush. She should have called him when she got home to let him know she was okay. Had intended to, but for the fact that every time she palmed her phone, the urge to call Lance instead hit her with a nearly overwhelming force.

"Who are you, girl?" She scowled at her reflection. "Mom would be mortified."

Actually, to the point, Sophie was a bit mortified. Especially when she looked back over the day and landed on the moment Lance had slipped his large hand over her hip as a means to steady himself, and she'd thought seriously about closing the dwindled gap between them to test the firmness of his determined mouth.

With both hands on the countertop, she leaned toward her own face. "Wow. You about lost your mind there."

Yes, she had. And to make it worse, she rather regretted the fact that she hadn't yielded to the impulse. There was something really ridiculous going on with her.

"Not just ridiculous. Flighty. Stupid. And undignified." Her mouth twisted to one side, and she stared herself down with a look she knew she'd leveled on a few wayward students. "Knock it off, Schultz. You don't treat men that way, because that's not what you'd want from them."

There. That should settle it. A sense of rightness—and a return to self-control—settled in her and eased that crushing grip of guilt as she turned away and dried herself. Hurrying, because she hated the chill that rippled over her skin when she left the warmth of her steamy bathroom to dress in her bedroom, she wiggled into her comfy jammies and reached the book she'd been reading from her nightstand. Her phone, sitting beside the book, lit up.

A text. Likely from Craig, who would surely be checking on her now that it was after dark.

*I pulled your car out. It's in my driveway, cleaned up and shiny.*

Sophie replaced the book as her heart gave a little squeeze of delight.

*You pulled it out already? It was nearly dark when you dropped me off.*

*Roads were good. Not a problem.*

*Why is it clean and shiny?*

*The car-wash fairy likes to visit my place. Why orange?*

Sophie snorted. Why orange...ah. Her Renegade. *My favorite color. One of them. The other is yellow.*

*Because...*

*Because it's bright and happy. Like spring tulips, and a summer sunrise, and a good bonfire.*

There was a long wait between her response and his, the span providing Sophie with time to imagine the way his face smoothed while he thought, a look of consideration giving those mossy-green eyes a dignified look of intelligence.

*All good reasons.* His response finally came up on her screen, followed by another expanse of nothing. What could she say into that space? She wasn't done with the conversation, with the day that they'd accidentally spent together.

Was he?

*I've heard we go to the same church.*

Apparently not.

*We do? How, in a town this size, and a church even smaller, have I not known that?*

*I haven't been consistent in attending, and when I have gone, I've been, uh, discreet.*

*Are there reasons?*

*Yes.*

More waiting in the dark.

*I was thinking that I'd go tomorrow. Maybe.*

That was not an explanation, tantalizing though it may be.
*Oh?*

*And that perhaps after, you'd come out to the lodge for lunch.
Maybe?*

To get her car, of course. And for lunch. Like a date?

Oh goodness. She wanted, more than she'd wanted anything in
quite a long time, to say yes, and for it to be a date. But there was
that Craig thing.

She and Craig never had a DTR—a *define the relationship*—
talk. So maybe there was no reason she should have this gut-
twisting sense of shame. But she did, and it wasn't something she
would be able to ignore. Or justify.

Sighing, Sophie flopped onto her bed and squeezed her eyes
shut. *Why now, God? Why couldn't he have introduced himself
three years ago? Or even three months ago? Why'd Lance have to
wait until after Craig came back to Big Prairie to make his
presence known?*

Answers didn't filter down from heaven. Even still, she knew
what her answer to Lance needed to be—at least for this request.
Resolved and disappointed, Sophie rolled onto her stomach,
propped herself up on one arm, and pecked at the phone.

*Can I take a rain check (LOL—the irony, right?) on lunch? I'll
need to come get my car, and I'd love to see you in church on
Sunday, but I have some other things to take care of.*

She exhaled after she sent her reply, praying he'd take her
seriously about the rain check. As soon as she could talk to Craig,
she'd say yes to Lance. Guilt free.

*Another time.*

What did that cryptic two-word answer mean? *So...I'll see you
at church?*

Another long space of nothing filled nearly a minute as she
stared at her phone. Then finally, a simple, show-no-cards reply.

*You will.*

She hardly felt better and almost wished she'd not had a
conscience, because spending another afternoon with Lance

Carson at his gorgeous vineyard and lodge now seemed like the only thing she really wanted to do with her Sunday afternoon.

Even a good book like the one waiting on the nightstand would not be able to distract her from the growing disappointment.

# Chapter Five

LANCE SAT IN HIS PICKUP, SHOULDERS CURVED IN,
STARING AT THE BRICK BUILDING IN FRONT OF HIM.

He'd told Sophie he'd come. Why, he wasn't clear about, since she'd turned him down for lunch. Nicely—said she had some things to do—but it was still a refusal. Polite, but clear. He'd been civilly rejected before. He knew how it went.

*She asked for a rain check.*

The hopeful reminder running through his mind annoyed him. Especially as he'd witnessed Craig meeting her at the front door to the church before they passed through the entrance together, Craig's two young charges bouncing along beside him. Though there was no discernable PDA between Sophie and the hometown football star, they were both all smiles and easy familiarity. Not to mention, made quite the charming family-like picture together.

No. Lance knew a polite rejection when he'd been handed one, and Sophie had done that. She was seeing Craig—and why would she want to change that? So really, he didn't need to show up in town for church, even if he'd told her he would.

*How about to worship Jesus?*

The internal question weighed hard against his heart. Lance had been a believer in Christ since he'd been a confused, hurting fourteen-year-old, witnessing the quickening slide toward the end as his mother lost her battle with lupus. Tearfully she'd shared her hope in Jesus—and His promise of eternal life in Him— something Mom had done periodically over the years of her sickness. Why Lance suddenly took it personal in that conversation, he couldn't say for sure. Maybe it was the heartbreaking realization that his mother would really die, and soon, from something they'd first thought was manageable and not fatal. Or the longing to know for sure that their goodbyes wouldn't have to be final. In any case, Lance had confessed that Jesus was Lord, believing that He'd been raised from the dead after He'd paid the price for Lance's sins, and he'd asked for the salvation that came through faith.

He'd really, truly believed back then—and that comfort of faith saw him through the agony of his mother's death. Then again through the second trial of losing his dad only six years later.

Truth be known, Lance still believed. He hadn't lost the faith that promised joy and paradise with Jesus in eternity. But he'd become mixed up about how that faith played out in life, in the here and now.

Thing was, the turns in his world had him wondering which direction was true north, so to speak. The grief he'd shouldered had led to some hefty responsibilities as well as some estrangement. From his brother first. And now, as he tried to figure out a way to stitch that relationship back together, the separation extended to the town, including the members of his church.

Thus, his sporadic attendance. At best.

Nearly convinced he should start his engine and go back down the road he'd come, Lance watched as a few last-minute attenders hustled toward the door. A check of the digital clock on the dash told him it was 9:56. If he waited a couple more minutes, he could slip through those double doors after the appointed greeters left their posts and sneak into a vacant back-row seat.

Might be okay. Maybe they'd even sing "In the Garden"—a favorite of his mother's and a song that could lay him flat before Jesus like nothing else. It'd been a long time...

Or, he could leave.

*You said you'd be here.*

That was because it was the polite thing to say—and who was he arguing with here, anyway? Besides, she'd not see him if he snuck in the back late and slipped out the same way before the closing amen. Basically, it was the same either way.

Though he knew that wasn't true, for more than one reason, Lance sat up and reached for the keys. The moment he moved to turn them, however, a solid *tap tap tap* sounded near his shoulder. He nearly jumped.

He had to look downward out his window to find Miss Jane standing beside his vehicle, staring at him.

Great. One of several people he'd hoped to avoid.

With her piercing blue eyes zeroed in on him, Lance shivered to think the elderly woman might actually be able to see into his soul. He rolled his window down, swallowing and praying that his voice wouldn't crack like a nervous teen caught doing wrong. Miss Jane cocked her head, causing her loose silver-white hair to brush her bony shoulder. Simply watching him until his window descended completely, she didn't move from her perch beside his door.

"Well?" Her salt-and-pepper brows lifted.

Lance felt like a moth pinned to a display board. He cleared his throat. *Don't sound like a guilty kid. You're not.* "Good morning, Miss Jane."

"I think so. Glad to hear you do as well." Her thin, pink-glossed lips closed in a line. Not a frown. Not a smile either. Not that he'd expected a smile from her. Actually, he *had* expected the frown. Wouldn't blame her for it—not that it'd change things much.

"Have you made up your mind, then?"

Lance stared at her. What was the woman talking about?

"Young man, the service is *inside*." She huffed. Maybe it was a chuckle? "Seems if you made the drive into town, you might as well go the whole way. Heaven knows, you're long overdue."

"Oh," he said on an exhale. Because that was all he could manage.

"So." One thin, aged hand perched on her hip while the other clutched her Bible. "Are you coming in or aren't you?"

"Oh." This time he wrangled up a smile. He hoped. "Well, I suppose—"

"Good. You can sit with me. I hate sitting alone, but the darn ducks got out of their yard this morning, and old Hank has it in his feathered head that it's time to head south. Never mind that he's domesticated, and he's too fat to fly more than ten feet. He's bound and determined to lead his ladies on a migration that is certainly doomed to end in a fox's den. And those girls are witless enough to follow him. They'd never survive in the wild, I tell you. Anyway, now I'm late, and I don't want to walk up to the third row in the middle of service."

Lance felt his lips part somewhere in the middle of the duck story, and by the end, he was certain his eyes had become the approximate size of Frisbees.

"Well, don't just sit there, young Mr. Carson. Get your hat and Bible, and escort an old woman into church. And if I smell like duck, don't say anything. Simply forgive the fowl." She winked, a small cackle lifting from her lips.

"Uh, yes, ma'am." Lance slid his hat overtop his hair and snatched his Bible.

She tilted her head up and smiled at him as his feet touched the ground, and relief filtered through his veins. Miss Jane didn't hate him. It surprised him to discover how much that mattered.

\*\*\*

Sophie had spotted Lance somewhere between the last song and the beginning of the message. Because she'd been looking for him. Sitting right there beside Craig and his foster boys, she'd been surreptitiously watching for Lance Carson. Her mother would not be impressed. Daddy either, for that matter.

She felt an explosive contradiction of reactions when she spotted Lance in the back row next to Miss Jane, who was oddly out of her normal seat across from the row Brenna and Grant typically shared. Usually. Where was that predictable-as-clockwork guy? Seemed the doings of the Big Prairie community were sliding topsy turvy that Sunday morning.

Or maybe that was her. Sophie refocused on the doings at the front, where her attention ought to have been the whole time. But oh, it was sure hard not to steal another glance over her shoulder.

How could a simple glimpse of a man she'd only met once be this thrilling? And what was she supposed to do with that sitting in church next to Craig Erikson? Ugh. They needed to talk—clear some things up and cut some implied (maybe?) ties.

This. This was why Sophie hadn't dated much. The few times she had, things seemed way too complicated, more trouble than it was worth. Well, it wasn't the only reason. There was a whole hill of fear mixed in there as well. But she had too much running around in her mind at the moment to figure that part in too. Suffice it to say, she was better off as the eternal friend of the male species and nothing more.

Interesting. That claim seemed to stick about as well as wet slime on a buttered pan when it came to her thoughts and inclinations regarding the tall vineyard cowboy sitting in the back.

Pastor Lander concluded his sermon over Matthew 8—something Sophie should have been paying attention to. The peace that would result from trusting Jesus, who even the wind and the waves obeyed, would be a good thing regarding her unintentional love triangle.

Oh, for heaven's sake. Sophie had not landed herself in a *love triangle*! She and Craig weren't technically dating. And she and Lance were simply...

New friends.

Craig pushed off the chair beside hers after the last amen, rising slowly to his feet. He stared forward for a moment, as if gathering his thoughts, glanced toward the general direction Brenna and Grant would be (or rather, where Grant should have been, if he'd attended), and then settled a gaze on Sophie's face. "Everything work out okay yesterday?"

Sophie's smile felt full. Maybe too full. "It did." Why was heat touching her face? For heaven's sake. "I got to see the vineyard and hang out at the lodge for a bit. It's lovely."

This news didn't seem to bother Craig in the least. "I hear it's impressive."

"You haven't been?"

"Haven't been around Big Prairie much, remember?"

Right. He'd left seven years ago following an accident that took the life of Brenna's younger brother. Craig had told her some of the story, including the part where he felt like it was his fault. It hadn't been, of that Sophie was sure, and seeing the confident, mostly happy, easygoing man that Craig usually was carry that kind of burden made Sophie's heart ache.

Also made her a touch mad at her good friend Brenna, who seemed to hold the past against her ex-boyfriend. The ex-boyfriend part was only recently known to Sophie. That too provoked a bit of irritation toward the other woman. Sophie wished Brenna had told her about it when Sophie had asked about Craig before the first week of school. Instead, all Brenna had claimed was that "everyone in Big Prairie knew Craig."

Now things felt awkward. Why would Brenna have kept her history with Craig such a big secret? Sophie had some suspicions. Ideas that were confirmed on the occasions Sophie had witnessed the tricky, though electrified, interactions between Craig and Brenna.

All the more reason to have that talk with Craig.

"I should have called you last night." Craig angled his stance to face her. "I'm sorry."

"Don't be. I told you, you don't owe me anything." Was this the time, or the place, to have that discussion? Ashton and Trent, Craig's foster boys, waited behind the former football star's large frame. Trent, the older of the pair, threw air punches, though the grin on Ashton's face proclaimed it was all play. Still, it gave her the answer. Not now. Not there.

Craig gripped his neck and looked toward his shoe. One of his more subtle tells—he felt either bad or uncomfortable—and as much as she found it amusing when the big man blushed, she didn't want him to feel either about this situation. Reaching, she touched his elbow with the tips of her fingers.

"Craig, truly, I was fine. Lance took good care of me." And now she might be the one to blush.

His firm mouth softened, and those bright-blue eyes sought hers. "I'm glad. I haven't spent much time with him, but he had the respect of everyone back in high school. Smart. Hard working. Honest. Sure hated to see him go through the things he did."

Sophie's ever-ready smile froze. Then melted. What things? Tempted to blurt out the question, she seamed her lips. Lance's mom had died when he was a teen. That must have been it. Right? Goodness, this sweet country town carried its share of mysteries.

Those air punches being tossed by the brothers near Craig's legs turned into contact hits. Probably by accident, but the result was the same. Ashton yowled. Trent froze, his tense little body all defense as he clearly expected the gavel to drop on him. Knowing Craig's tender care for the boys, Sophie sagged with a deep empathy for all of them. This thing Craig had come home to—a sick mom and two foster kids—it was. Just straight up hard.

And she might possibly add to Craig's load of disappointments and burdens. Wasn't she a peach?

*Smile, it'll help.*

Doubting the truth of that well-worn mantra, Sophie grinned anyway. "Never a dull moment, hmm?"

"Not ever. You'll have to come see the handprints we've gained on the back door."

"Handprints?"

"In yellow paint." Craig pushed up a half grin. The kind that was both tired and surrendered. "I'd best get them out of here while we still have a shot a peace. See you at school tomorrow?"

"Sure."

His back was to her before she had the response out, and within two heartbeats he was escorting his short charges toward the exit, one on each side and his hands on their slim shoulders. His posture curled in a way that read *defeat*, making Sophie want to run to his side, give him her peppiest of pep talks, and assure him he was doing fine. More than fine. Craig was doing good work, even if he couldn't see it through the weeds he'd fallen into.

But maybe she wasn't the one he needed to cheer him on. That electrical undercurrent she sensed between Craig and Brenna came to mind. She refused to ponder it, as thinking about it would not be helpful. Instead, Sophie switched her thoughts to prayer.

*Father, lift Craig's spirit. Give him Your strength for this hard thing he's doing.*

She trailed behind them, exiting first the worship center and then the building. The sun embraced the warmer autumn day with a cheery brightness, and Sophie squinted as she moved past the building.

Craig and the boys stopped at a familiar mud-splattered pickup, and the man he addressed nearly matched his tall build. Knowing both the red truck and the hat on the man's head, Sophie held her breath.

She had no reason to fear. *You've done nothing wrong. And they're both reasonable men.* Still, her chest strummed like a well-practiced musician was picking his way through "Dueling Banjos," and her heart was his banjo. Especially when Craig glanced back at her.

He smiled. She exhaled and at the same time scolded her ridiculous reaction.

Lance tilted his head enough to make eye contact with her around Craig's shoulders. Ah...those eyes. She felt her expression go mushy—and hoped neither man still watching her noticed.

Straightening her shoulders, she approached the pair—well, actually the quartet, because the Fulton boys were still beside Craig—with her ready smile. "I see you've made it back down that muddy road, Lance."

"I did, though it's pretty solid now. Mostly rutted, which also makes for a jarring ride."

"Ah." She stopped beside them. "I'm glad you made the trip."

"See." The comment drifted from a spot behind Lance, from a woman Sophie rather adored. Jane Hopewell, or Miss Jane, as everyone in Big Prairie called her, strode the length of Lance's pickup bed and rooted herself beside the small circle they'd made. "I am not the only one happy you've made an appearance, Mr. Carson. Which means you must do it again."

Lance shuffled back a couple steps. Perhaps to allow more space for Miss Jane. Or maybe to gain a moment to school his response. Miss Jane had a reputation for being direct. Wise, loving, and welcoming. But also, direct.

"Yes, ma'am."

Miss Jane grinned up at the tall cowboy with a look you'd expect from a proud grandparent. She slid her long fingers through the crook of his elbow. "Excellent. And I have another brilliant idea. How about lunch? All of you?"

Uh. Hmm. Might be fun. Might be terribly uncomfortable. Lance's glance slipped from Miss Jane, bounced between Sophie and Craig, and then stopped again on Sophie. Clearly uncomfortable.

"I appreciate the invite, Miss Jane," Craig said. "But I'm going to take the boys home. Mom wasn't feeling well enough to come to church today, so I think I'll find something to throw on the grill. Thanks though."

"Of course, Craig. And you tell your mom I'll be by tomorrow with a jar of soup and some of my homemade jam."

"She'd love that, Miss Jane." Craig nodded and then moved away, tossing a small wave toward them.

"Well." Miss Jane slipped her free hand around Sophie's arm. "How about it, you two?"

Sophie looked at Lance. Though appearing less uncomfortable, he still looked unsure.

"I have to go get my car from the vineyard." Um... Oh dear. Did that sound...uh, questionable? She rushed to explain herself. "I went for a drive yesterday, not realizing how muddy the roads would be, and got stuck. Lance rescued me, and then my car, and now it's out at the lodge."

"How serendipitous." Miss Jane's eyes brightened, which was notable because they always seemed to smile, as if she had some kind of joy gene that made her expressions sparkle. "And if I join the two of you, will I be intruding? We could go by the café and put together a picnic of turkey on rye and fresh peaches."

"You wouldn't be intruding at all." Lance finally used his voice, and Sophie rather thrilled at hearing it. "But I have food at the lodge. You don't need to—"

"Nonsense. I invited you to lunch, and I will provide it. With delight. Shall we all ride out together?"

Lance looked at Sophie, one corner of his mouth playing at a smile. "Sounds good. Sophie?"

"Perfect." Sophie directed her own grin at Miss Jane.

There was something about the woman. Calming and yet challenging—in a good way. Like her very presence lent the strength for a person to be their very best self.

Who couldn't use some of that?

***

"This, Lance Carson, is stunning." Miss Jane leaned back in her chair, her attention a sort of far-off gaze set on the view beyond the large lodge windows. "Have I told you that before?"

Lance watched the older woman to his right, looking for the sliver of rebuke he felt certain Miss Jane would be dealing him at any moment. "I believe you said something like that at the grand opening two years ago. And perhaps last year at the pickers' picnic."

"Ah." Miss Jane's satisfied expression didn't rob her of the wonder she carried with her everywhere she went. "Well, it is as true now as it was then. Simply splendid." She turned her eyes, complete with smile lines, toward him. "I am proud of you."

At that, his gut clenched. *Just say what you are really thinking.* Surely she had more behind her lunch agenda. Something to discuss. To deride. Certainly she'd heard of his plans for investment, and she would have an opinion about that. Lance inhaled, willing calmness into his roiling stomach.

What if sincerity propelled Miss Jane's loving compliments and not an underlying motive of reproach? Perhaps Miss Jane hadn't heard the rumors rumbling among the business owners in town. That would leave room for the heartfelt possibility, and Lance had only ever known Miss Jane to be honest.

Somehow that didn't make him feel much better.

"I appreciate that, Miss Jane." Lance surveyed the view of his land before brushing a glance at Miss Jane.

She met his response with a small nod and shifted her attention to Sophie, who sat on his left. "And let's talk about you, Miss Shultz."

With a quick move of his neck, Lance found Sophie nearly choking on the lemonade she'd sipped. After brushing her lips with a napkin, she cleared her throat and sat forward. "Me?"

"Yes. I know only of the surface data on you, as you did not grow up here. Seems a shame—and that would be mine—as you've lived here for what? Nearly four years?"

"A bit over three." Sophie's eyes slipped upward toward Lance, a look of uncertainty.

"Well." Miss Jane's jawline firmed with determination as she dipped another firm nod. "Let's become actual friends, shall we? I cannot reconcile not knowing my neighbors. How am I supposed to love them if I don't even know them?"

"You're Sophie's neighbor?" Lance asked.

Miss Jane stared at him quizzically. "In literal geography? I have no idea." Her brows went up, and she shifted back to Sophie. "Are we?"

"I don't think so."

"Hmm." Miss Jane leaned in. "Doesn't matter either way. That wasn't what I was talking about. Now, let's begin."

"Oh." Sophie seemed to contain a laugh. "Okay then. Where?"

"At the beginning, of course."

"Of course. I was born on a quiet summer morning—which was good because my mom didn't have classes in the summer. She was still in college, you see. And single. Her ex-boyfriend—my biological father, whom I've never met—didn't stick around long enough to even know she was pregnant. Apparently he didn't care, as she contacted him and he simply stated that he could not be responsible."

Whoa. Sophie was taking that *begin at the beginning* thing seriously. Lance inhaled as a prick of sympathy jabbed him. At least he'd known both of his parents, even if they were gone now.

Sophie had paused, her gaze fixed on Lance. When he connected with it, she shifted back to Miss. Jane. "Too much?"

"Not for me. Too many stories begin this way. But the good news is, our beginnings never have to dictate our middles or endings. I, for example, was an orphan. I have no idea why my parents didn't raise me, as in my time, those sort of questions were often not asked. I was delivered to the front porch of the local doctor—Dr. Jacobson. But that is a story for another time. We want to hear yours."

Actually, while that had been true, now Lance had wanted to hear both. How had he not known that bit of history about Miss Jane? The woman had been his Sunday school teacher when he was seven. A faithful friend to his parents while his mother had been so sick. Had delivered meals to him, even well beyond the typical casserole parade timeline after his dad's funeral. Sitting there listening to the two women, Lance suddenly realized how little he knew about many of the people in town.

*Love your neighbor as yourself.*

He didn't even know them.

The sting of conviction. Especially when it came on the heels of an early twinge of guilt. Both legitimate. Both things he'd rather find a way to ignore.

"...so we moved in with my grandparents—my mom's parents—until she graduated and found a full-time job. Mom was determined that I would not suffer for her bad choices, and in that, she decided I needed the best opportunities. The best school district. Music and dance lessons. Every opportunity she could pry open, she did it. I feel like sometimes she was operating out of guilt. Like she was doing penance before God or something. But mostly, she really loved me. That's precious, you know?" Sophie had leaned toward Miss Jane, her expression so full of depth and love as she talked with Miss Jane like they were long-lost best friends, exchanging the joys and burdens of life.

"I do know. Love is mighty powerful." There was that firm nod of Miss Jane's again. "And you love your mother back. I can see that as plain as I see this wrinkled old face I meet every morning in the mirror."

Sophie chuckled softly. "Smile lines are not wrinkles, Miss Jane. And you are one of the loveliest people I've ever met. I've thought so for quite some time."

With a wave of her hand, Miss Jane dismissed the compliment. "And now? Is your mother all by herself since you've left Omaha?"

"Oh, no." Sophie fingered the rim of her lemonade glass, a fresh look of soft joy wreathing her expression. "No, Mom married a man who I thought might be the best prince charming the world could offer."

"Ah. How old were you?"

"Almost fourteen when they married."

Miss Jane laughed. "You adored this man as a teenager! He must be quite something."

"He is. He's my daddy." Sophie's confident, smooth speech cracked there, and a sheen made her dark eyes sparkle.

There was quite a story there, Lance was certain. And he hoped Sophie would share it.

She sniffed, sat back, and looked over the vineyard beyond the lodge. "That's when I learned—well, maybe really grabbed—on to what my mom and my grandparents had been trying to teach me."

"What's that, lovie?" Miss Jane asked.

"That God takes the bad and He turns it for good. He has such a tender, personal way of making His presence known." Sophie's throat bobbed. "Miss Jane, I hated that I didn't know my dad. That I didn't have one. More, I hated that in the place I'd been put, I was...alone. Very few people looked like me. Had my skin color, my dark curly hair. And my backstory that went with it. Made me pretty lonely, and honestly, resentful, in here." She tapped her chest.

Miss Jane crossed her arms, anchoring her elbows to the table. "And in that hard place, God sent you your daddy?"

"He did. A superhero if there ever was one."

Miss Jane lifted her chin, a lovely smile on her profile, shut her eyes, and then hummed. "Mm, yes. You are good."

The space between them held with a kind of sacred silence.

"Amen," Sophie whispered.

It was then that Lance realized that had been a prayer. A praise. And to him, it seemed, heaven replied with a whisper, straight to his heart.

*You will see it too.*

He was almost too scared to believe it. More, that was crazy. He'd never heard God speak to him in such a way—tender and personal as if only to him.

Not once, in any of his hard places.

# Chapter Six

Sophie fiddled with the remote as she curled up on her small brown sofa, a mug of honeyed citrus tea in one hand and pleasant thoughts drifting through her mind like butterflies on a warm August afternoon.

For all her trepidation, the day had turned out pleasant. Even with the discomfort about the Craig situation, and the awkward way in which she did end up at the vineyard for lunch, it was as if it had all been meant to be. Choreographed by the Master himself.

Sweet Miss Jane. Sophie had liked her to begin with, this older woman with more energy than most of Sophie's high school students, more zeal for life than several of her college classmates had shown, and more industry than many workers and business owners half Miss Jane's age. With all that, it shouldn't have surprised Sophie to discover that Miss Jane lived with a Christian authenticity that was unique. Surprised she was though. Pleasantly.

If ever there was a woman to imitate, it was Miss Jane.

A humble gratitude fell over Sophie as she ruminated about the afternoon. Though she knew Miss Jane was kind, loving, and blunt, she couldn't help feeling that there was a special bond between them during the course of their conversation that afternoon. Truth was, Sophie was certain everyone who sat with Miss Jane likely felt that way—which somehow did not rob that joyful sense, but rather expanded it. Miss Jane was a special person indeed.

Laying aside the remote, Sophie instead folded her hands, leaned back against the cushions, and reviewed the conversations and emotions of the day, and as she did so, her heart turned toward gratitude. For new friends—including both Miss Jane and Lance, who proved himself again to be a gentleman. A quiet one, but a kind one. For the redemption of her mother's story, which obviously bled into her own. For the gift of her daddy, a man who continued to show the heart of God's great compassion and generous love, as he had from the beginning. For this quiet small town of Big Prairie, which claimed her as its own as she claimed it as home.

With so much to praise God for, who needed to binge on a distraction via a screen? It'd been too long since Sophie had set aside a quiet evening to write out her thoughts. Tonight they would be more words of thanksgiving that would revive her spirit, make that smile she always aimed for more authentic, and give her heaven's perspective on her students, her colleagues, her friends, and her ambitions. So rather than reaching for the remote again, Sophie left the sofa to retrieve her journal and a gel pen, then returned to do exactly that.

After settling under the white crocheted afghan her aunt Laura had given her as a graduation gift, and taking a warming draw of her tea, she put pen to paper. The beginning came easily. She started as she often had before, with a psalm.

*Bless the Lord, oh my soul, and all that is within me.*
*Bless His holy name.*
*Bless the Lord, oh my soul, and forget not all of His benefits.*
*He who redeems your life from the pit,*
*Who crowns you with lovingkindness,*
*Who heals all your diseases and satisfies your soul so that your strength is like that of the eagles.*
*Bless the Lord, oh my soul. Bless the Lord...*

As she did often, because she must, Sophie paused there. Marinated in the simple pleasure of praise. Of remembering the goodness of her Father in heaven. And then her pen took on life, scrawling the overflow of her heart.

*Ah, but what about when hard things come?*

> *Bless the Lord.*

*Yes, but when sickness takes hold?*

> *Bless the Lord.*

*Still, there are times things go wrong and turn out badly.*

> *Bless the Lord.*

*Will you always cling to this?*

> *With all my heart.*

*Why would you do such a blind thing?*

> *Not blind at all, because we see with faith. I know my Savior lives. I will rest with quiet trust in His goodness, because His faithfulness never fails.*

*So then?*

> *Bless the Lord, oh my soul. Until I see with both faith and eyes. For what is now is only a shadow. Someday, my hand in His, I will walk in the brightness of His light.*

*Bless the Lord.*

The ink glided over the page as Sophie penned the words of her own psalm, her mind ever bent toward music, composing a simple melody that would suit the words pouring from her heart.

Should she put the verse to tune?

Perhaps.

Maybe a project to work on with Craig?

*No.*

The answer came to mind with strength, as if not her own.

*Let that one go.*

Indeed. She should. She would. As soon as she figured out what to say.

In the space that settled in her heart, one of peace about what must be done, there came a beat, and then her mind turned toward Lance.

*Lord?*

Gentle silence. Sophie wasn't sure how to interpret it, but when she closed her eyes, there waited an image of a tall cowboy whose green eyes were both kind and electrifying. Whose shy smile set her heart to music.

He'd been quiet that afternoon. At moments, perhaps even withdrawn, as if he felt out of place in his own lodge. Or worried about something important. But he listened well, and when she spoke of her backstory, he seemed intent on listening, absorbing. As if he felt as much as he heard. A quality she had always adored in her daddy—a man of empathy.

Sighing, Sophie laid aside her pen and journal, took another sip of her tea, and then settled deep into the cushions of the sofa. Eyes falling shut, she couldn't help but grin as she pictured Lance again.

*Bless the Lord, oh my soul...*
*Bless Him for good men.*

***

Seemed Miss Jane had set her mind on him for the long haul.

Lance laid his cell phone down beside the keyboard on his desk and looked up at the ceiling. He'd opted to set up his office in the loft space over the kitchen in the lodge, though he'd have a better view of the vineyard from the old office back in the house. But up there, with only the dormer window that faced toward the pasture lands to the east and across the bend of the river—the opposite direction from the vines—he could look out and remember the long game. He had more to do, because responsibility demanded it.

With a roll of his neck, he looked toward that window and to the view beyond.

If Lane would listen—just try to understand. If his younger brother would come home, stand right there in that lodge he hadn't even seen yet, then Lance could *show* him what he envisioned. It wasn't what Lane assumed.

But Lane refused. Stubbornly remained in Wyoming, roaming the backcountry like a half-wild man without a home. Wouldn't even entertain a phone call—*out of range*—was usually the texted explanation, sent hours past every attempt Lance had made.

None of that had anything to do with Miss Jane. Well, actually, in a very roundabout way, it sort of did. Because she wanted to meet with Lance again, to talk. Certainly this time, without the innocent and lovely company Sophie Shultz had been at lunch three days before, Miss Jane would let him have a real piece of her mind.

*You always assume the worst. Do you know that? Lighten up, brother. You'll die young at this rate.*

Ha! Words of wisdom from the nineteen-year-old Lane had been back then. Little had either Carson boy known that in less than twenty-four hours, when they finally did hear an update about their dad, their lives would unravel for the second time in six years. Afterward, their relationship had come completely undone. Seemed there was no mending of that mess, no matter how much Lance ached for it.

But. Lane had a point back then. Lance did assume the worst—of people and situations—and he was on ulcer meds to prove it. Blame it on all the responsibility. All the weight of needing things to go right if he had any shot at all of bringing Lane back. And all the disappointments of the past that proved to him how quickly and disastrously things could go wrong.

But there was something about Miss Jane...

The way her face nearly glowed as she tipped her chin up, eyes closed, and whispered, *Mm, yes. You are good.* Words so beautiful and simple he couldn't help think on them. Yet so powerful his eyes pricked with emotion.

It was longing. That was what the emotion had been. A longing to believe that what Miss Jane had said was true—that God was good. And a fear that he would discover, as it seemed life had implied multiple times before, that while that may be true for some, it wasn't for Lance Carson.

God was not good to him.

Well, that wasn't entirely what he thought. He didn't believe God wasn't good to him, but rather that to God, Lance was easily overlooked. Maybe even forgotten. And that hurt more than a man wanted to claim. It cloaked him in a cold loneliness that made him want to curl up away from the world and wish that life was different. That *he* was different. Somehow that he was more noticeable to God, less awkward to people, and better at life in general.

Lance looked back down at the phone, resting near his hand, and came back to the conversation he'd had minutes before with the lady in question. He'd meet with Miss Jane. Listen to her as she laid out all the reasons that what he was pursuing behind the backs of the local Big Prairie businesses was wrong. He'd nod. Hear her out politely because one of the lasting lessons he learned from his dad was that a gentleman and a good businessman needed the ability to listen well—and then he'd leave her with a simple apology.

"I'm sorry, Miss Jane," he'd say. "But I can't withdraw on this deal. Please know, it's not personal, and I have all the respect in the world for you, and the Garretts, and for Wes and Jaycee. But this is business."

Business he desperately needed to succeed in if he'd ever have a chance to mend things with Lane.

That was all he'd offer—sans the last part. Because he was certain that even if he tried to explain, Miss Jane wouldn't understand.

\*\*\*

She'd been thinking about it for over a week. Avoiding it, if she was willing to admit the truth. She'd rather not.

But it was time to wiggle into her big-girl pants and go have the *talk*. The DTR talk that would end the mild guilt that irritated her every time she thought about texting the handsome cowboy vineyard owner who lived down that fateful dirt road. Well, she didn't only think about *texting* him. She thought about how much she'd like to stare into those green eyes while he listened to her as if she had the most important things to say that he'd ever care to hear.

Goodness, her mind had gone from sensible to romantic mush within the space of a week. That couldn't possibly be good, could it? Ah, but who could help such hopeful imaginings? *Stable, level-headed people who didn't get swept up in ridiculous whirlwind romantic notions.*

There was that—and for her whole adult life, she'd been that stable, level-headed girl. Which was likely why she was ever the *friend*. What if she threw that restraining order to the corner and gave this...whatever it was she imagined with Lance...a real, mushy-hearted shot?

This time, she was gonna do that. Right after her talk with Craig.

Resolved, Sophie gripped her candy bar latte, fresh from Garret's, and walked herself through the halls of the middle school where Craig's classroom—such as it was—had been assigned. Once she reached the doorway, she paused and drew a long breath. *Smile. It'll help.*

She smiled, then knocked on the open door. "Morning, Mr. Erikson."

Craig swiveled in his chair and looked up from his computer where, by the appearance of the program the district used on the screen, he had been catching up on grades.

"Morning, sunshine."

Her mouth wobbled. Ugh. Why was this always so hard? And with Craig, with everything going on in his life, this time was even more difficult. But Mom always told her honesty was the best policy.

"I'm sorry I haven't seen much of you." Craig stood, shoving his hands into his pockets while he sauntered toward her. "You must think I'm—"

Sophie held up a hand. "The thing is, Craig..."

Head tilted, shock registered on his face, along with immediate understanding. Sophie wanted to groan at the tightness in her chest when a flash of red raced up his neck and tinged his cheeks.

Usually she found it amusing when the giant Craig Erikson blushed. Not today. Today the effect her words had on him made her miserable. His gaze wandered toward his shoes while he gripped his neck with one hand.

She'd vastly underestimated their relationship.

"Oh dear," she breathed, a catch in her words. "I really, really don't want to say this..."

Recovered, he lifted his gaze to meet hers. "It's okay, Sophie. Actually, if you're going to say this isn't working, then you should find some comfort in knowing that it's mutual."

She drew up straight. "What?" The shock swiftly ran into relief, and this time she didn't have to remind herself to smile as she stepped forward. "Oh my goodness, are you serious, Craig? I've been agonizing over this!"

"I'm sorry for that." His hand fell from his neck and met her elbow.

"Yeah, me too!" She breathed a shaky laugh.

"I should have said something sooner." That hand still on her elbow squeezed. "I just...really do like you, but—"

She gripped his elbow in return and then leaned her forehead onto his shoulder, her heart throbbing with absolute relief. "But we're not going to make it past friends."

"Right."

They stepped apart, a mutual understanding now solid between them. Thank heaven! Sophie stepped back and grinned up at him and then wiped her brow. "Whew. Glad to have that established."

"Me too."

She lifted her coffee cup. "But we're still good for morning coffee sometimes, right?"

A sheepish expression made him look adorable as he shook his head. "I'm actually not a coffee drinker, Sophie. But I'd be disappointed if I didn't see you with your mug at seven forty-five at least two or three times a week."

Not a coffee drinker? All these weeks of morning coffee, and he wasn't a coffee drinker? What did she put in that Yeti he carried all the time? Plain old boring good-for-you water? Clearly they were not a match made in heaven.

She wanted to giggle. "Right. And I'll still get a dance or two out of you at homecoming, right?"

Homecoming...hmm. What would Lance say? Strike that. She was *not* asking Lance Carson to a high school homecoming dance. Returning to her adult self, she waited for Craig's response. It took a while. Why did he look so uncomfortable? Surely he hadn't banked on her as his date. They weren't actually *in* high school.

"Craig?"

"Yeah." The response came out rushed. "Yeah, we'll definitely have to work the floor."

What was going on with that? Her gut hinted that it had something to do with Brenna Blaum, and as she remembered the way the two of them had acted right after the adventure race a few weeks back—all close and adorable, immediately followed by stiff, cold, and awkward—her mind became convinced.

Oh boy. Things could get real sticky, since she knew Brenna and Grant had been acting weird lately as well. Mom was right—honesty was the best policy. She hoped her friends had the courage to try it and that things would work out without anyone getting too damaged.

Setting that all aside, because, really, she was no longer involved, Sophie met Craig's eyes. "I'm glad we're friends, Craig Erikson."

And that was the bare-bones truth. Relief set her free, even as her mind drifted back to Lance Carson for the rest of the day. She'd text him that evening and see where it went from there.

***

Lance patted his freshly shaved face with a towel and met his own gaze in the mirror. *Get it over with.*

He'd rather have the flu.

Raising his arm, he rolled his watch to face him and checked the time. There were forty-five minutes until he was to meet Miss Jane at her café in town. He only needed twenty to get there, which left him more than half that to fill with...

What?

He could pray. That was what Dad would advise. He hardly knew what to ask for, though, and wasn't convinced that it mattered much. Even if he had the gall to ask God to make the business owners in town not despise him coupled with a plea for this next endeavor to work out—a contradiction if ever there was one—he wasn't sure he'd be heard.

With a backward step, he met the wall and leaned against it and shut his eyes. Why had everything gotten so complicated? All he'd wanted back in high school was a small section of river land where he could try to grow some dreams. He hadn't wanted everything else. Didn't need it.

*You're the oldest, Lance. And frankly, the more responsible of my two sons. But remember what an inheritance is for. I mean for you to be the provider, to take care of the land and the family. It's to be a blessing, but not one that you squander on yourself. Understand?*

Yeah, Lance had understood. Even back then, when Dad had revealed the details of his will—not thinking it'd be necessary within a year—Lance felt the weight of it like the universe had been anchored to his shoulders. Strength he didn't have in the first place failed him. He'd wanted to argue, to tell his dad to change his official wishes, but Dad wasn't one to bend. Especially not on something he was convinced about. A last will and testament fell into that category.

Hadn't known back then Dad hadn't explained things to Lane.

"Thanks, Dad." With eyes shut, Lance muttered under his breath.

The beep-beep-beep tone of his phone drew him away from the bathroom and out of his niggling resentment. Finding it on his dresser, he checked the screen. A text. From Sophie.

He ignored the leap in his chest as he tapped it open, vaguely conscious that he held his breath.

*Hey, stranger. Didn't see you at church yesterday.*

Something spread wide and warm in his chest. She'd noticed. And missed him.

*Didn't make it in.*

*Everything okay?*

*Yes. Everything out here is good.*

Several long, pulse-throbbing moments went by without her responding. Ah! How he wanted her to respond. Was this a friendly check-in—maybe something the pastor at church had encouraged the people to do to get straying souls to come back? Man, he really hoped not. *Come on, Sophie. Don't be—*

A fresh beep cut off his plea.

*I keep hoping I'm going to bump into you again. Seems you're never in town.*

Lance dropped to the edge of his bed as relief crashed over him.

*I'm heading that way in a few minutes.*

*Yeah?*

A hopeful grin poked on one corner of his mouth. *You could bump into me at Miss Jane's in about thirty.*

*I could, huh?*

*It's an option.*

*Any other options?*

Wow, was she flirting? Really seemed like flirting. Maybe he really wanted it to seem like flirting. How could a guy tell on text? He'd been bad at gauging the flirt in a live-and-in-person situation. This was a whole new level of—

*How about I see you in thirty and we can talk about it?*

Lance rubbed his jaw and grinned like a fool at the phone. That was flirting. Had to be, right?

Guess he'd find out in less than an hour. And bonus, Miss Jane wouldn't have the private audience in which she would have opportunity to give it to him straight.

He barely cared that his conscience named him a coward.

# Chapter Seven

Anxiety rolled through him. Miss Jane set a mug of strong black coffee in front of him—his preference when she offered him a long list of fancy-flavored frou-frou coffee options.

"There now." She nodded in that firm but pleasant way of hers and eased her wiry frame into the chair across from him. "An easy keeper. I like that. Wouldn't have guessed it, with that vineyard and fancy lodge of yours. But you can't tell about people that easy, can you?"

"I guess you can't." With that clear blue gaze fastened on him, Lance fought against the instinct to squirm in his chair. If he could distract Miss Jane with small talk for a few minutes, Sophie would waltz in to his rescue. *Hurry up, lovely lady.* "I wouldn't have figured you for a lady with a taste for sweet rich coffees, so there we go."

Laughter lit her face. "There we go indeed. Actually, I'm not usually one for such." She lifted her mug. "This is peach and ginger tea, with a touch of honey. I only have the rich loaded caffeine on occasion. Perhaps that means you have got me figured."

"I'd guess not. I'm not very good at understanding people in general."

"Ah." Miss Jane's smile tamed as she tipped her head. "Is that what keeps you away?"

"Away?"

"From town. Church. All of us."

Great. Blew that whole small-talk mission, didn't he? He looked to the table, his big hands gripping the warm mug in front of him because he didn't know what else to do with them.

"I've wondered if it was lingering grief." Miss Jane's voice drifted like a warm August breeze. "But maybe not? I've been pondering the assumptions we make of people and their actions. Thinking that we try to calculate too much, simply accept too little."

"Why?" He wasn't sure why he'd let that question slip out. Wouldn't lead them back to the security of small talk.

"Why have I been thinking about that?"

Lance nodded, curiosity pushing harder. It was an interesting thing to ponder.

Miss Jane inhaled, her gaze wandering toward the wide window that framed Main Street outside. "I wonder what we really gain when we dissect another human. We say we're after understanding, but lately, I guess I'm not sure. I wonder if it wouldn't be safer—and kinder—to simply let people show us themselves as they feel comfortable? That way seems so much more...I don't know...natural and gentler. Like the difference between slicing an unopened bud so that we can investigate the color of the bloom and allowing that bud to burst forth on its own. With the first, you gain information. The second, the beauty in its own time, along with some answers."

Lance visualized the comparison. "The second would be better for the bud, no arguing that."

"Yes." Miss Jane lifted her tea to her lips, inhaled the fragrant steam, and then sipped.

Though still antsy for this interview to be over with, Lance wondered where all of it was leading.

After lowering her mug to the table, its landing a dull thud, Miss Jane straightened. "I'm a bit of a sparrow sometimes, Mr. Carson. You'll have to forgive me for flitting from one thing to another."

"That's all right." Though he did still wonder...

"The thing is, I wanted to change something, if you're willing."

And here it came... He swallowed, grabbing hold of the resolve within that he'd need to stay his course.

"I was thinking about our luncheon two Sunday's past, and I think it should be a regular thing."

"What?" Lance snapped his lips shut, certain he'd allowed his mouth to swing open in shock.

"Our Sunday afternoon lunch. I very much enjoyed it, and I was thinking about how lovely it would be if it became a habit between us. Perhaps not *every* Sunday—wouldn't want you to grow tired of me." She chuckled. "I would provide the food, of course, if I could come enjoy the lovely view at your lodge, as well as your company?"

Talk about whiplash. What was she aiming for with all this? "I...I..."

A tinkling bell from the front of the café saved him from continuous stutter.

"I thought that was you." Sophie waltzed in, charming as you please, with that infectious—not to mention beautiful—smile and all the relief he required.

"Well, my new friend, Sophie Shultz." Unpretentious as ever, Miss Jane rose to her feet.

Sophie waved her down. "Don't get up. I don't need anything. I saw this man with a cowboy hat resting on his knee, and knew I'd seen him somewhere before." She winked. "Now remind me again. Where was that?"

"On a muddy road?" he answered dryly.

"No, that's not it. I think it was at church." She snapped. "Yes, that was it. At church."

Miss Jane clapped. "Girls tend to notice a good-looking cowboy at church."

Sophie smirked while a rush of heat raced up Lance's neck. He cleared his throat.

Snagging a chair from a nearby table, Sophie joined the pair.

"Can I get you something to drink?" Miss Jane asked.

"No, ma'am. I'm good. Am I interrupting though?"

"Not one bit." Miss Jane nodded. "In fact, I think that you should have a say."

"A say?"

"Yes, because the idea involves you too."

It did? Well, then...

"What idea is that?" Sophie asked.

"Our luncheon that Sunday at the lodge. I think that it should be a regular thing with us. Don't you?"

"With you and Lance? Absolutely."

"And you?" Miss Jane leaned forward to grip Sophie's hand, the gleam in her eyes rather suspicious. "Don't you want to join us?"

Lance knew the exact moment Sophie turned to gauge his reaction, because he was watching her. And in that exact moment, when her eyes connected with his, he also knew life had somehow changed.

"Do you want me to?"

He heard her question clear enough, but in his mind it became shorter. Simpler. More profound. Something more like *do you want me?*

"Yes."

And the world shifted.

\*\*\*

Sophie nearly floated.

She couldn't have merely imagined the chemistry firing between them before. Not with the way he'd held a look on her as if their souls had connected.

"Well."

Oh. Oh my goodness, they were being so...rude. Even still, Sophie twisted her chin to find Miss Jane sitting across from them, right where she'd been the whole time, brows raised in mild amusement.

"It's settled, I think." Laughter edged Miss Jane's voice. "Unless Lance has any objections, which clearly he does not."

Sophie was not prone to blushing often. Not the way Craig Erikson had been. But by the scalding of her cheeks right then, she was definitely blushing. A quick peek at Lance told her he was too.

So then it *was* mutual. Praise heaven! She caught her bottom lip, tucking in a sheepish—but victorious—grin.

"I think it will be lovely." Miss Jane tipped her mug to her lips, her eyes dancing with merriment. "Three new friends becoming three old friends. Oh, the possibilities!"

Glancing at Lance, Sophie wondered if his expression of deep thought meant he was already having regrets. He met her look, and his lightly furrowed brow smoothed. Then the corner of his mouth poked up.

"I suppose this was planned by the two of you?" he said.

"What?" Sophie said.

"To get me into church more often."

"Psh." Miss Jane slapped the table. "You're a grown man who can get himself to church. I told you why. I simply need to know my neighbors more. Including the young man who grew up and out of my little old Sunday school class."

Lance crossed his arms. "Is that right?"

Miss Jane pinned a challenging scowl on him. "Are you dissecting me even after our conversation?"

Lance loosened his arms, looking down to his lap as he did so. Sophie wondered what she'd missed. His pause wasn't long enough for her to ask.

"No, ma'am. I mean, yes, ma'am, I guess I was. I'm sorry."

"Accepted." Miss Jane held him in a firm, approving gaze and nodded. "And for the record, a person is responsible for his own relationship with the Lord. Getting to church has only small bits to do with it, and I'd die to think that you heard from me that church attendance equaled salvation. It most certainly does not." She thumped a spot over her heart. "What's going on in here and here"—she tapped her temple—"that matter's a whole lot. And so does what we do outside the church. In our everyday. In fact, there's a part in Jeremiah where God tells the prophet to go out to the gates and warn the people that they were not supposed to think that because they had the place called 'the Lord's house' that they were free to do whatever they wanted. He told them to *walk with Him!* When they didn't listen—didn't obey—well. Not good. All of it is about your relationship with the Lord. Is Jesus your savior? Do you act like He is your lord? That's what matters most."

Lance's mouth firmed, and Sophie could see him visibly swallow. Another something she wanted to ask him about. Later. After a long-drawn breath, Lance nodded and then moved a curious look to her.

"He's mine," Sophie said, not sure if that questioning glance was about that particular matter. "Jesus is my Savior, and I'm thankful."

It was good to have that out there. Maybe people should be more blunt about what they believe, anyway. No one could doubt where Miss Jane stood. She was about as subtle as a sledgehammer when it came to her loving and following Jesus—and she didn't need words to prove it. Sophie could use some more of that in her life.

With those thoughts melding in her mind, Sophie returned Lance's silent question with her own raised brow.

"Mine too." His sounded less confident, though he didn't look away. At least not until he looked at Miss Jane. "Since I was fourteen—although I always believed in Jesus, since I was a short guy in your class, Miss Jane. But it wasn't personal until a bit before my mom died."

Miss Jane reached for his hand, her sinewy fingers looking small against the tanned meatiness of his. "You were a young man in a fiery place back then." She paused, shook her head, and made a small grunting sound. "You've been in several fiery places, and you're still a young man. I'm glad to know you have Jesus right there with you—like those three young men in the book of Daniel."

While her eyes misted, Sophie looked away. Wow, Miss Jane had an armory of biblical knowledge to draw on. And goodness, Lance must wear some scars beneath those broad shoulders.

A silence fell over the table, one of reflection, and maybe a touch uncomfortable. But sometimes, when forging an honest friendship, wasn't that necessary? Seemed to Sophie that Miss Jane thought so, as the older woman allowed the pause to linger. As Miss Jane had clearly gained heaps of wisdom with her lovely silvery hair and pleasant wrinkles that bespoke of many smiles, Sophie was willing to follow her lead.

Lance sliced through the quiet moment with a subtle clearing of his throat. "Though it seems this was not a ploy"—he moved his chin toward Miss Jane—"I'll be in service on Sunday, and the two of you can ride back to the lodge with me after, if you'd like?"

"I'd like that quite a lot," Miss Jane said.

Sophie would too, but the plan wasn't entirely practical. "How about I follow you and Miss Jane out? Unless the road is muddy, of course, because we all know how well I handle that."

"What for?" His furrowed brow looked more disappointed than mad.

"So I can bring Miss Jane and me back to town." Sophie shrugged. "Less inconvenience to you."

"You're not an inconvenience." He directed his words to Sophie, and then, as if feeling caught in something too personal, he scooched backward and widened his glance to encompass both her and Miss Jane. "My dad always told me to keep to what God said about rest. Though Sunday isn't the sabbath, he said the principle didn't change."

"Your father was a wise man. And a good one," Miss Jane said.

Lance stopped on that for a breath. "Anyway, I'm happy to see you both to and from the lodge. If you want." With both palms, he smacked his thighs and unfolded himself from the chair, snagging the hat that he'd hung on his knee as he went. "That being said, tomorrow *is* a workday, and I'd better head back."

Miss Jane grinned at him like a proud parent while she remained seated. "I'm glad you took time to come visit. You'll do it again?"

"If you'd like."

There was that firm nod that seemed to be Miss Jane's signature of approval.

Sophie slipped from her chair as well. "I'd better be going too. Thanks for letting me butt in here."

"Not at all." Miss Jane reached for Sophie's hand. "I'm glad you did. You're always welcome, and I'm sure looking forward to Sunday afternoon."

Sophie smiled and pivoted toward the exit, finding as she reached it that Lance had been near her heels. He reached for the door around her, placing a warm palm on her back as he did so. With other men, Sophie might have ducked with a sense of hesitancy, but with Lance, she met his eyes.

"Walk you to your car?" he asked softly.

"Sure."

And he did. All the way up Main Street near the old Limestone Hotel, and as they meandered together, his fingers brushed hers.

"I liked bumping into you like this," Sophie said.

They neared the nose of her Renegade. Lance stopped, and when Sophie did the same, she turned to face him. His study was somehow smiling but intense beneath the rim of that white cane hat.

"Did you?" He slid a half step toward her.

She had to tip her chin up as he closed the gap between them. "I did."

"Want to do it again?"

"I do."

"Tomorrow?"

She bit the side of her bottom lip, feeling playful. "With Miss Jane?"

"She is good company."

"That's true. I like her a lot."

His head cocked to one side, and then slowly he shook it.

"No?" Did that sound a little breathless?

She lost herself there, under that gaze. Just the pair of them, sheltered by the brim of his cowboy hat, the cool fall evening, and the dusky light of near sunset. Some moments should last forever...

His fingers settled beneath hers, and he lifted her hand slowly. As if unsure, though those green eyes never strayed from her face. With a feather softness that made her wonder if she'd only imagined it, he brushed her knuckles with a kiss.

*Ah, Brenna, your Captain Wentworth has nothing on this cowboy.*

The next thing she knew, Lance was holding the door to her car open and she was slipping inside.

"I'll see you tomorrow." His low tone made her spine tingle.

Yes. Yes he would. And the next day. And the day after that...

Her heart skipped with giddiness at the thought. A girl could hope.

# Chapter Eight

Lance savored the feel of her fingers in his, the thrill of this evening, this moment more amazing than the sunset they were watching over the river. This had been his favorite spot since he'd been a quiet kid trying to understand the unstable world he was a part of. A spot he hadn't shared with anyone. Aside from his dog, not another living soul.

He loved sharing it with Sophie.

Three dates in one week—not counting the bumping-into-you thing he'd arranged at Miss Jane's Monday night. That might be excessive. It was definitely a personal record. He might be moving too fast.

That thought—so Lance-like with all of his calculated caution and fear of people and relationships in general—got caught in a rapid replay of the time they'd spent together that week. Easy dinners, twice at her small house near the schools. Relaxed walks through town and down by the river. All of it feeling as natural as putting on his boots every morning.

Sophie loved Mexican food and pudding. She preferred eighties music but wasn't particular about the genre. Her joy in music and delight in kids had launched her into teaching, and she loved her job. The transition from the more urban culture of Omaha to the small-town niche of Big Prairie had come with its set of challenges but had been a welcome surprise to her as well. She planned to stay.

She was kind. Sensible. Talented. Joyful.

Beautiful. In every way.

Too fast? Nah. This was perfect. There was nothing about her that he didn't like. Sophie was perfect.

She leaned her head against his shoulder, quiet as she took in the view. Lance shifted his attention from the pinks and oranges streaking the skyline, creating a pastel canvas of color and hope behind the foreground of fall-splattered trees. Ah yes. This woman, with her contented smile, dancing eyes, beauty that reached to a depth well beneath her lovely face...he thought her perfection as she burrowed further into his heart.

"You keep this spot from all your visitors?" she asked, as if feeling his study on her. Absently, she stroked Mutt's head, which lay on her lap, as if his dog was falling for her harder than Lance was.

Well, no. That wasn't likely. But it was sort of a confirmation that Mutt had taken to Sophie and Sophie to Mutt. His two best—and only—girls.

"Yes. There are other vistas tourists can visit. Several of them. This one's mine." The ground where they sat was raised a little from the river, the small hill to it requiring a bit of a hike. It marked the western boundary of the Carson family land and lay a half-mile's walk behind his house, which sat as the barrier between what he was willing to share with the public and what he held back.

Sophie tilted her face toward him, her fingers unwinding from his. "But you'll share with me?"

"Mhh..." Too much to resist. Lance shifted to hold her under his arm, the move closing the slim space that had barely existed between them. For three evenings now he'd resisted. Told himself to be a gentleman, not to rush. Not to fall too fast.

He'd fallen, and there was no help for it. The longing to know her mouth, to share the breath of life and thrill of romance between them had become more than he could defy. With a hunger tamed by the quiet reminder to be gentle, he tested her upturned mouth. On a sigh, she responded, her kiss a timid invitation as her palm slipped over his jaw, fingers feathered over his ear, dancing in his hair. Every touch a tingling sensation that pulled him in deeper. He lost himself there, allowing, as he rarely did, himself to only feel without calculating the next thing.

"Lance." His name was a warm whisper near his lips.

His breath shivered. "Yeah?"

"I'm not good at—" She moved away. Not out of his embrace, but from his kiss. When she looked down, as if somehow ashamed, he felt she misunderstood.

"Sophie, I'm not..." He laid a palm on her cheek and coaxed her gaze back to his. "I'm sorry if that was too much, too soon."

"No." Her teeth sank into her bottom lip, an innocent temptation. "That's not what I mean. I trust you."

"You do?"

"I'm out in the middle of the country, alone with you on the bank of the river. Yes, Lance, I trust you. You've given me no reason not to."

"Then?"

"I'm not good at...um, dating. I guess. I've usually only ever been good friends with a guy."

She stumbled through that like it was a confession. Like it was some kind of shameful history she needed him to forgive. He welcomed it like the best news he'd heard since he'd landed the grant to expand his vineyard.

"You're saying you haven't dated much?"

"Yes. That is what I'm trying to get out here."

He leaned back, one hand anchored to the ground right behind her. "What about Craig?"

"Craig?" She breathed a small laugh, shaking her head. "That was hardly dating. It was a few coffees—except he doesn't drink coffee—and me figuring out really fast that his heart is definitely not available."

"Really?"

"Truly."

"Was that disappointing?"

"Not at all." She met his eyes again. "See, I met this vineyard-cowboy guy, and he has kind of been all I can think about."

Her expression turned shy, and Lance wondered if the woman taking him under her spell ever blushed. She looked vulnerable and bold at the same time, an irresistible combination if he'd ever seen one.

He chuckled and feathered a thumb along her cheekbone. "I haven't dated much either."

"Oh." Her brow furrowed. "I'm not sure I believe that. You're too good looking to not have dated."

"People in general make me nervous. There's a reason I don't go to town much. Women flat out scare me."

"I scare you?"

With a finger, he traced the soft fullness of her top lip. "Yeah. A little."

She turned her mouth into his hand and kissed his palm. "So we're being brave?"

Sweet heaven, she was killing him with this. "Quite." Cradling her face, he sought those lips again.

"And this..." She covered the reckless pounding of his heart with her palm. "Between us?"

He rested his forehead on hers, waiting for her to clarify the question.

"Lance?"

"What are you asking?"

"What are we?"

*Gone.* He was gone, in way over his head. Completely submerged and had no desire to surface. Could a man tell a woman that after three dates? Seemed like too much.

Sophie leaned away, a sigh drooping her shoulders. Maybe he should have told her exactly what he'd been thinking. Why was navigating relationships like searching for a clear path in the dark? As always, Lance found himself feeling *less than* whenever it came to human interaction. The awkward one who probably should have kept to himself.

"I scared you too much, didn't I?" Sophie's words were aimed more at the cool ground beneath them.

Aw, man. The mild hurt in her tone broke through his sense of self-preservation. He covered her slumped shoulder with his palm, slid it down her arm until the trail of his fingers found her hand, and then squeezed. "I'm not messing around here, Sophie. I told you—I'm not good with people, so it wouldn't be worth the risk if I wasn't serious." His heart hammered at that bold confession, and swallowing seemed impossible around the thickness of his throat.

What on earth was he doing?

Her expression seemed more cautious, though her hand remained warm in his. "Then we're dating?"

That was all she'd been asking? Good grief, he'd made too much of it. "I sure hope so."

That smile that warmed him from the inside out broke over her face, making the eyes she lifted sparkle. "Oh." She moved forward and pecked his cheek. "Good." Now his lips.

Lance chuckled. Relief. And delight.

"Don't laugh at me." She landed another kiss on his jaw. "I told you—I haven't done this much."

Laugh at her? She had a lot to learn about his ineptness. He'd be the last one to laugh as he stumbled through. He caught her in his arms and pulled her in a hold that was playful and secure. "I'm glad."

"Hmm." She settled her head against his chest. At her side, Mutt readjusted her lazy position, cocked her head as if she was mildly concerned about the pair of humans she'd claimed as her people, and then resettled her head against Sophie's knee with a doggy grunt.

Lance patted Mutt's head while he continued to hold Sophie, an unfamiliar sense of belonging fortifying his heart. The moment stretched into several as the colorful display along the horizon faded.

Sophie sighed. "I should head back to town."

Instinct had him flexing his arms around her. He'd rather she stayed. But that was definitely getting ahead of things. So after pressing a kiss to her temple, he unfolded his legs to stand, handing her up to her feet at his side. Mutt let out a small whine of protest—and Lance could hardly fault her for it—and then stood with a wagging tail between them.

The walk back to his house and then to her car—she'd insisted that she drive herself out, against his intentions—was done with her fingers woven with his in a comfortable silence, Mutt roving her way back down the trail ahead of them, sporadically bounding back between them, as if to make sure they were good.

"Will you tell me what happened to your parents?" Her question sounded timid.

Lance lifted their laced fingers and kissed her knuckles. "My mom died when I was fifteen—complications from an autoimmune disease that everyone thought was under control. Officially, she died of pneumonia, but..."

But it was the lupus that had both welcomed the illness with a neon sign and then suppressed her ability to overcome it.

Sophie's eyes turned up to him, big and so full of sympathy his heart warmed, driving away the chill of that memory. "I'm so sorry, Lance."

In the place of words he couldn't find nor form, he squeezed her fingers. After swallowing, he continued, feeling almost disconnected from the tale he was sharing, though he wouldn't be able to say why. "A few years later, my dad died in an interstate pileup. He was a trucker—that was how he supplemented the farm income. One night he just..."

"Just didn't come home?"

Nodding, Lance pushed away the potency of that memory, preferring the disconnection he'd felt moments before. "Usually he'd check in every evening. That night, he didn't. We didn't get a phone call from anyone official until the next day."

The trail wound around the big yellow barn, where Lance had installed three large vats but also kept the equipment he needed for his farming and ranching operation. Sophie absorbed his sad life story in silence.

Finally, she asked, "How long ago?"

"Five years."

She stopped as they were halfway between the barn and his house, and she gazed up at him with glazed eyes. "I'm so sorry."

He little knew what to do with her sympathy as he stood under her steady watch. A yawning of want cracked within him—the desire to be seen like this, known and deeply cared for. That yearning had been with him through the years, but always before he'd suffocated it with the distractions of hard work and determination. Now, with Sophie, the longing opened wide and strong with incurable need.

And she stood there, meeting that silent, powerful ache within him, with an intimately tender look that somehow made him feel safe at last. Again lifting her hand, he brushed his lips over the back of it and whispered, "Thank you."

He couldn't fathom how she moved within him so deeply, so quickly, nor did he care, which seemed a contradiction to who he knew himself to be. They continued the path back to the house and around to where she'd parked.

At the car, Lance turned Sophie back into his arms.

*Perfection*, he thought.

"Will you come to the game tomorrow?" she asked.

He loved that she hadn't tried to peel back his heart further with more questions of his emotional history. "The football game?"

"Yes. It's homecoming, and my pep band is doing the field show."

"Ah." Homecoming? The irony. Timid as he was, he hadn't ever been to one of those—not the dance part, anyway. He chuckled, the sound muffled by her hair. "It's been a while since I've gone to a game. Let alone homecoming."

"Oh." She stepped back.

He caught her chin with the tips of his fingers, flinching at the disappointment in her voice. "I'll be there."

She smiled, held his gaze for a moment, and then moved to brush her lips on his jaw. "I'll see you then."

Within moments, she was safely in that orange Renegade and driving out of sight. It didn't occur to him until much later that she would likely be going to the dance that weekend as well. She was school faculty. And she hadn't asked him to go. Likely his fault.

He looked down to Mutt, who lay in a stretched-out line at Lance's socked feet, already having called it a day. "What do I do about that?"

The dog merely looked at him, her chin barely lifting off the living room floor, and then grunted. Then with a roll of her eyes, she dropped her face back down and returned to her nap, clearly unimpressed with her owner.

Man. Even his dog agreed. He was really bad at this.

\*\*\*

Sunday came as a relief.

Sophie stepped into her comfortable polka-dot skirt—the long one that brushed the ground and looked dressy and casual all at once. A much-preferred choice to the fancy dress she'd worn the night before. What a long deal that had been. Between acting as chaperone for the dance—and who really enjoyed telling pairs of hormonal high schoolers to come up for air at any point in time?—and feeling caught in the Craig-Brenna-Grant drama that continued to unfold before her, Sophie felt nothing but relief that homecoming was now, once again, a full year away.

Not that she was irritated with her friends. Truly, she hurt for them. Even not understanding all the history between Craig and Brenna, she could see plain as anything that they hadn't healed from past wounds, and now, though unintended, Grant had been sucked into much of it as well. As for Sophie, she had only to step back. And to pray for all of them. Which was her normal position in most of her relationships. The distant prayer warrior.

The stand-by friend.

That was okay. Except last night she'd really wished for someone at her side—to have her own fairy-tale distraction, rather than watching everyone else do life. This time the longing wasn't for just any someone. She'd wanted Lance. Cheesy though it may be, she'd really wanted to ask him to the dance. But he'd laughed about her asking him to the football game, thereby stretching the length of her courage. It was silly that she felt so disappointed, anyway. They weren't high schoolers, after all, and even if they were, she'd have to consider the fact that the Lance she was coming to know was an extreme introvert. Homecoming—or any public dance—was likely not within his comfort boundaries.

Catching her profile in the full-length mirror on the back of her bathroom door, Sophie ran a quick check over her appearance. Good enough.

Ack. She hated *good enough*. Especially when the slithering coils of self-doubt gripped her. In those moments, she'd compare herself to those around her—typically the pretty blondes who owned jewel-toned eyes and pale skin. Made her feel like dull background filler. Fighting against that feeling of less-than, she shut her eyes and found the replay of a conversation she and Lance had on their first shared afternoon.

*"I thought you were beautiful, and I wanted to know your name."*

Even at the memory, her pulse skipped, sending shots of tingling delight through her middle. She met her own gaze again in that mirror but imagined it was her mom standing across from her. "You'll think I'm crazy," she whispered to the illusion. "But I might love him."

Yes. Mom would think she was crazy. Not to mention acting very much out of character. Then again, Mom hadn't met Lance Carson yet.

Sophie shook her head, rolling her eyes at her own ridiculousness. It was because this was new. All of it. That was why she was being nonsensical. Mom would warn her to be cautious, not flighty. To be prudent, not foolish. One week was not enough to know a man. Certainly not enough to fall in love.

Lance would certainly agree, level-headed man that he was— not that she planned to bring any of *that* up with him.

Besides, she hadn't even had the courage to ask him to the dance. Which, to be honest, was fueling the frustration.

Skip it. She smoothed the back of her hair, ensuring the spirals hadn't frizzed, slipped into her denim jacket, and grabbed her Bible on the way out the door.

Lance was there, waiting in his truck and looking like he wished he could make himself invisible. How could a guy that good looking, and that smart, and that successful feel so out of place? Sophie couldn't understand, and since she was already annoyed with herself for reasons that she wasn't sure she could pin down, the emotion spread toward him.

They were only people, she thought. People he'd grown up with. This should not be that hard.

That'd be a fine pep talk. He'd be sure to come back next week, wouldn't he? Sophie shoved the irrational bite out of her mind as much as she could as she crossed the parking lot to Lance's truck. With the familiar *smile, it'll help* mantra in the back of her mind, she met him with a grin.

"Morning."

"Hi." Rocks crunched under his boots as he dropped out of the truck to stand beside her. "How was the dance?"

*Not great, and thanks for being there...* Her lips pinned shut, and she glanced toward the door. "We should go in."

Lance caught her hand. "Sophie?"

After two steps, she stopped, their arms stretched between them because he hadn't moved. "Yes, Lance?"

"You okay?"

"Yes."

"You look, um..." He closed the gap between them.

She lifted her chin as both brows rose. *What is wrong with you, girl? This is ridiculous.* That may be true, but she felt...miffed. Yes, miffed that Lance hadn't known that she would want him to go to the dance last night. That instead he spent the evening doing...whatever he did with his evenings alone. What did he do with all that time, anyway?

"How was your evening?"

His brow furrowed. "Mine? Fine, I guess. Watched Jack Ryan while I worked on some order projections."

Huh. Sophie didn't know who or what Jack Ryan was and didn't care. "I see."

"Are you"—he dipped his head, the wide brim of his hat shading her face from the midmorning sun—"are you irritated with me?"

"No." That would be silly. Uncalled for. Un-adult. Know what else was uncalled for? She'd lied to him. *Oh Lord, what is wrong with me?*

She was a bundle of pent-up emotions and had no previous experience that would help guide her in how to deal with them. With a long draw of clean, cool autumn air, Sophie began again. Stepping forward, she laid her free palm on Lance's crisp white button-down and fixed her smile. "I'm sorry. Can we start over?"

"Okay...but if I've—"

"Good morning, Lance."

His words died as his lips seamed, but his gaze on her bore the same intensity. They were both hopelessly blind in this new thing. How had they both missed the Relationship 101 course that every other adult seemed to have passed?

"Will you sit with me in church?" she asked, perhaps a bit overly bright.

Finally his stern brow eased, and he nodded. "I hoped to."

With that, they moved toward the church. Sophie mentally dusted off her hands. First tiff—if you could call it that—fixed. Relationship 101? How hard could this dating deal be?

# Chapter Nine

Miss Jane supplied soup for their Sunday dinner. Her butternut specialty that was creamy with a hint of heat and a touch of cinnamon from the candied pecans she used to garnish the bowls. It'd be a perfect entrée for one of the lodge's evening offerings, but Lance wasn't about to ask if she'd be willing to share the recipe. Or supply his restaurant. He'd have to talk with Clint, the part-time chef who worked for the vineyard, about finding an unusual soup for the lodge, to mix up the typical menu of steak or salmon they served on Friday and Saturday evenings during the season.

"What did we think of our start in Matthew?" Miss Jane held her spoon above her bowl, ready to take another dip into the soft orange creaminess.

"I like the plan of it." Sophie dabbed her mouth with the deep-purple cloth napkin. "I'm not sure I've ever read through all four gospels consecutively. Honestly, I think that I'm prone to hopping around the Bible searching for snippets that fit my current need, rather than dipping into a whole book to see what God shows me."

"Hmm." Miss Jane hummed around a mouthful and nodded. Her attention turned to Lance.

What did he think? She put the silent question to him as plain as if she'd spoken.

He hadn't thought much about it. Through the hour-long service, he'd been more wrapped up with the flash of irritation he'd seen in Sophie, the confusion of it mixed with the familiar discomfort of being in a large group setting and feeling like he didn't belong.

But Miss Jane waited for an answer.

"I think..." Uh. What, exactly? He glanced at Sophie. She watched him with sincere interest. Like it mattered what he thought. "I think that you can't go wrong reading the Bible, whichever way you do it."

Was that right? Honestly, he hadn't a clue.

One dark brow slid up into Sophie's forehead. "Like *a verse a day keeps the devil away?*"

Yikes. That sounded like a test.

He cleared his throat. "I don't know about that."

"There are certainly those who seem to believe that." Miss Jane's matter-of-fact tone didn't give away her opinion much.

"And you?" Lance was all too glad to turn the attention away from himself.

"Hmm." A thoughtful bend of Miss Jane's mouth made her look both wistful and wise. "I think that your approach to study reveals the depth of your relationship."

Lance felt like he needed to take a deep breath, as it seemed the upcoming explanation would require careful thought. Not that he didn't want to think carefully. He wasn't accustomed to it. At least, when it came to church sort of things.

Resting both forearms on the table, Sophie leaned in. "Yes, I think that's it. Like the scatter-and-gather approach I've usually leaned on is more superficial than I want. To go deeper, I need to dive into the whole story. To know this Jesus I'm claiming to love, I need to see all of Him. Does that make sense?"

The pause at the table lengthened when Lance thought Miss Jane would answer. Needing something to do, rather than simply feeling awkward about not knowing how to answer, he gripped his glass of lemon water and lifted it to his lips.

Finally Miss Jane broke the silence. "I'm looking forward to it." Her joyful expression eased some of Lance's anxiety. But then her insightful blue eyes pierced him. "We must *know* someone before we can really understand what they do."

That he couldn't argue with—but he was certain that her statement was intentionally layered with meaning. His chest tightened as he expected Miss Jane would give a *for example* right then and there—outing him in front of Sophie, revealing what would only be seen as selfish and heartless before he had an opportunity to at least try to make her see his reasons.

*Please let's not talk about the franchise now.*

If Miss Jane chose to, she could put him on the spot when he was vulnerable. The woman was not a successful business owner by mistake—she was savvy and knew how to make the most of opportunity.

As Lance fortified himself for the coming onslaught, he forced himself to meet Miss Jane's gaze. A sad curiosity softened the old woman's look, and as she tilted her head, he felt nearly certain that she'd like more than anything to wrap him in a gentle embrace.

Which did not make sense.

Miss Jane's silent connection drifted from him, and she scanned the view of the vineyard. Her mouth regained that easy smile. "The pickers' picnic is always a favorite. Should be perfect weather for it this year."

"Yes." He grasped her change in subject like a line tossed to a falling man. "I hope so."

"It's lovely out today."

"Would you like to go walk the rows?" He dropped his napkin and rose.

"I think"—Miss Jane sent a knowing glance toward Sophie—"the two of you should do exactly that. I'd prefer to find myself a seat in the sunshine, right there in the window." She pointed to a splash of yellow-white light painting the pinewood floor.

Lance met Sophie's look as she turned her face toward him. She smiled, easing him further from his earlier discomfort. Then she turned back to Miss Jane. "You're sure?" she asked. "It is a good day for a walk."

"I am," Miss Jane said. "An afternoon snooze in this beautiful lodge sounds perfect to me."

Pointing to one of several gray upholstered chairs that he'd scattered in groups around the perimeter of the lodge, Lance moved around the table toward Miss Jane. "Can I move that into the sun for you?"

"That would be lovely."

With little effort, he had the more comfortable seat arranged. Moments later, Miss Jane settled into her spot in the sun, her Bible spread open on her lap, and he and Sophie were slipping on jackets. Mutt sprang from her spot in the sun on the deck and joined them, weaving herself around their legs, as if she needed to be sure they knew she was there.

The afternoon smelled of damp leaves, fertile soil, and the river. A chilly breeze cut through the sun-warmed air, toying with a few stray wisps of Sophie's black curls. Lance reached for her hand and delighted in that sensation of being wanted when she tangled her fingers with his. Through the first two rows, they stepped in slow, settled quietness, his trained glances checking the leaves and vines for mildew, disease, breakage, or distress as they meandered past.

"There aren't any grapes left," she said.

"No. Harvest is over. The last of the wine grapes were taken to a larger vineyard near Lincoln last week."

"You don't use them all?"

"No, that was never my intent. We make three house wines—two of them dessert, and one dry red—using the vats I have in the big yellow barn. But only about half of my produce are wine grapes. I grow concords that go to a juice producer—that's the other forty percent of my crop, and then table grapes that are sold locally. To make my mom happy. She loved them."

Sophie's trail encroached on his as she leaned her head against his shoulder. "You miss her?"

"Always." In that moment, he wished very much his mom was there. He felt certain she would have liked Sophie, with her ready smile and easy way with people. *Opposites attract.* Likely, that was what Mom would have said, then would have laughed and used herself and his dad as proof. Mom had a bubbly personality, very much like Sophie's, and had a way of drawing Dad out of his quiet, personal world. She'd balanced him, and Dad had loved her for it.

Lance settled a look on the woman at his side. She took in his work, the fields of his dreams and passion, with a visible appreciation that warmed him. Yes, this beautiful girl could balance him. And he could love her for it.

"Tell me about the pickers' picnic," Sophie said.

Lance cleared his throat—and his head. It was too soon to be thinking about love. "It's an event that grew out of my hands nearly the moment it started. My harvest manager suggested we have a picnic for the workers at the end of season about three years back. Since we employ a lot of teens during the harvest, it made sense to make it a family thing. But for scheduling reasons—mostly having to do with school—we had to bump the picnic back to the first post-harvest Saturday when there wasn't a football game, which means that it happens after the actual harvest season. And since it involved so many families in town, my manager thought we should open it up to all of Big Prairie."

She bumped his side with her hip. "That's generous of you."

Lance squeezed her hand.

"I hear it's quite a gathering," she said.

"It is. Like I said, it grew fast."

"Doesn't really seem like you though."

He stopped and turned to her. "It doesn't?" Maybe his solitary ways bothered her.

"No. I mean not the generous part. That fits. The gathering part."

Flinching, he ducked his gaze. *She doesn't like that part of me...*

She reached to lay her hand on his shoulder. "I mean that..."

"I know. It's okay. No, I'm not much for crowds. And to be honest, the picnic is a long night."

"Because it's tiring, or is there more to it?"

"Yes, it's exhausting. Especially after harvest season, which is full of twelve- to fifteen-hour workdays. But...um, I'm not sure you'll understand."

"Why?"

"Because being with people doesn't seem to bother you. Kind of seems like you thrive on it, actually."

"Yeah. But I get it, I think."

"You do?"

"Well, maybe. I think I do in my head, but then I guess maybe I don't really understand. I mean, you grew up here. These people are your friends. Don't you like being around them?"

"In small doses. But in a crowd..." He sighed. He was such an oddball. Had felt it keenly, especially during his late teen years. Particularly when he stood himself up next to Lane. Lane, the crowd favorite. Lane, the popular. Lane, who was so much more like his well-liked mother.

"Lance?" Sophie rested her hand on his arm.

Perhaps Sophie would have liked Lane better too. Either way, he determined he'd be honest with her. If she walked, at least it'd be early. He'd still have his heart. Sort of.

"It's like when I'm in the middle of a group, I feel like I'm intruding. Like I don't belong. And it's been that way my whole life. This"—he motioned over the acreage where they stood— "this has been my haven. My sanctuary, where I don't feel like a misfit or an intruder. I love working the rows, the quietness of the land as I pour myself into the vines. To have that disrupted is a little disconcerting."

She watched him, her dark eyes thoughtful as she absorbed what he said.

He was selfish. He knew it, but heaven help him, he couldn't seem to change.

A gentle grin moved on her mouth, and she rose on her toes to land a soft kiss on his cheek. "Then the picnic is very generous of you."

Not a rejection. Not even a rebuff. Relief barreled over him, and he tugged her into an embrace, shutting his eyes as he held her close.

"And I do get it," she said.

"Really?" Lance continued to hold her, not wanting her to leave ever.

"Yeah, the feeling like you don't fit part."

He loosened the embrace and stepped back. "You?"

Sophie's gaze drifted from him to the vineyard, and she swallowed. "Yes." In her thoughtful, hesitant pause, she ran her teeth over her bottom lip. "Back home I rarely felt like I fit in." As if forcing herself, she met his eyes. "I was the only African American girl in my class. And at my church, my dad is the pastor, and that is sometimes isolating. Even more so because, well, my mom is white. Some people..." Her words fell away.

A hollow ache for her expanded in his chest. Loneliness for him was bothersome—he didn't like *feeling* alone when he thought about it. But *being* alone didn't really bother him. It was the way he was wired. But Sophie? She was wired for people.

He tugged her back until she nestled against him. "I'm sorry, Sophie. That isn't fair."

Settled against him, her arms circled to his back, and she sighed. "It's okay. I mean, it wasn't always—for such a long time, I was afraid I'd never find a place that felt like home."

"But you have?" Dare he hope that he was part of that? Dare or not, he did hope.

Her quiet chuckle warmed him. "Yes. I love Big Prairie. It's not perfect, but it does feel like home."

She didn't offer more, and though tempted, he didn't fish. Rather, he held her while the afternoon sun seeped into his skin.

He savored the perfect feel of Sophie in his arms, the calming smell of coconut and almond, and the rhythm of her heartbeat against him. He didn't want the moment to end.

"I'm sorry I was irritated with you," she whispered.

"You were?" He didn't pull back but held on tighter. "I thought maybe you were, but I didn't know why."

"The dance last night was sort of miserable. I wished you were there with me."

"You didn't ask me."

"I knew you didn't want to go."

Well, that was true. "But I would have. With you."

Sophie stepped away, something beautiful shining in her eyes. "I know that." She cupped his neck and tugged, bringing his mouth down to hers. The kiss was soft but brief. "You're a good man, Lance Carson. I think I want to keep you."

He hoped—rather desperately—that she would.

# Chapter Ten

Those first days set a pattern for the weeks following. After full days in the vineyard or working the cattle on the ranch portion of his land, Lance drove into town at least three evenings a week and he and Sophie would share dinner. Sometimes he'd grab takeout. Other times, she'd cook. After, they would play a card game or talk about what she had the band doing, or the work he was doing at his place.

On Tuesdays they would snuggle on her sofa to watch the BBC drama she simply could not miss. Initially, he sort of napped through the hour-long miniseries. But by the second Tuesday, he was caught in the multi-threaded storyline, and they'd download the whole series so he could watch the episodes he'd missed. This thrilled Sophie, and Lance discovered that thrilling Sophie was definitely something he wanted to do on a regular basis.

On Fridays, he attended games with her. It wasn't so bad, as he knew exactly why he was there and that she wanted him. Though, if pressed, he'd have to admit that the waiting at the end of the game for her to wrap up, trying not to feel like a fool alone on the sidelines, was not his favorite thing. He did, however, enjoy watching her interact with her students during the game—she was quite a gifted teacher, and her easy rapport with the kids brought out the best in them.

"Big Prairie's band has never been this good, Ms. Shultz," he told her after a halftime field show. "How did we ever manage to snag such a talent?"

She pressed into his shoulder from her seat on the bleacher next to him. "Flattery will get you nowhere, sir."

"I'm completely serious. Three years in a row with superior marks? I looked it up with the district office, Sophie. Hasn't been done around here in over two decades."

"Hmm." He felt her sigh as she dipped her head onto his shoulder. The touch was brief—she was a faculty member and technically at work. "I wish I was better with the music."

"What do you mean? They're doing great."

"I'm better with the kids than I am with the music. To be honest, I was probably the worst in my college class of music ed candidates when it came to the actual music part. I'm jealous of Craig—perfect pitch and has much more natural talent than I've ever dared to hope for."

"Why did you choose music, then?"

"I love it." She laughed at herself. "That probably doesn't make sense. I had to work twice as hard as all the people around me who were loaded with natural music talent. I'm not kidding—twice as hard. I've never read music well, and my ear for it is less than ideal. I have to spend hours prepping new music—working out each part so that I know what I need to listen for and focus on. Lots of practice has made me better, but I still can't pick out a new piece and go with it. But there's something about music that grabs me, so it's worth it. And teaching..."

She didn't have to finish that—he got it. Could see it plain as the beautiful woman next to him. "That's your jam."

"Yeah. They're my vineyard. The thing that's worth all the hours of work and the times of frustration. I love to see them progress. To grab on to something and find value in it enough to keep trying. Ultimately to succeed. Every one of those superior rankings—Lance, I sit back behind them by myself and tear up when they announced that award, because I know how hard they've worked for it."

*Hard work inspires hard work.* Suddenly Lance knew exactly why Big Prairie's high school band did as well as they did. They truly had an extraordinary teacher.

He couldn't help it. With one arm around her, he gathered her close and pressed a kiss onto her temple. "That's my girl."

She sniffed, leaned into his side hug, and then sat up again. "Don't you think that it's amazing we get to do things that we love? Like it's this love note from God that says *to Sophie, just to see you smile.*"

So Sophie. She often spoke of how sweet God was to them. How he noticed them, provided for them, loved them. Usually, Lance nodded or would hum an agreement, while inside, her confidence in God's daily notice triggered nagging questions. That night he chose not to dwell on them. "I'm quite certain God does love to see your smile, Sophie, beautiful as it is."

She rolled a deadpan look on him. "There's that flattery again."

"Absolutely not." He resisted pulling her back against him again, choosing to respect her professionalism. "I love your smile."

The expression she shot to him was two-parts adorable, one-part tease. A combination that made him wish they were in a place where he could list *all* of the things he loved about her.

Or tell her the whole thing straight out.

He loved her.

***

"Hey there, stranger. Where have you been?" Brenna caught up with Sophie as she stepped out of Garrett's with her morning coffee in hand. Due to staying up too late with Lance way too often, Sophie had skipped what had been her routine coffee stop for several days, missing the unofficial walk she and Brenna shared as Brenna commuted by foot to her office on the other end of Main.

Sophie couldn't help a sly grin as they fell into step together. "Here and there."

"Oh yeah?" Brenna elbowed her as they paced down the sidewalk. "Here and there as in where, exactly?"

"Home. Football games." Sophie shrugged, that teasing smile growing.

"Vineyards?" Now Brenna's arm slipped through the crook of Sophie's elbow.

"Maybe."

"Eh?" Brenna laughed.

It was the following Monday, after the last home game of the season. Sophie and Lance had been dating for nearly a month by that time, and Brenna had only brought it up once, and that was through text right before the pickers' picnic. Sophie held her disappointment in check about her friend's lack of interest, knowing by observation that Brenna and Craig had been doing some serious work on the things that were broken between them.

Apparently, that work was paying off. Brenna seemed like a renewed person these days, and Craig was significantly more settled as well. Not to mention obviously in love. Whole-heart-gone in love, and he certainly wasn't alone in it.

Sophie bent her head toward Brenna, meeting her friend's temple in a sort of secret bestie gesture. "How about you, Miss Blaum? I rather have this feeling that the *Miss Blaum* thing is screeching toward a change at a breakneck pace. True?"

"Hmm." Brenna clutched Sophie's arm. "I can't say I have an answer to that. But to be honest, I've been worried you'll think less of me, because yes, things with Craig have shifted. Quickly." She stopped, not quite to her office yet, and turned to face Sophie. "I know that I've sort of made a mess of things. First, with Craig, and that's a long story that I don't have time to explain right now. Then, with Grant, but he swears he doesn't hate me. But also, I somehow got you involved in all of it, and I'm really sorry, Sophie. I truly hope you didn't get hurt and that you're not upset with me."

"Aw, Bren." Sophie stepped forward and took Brenna into a hug and then moved back. "That's sweet of you. But don't fret. I'm not hurt, and Craig told me a little about what happened with you two. I mean, not much, but enough for me to know that there's some stuff that you guys needed to wade through. I'm glad you are doing that. I'm glad to see you both happy." She winked. "And you both look *really* happy."

Brenna's cheeks shaded a deep pink, and her blue eyes danced. "Yeah. I wish that I hadn't let bitterness take so much control over me. I didn't know, didn't realize, you know?"

Sophie wasn't sure she knew, because she still didn't know the whole story. But she didn't need to, as it didn't matter for their friendship.

"I was afraid that you were upset though," Brenna continued. "Seriously, girl, I've barely seen you in a month, except briefly at church. Please tell me that your disappearance has something to do with that cowboy you've been sitting with on Sundays?"

Ducking, Sophie bit her bottom lip. "Something like that."

Brenna muffled a squeal. "Is it serious?"

"It's only been a month."

"Lance doesn't do anything casually, Sophie. I've known him pretty much my whole life, and while we're not close, I can tell you that he's intense."

"Yes. He is that."

"And he doesn't date. I don't think ever."

"I know that too."

"So?" Brenna gripped Sophie's hand.

Over the weeks, Sophie found herself comfortable with Lance, at ease with where they were. It was somehow both thrilling and oh so easy to be with him. And she was with him a lot. Maybe *comfortable* was a drastic understatement.

"He's quiet. Ambitious. Kind. And in almost every way in terms of personality, my opposite."

His best friend was literally his dog—not that that was necessarily a bad thing—and Mutt was definitely likable, so there was that. Lance loved the quiet of his property and the science of growing things, and he preferred that to the busy interactions demanded of him to make his business work. If he didn't see another human for days, he was pretty okay with it.

Yes. Very much her opposite.

"And?" Brenna prodded.

Sophie kind of adored him. Admired his quiet independence, his dogged determination, and his work ethic. She felt a special honor that *she* was the one he chose to bring into his world. She wasn't ready to say those things out loud though.

That heat that had been radiating from her neck up intensified. "And I can't stop thinking about him."

"Aw..." Brenna swung their clasped hands like there was playful music in the background. "Sophie and Lance, sitting in a tree..." She stopped, molded a serious face. "Wait. Have you kissed?"

"None of your business."

A knowing smirk lifted the corners of her mouth. "That's a yes. Then it *is* serious, because this is Lance Carson we're talking about here."

"I have to go to work."

Brenna giggled and whipped Sophie into a hug. "Me too. You can tell me more later."

"Right," Sophie said in a dry tone as she stepped toward her car with a backward wave.

"It's good to see you, my friend," Brenna called.

Sophie turned at the driver's-side door and sent her a sincere smile. "You too."

Sometimes things were perfect. Her life, for example, at that moment, was perfect. She couldn't wait to tell Lance.

\*\*\*

Mutt yelped a happy greeting, springing up from her cozy place beside the desk while her tail wagged a rabid *hello*. How his dog knew the sound of that approaching vehicle was Sophie, Lance had no idea, but he grinned as he followed Mutt down the loft steps, the phone call he'd finished with Miss Jane rolling through his mind. He'd ask Sophie what she thought.

"Your loyalty has shifted already, hasn't it, girl?" He chuckled as he reached the lodge's back door, where Mutt pranced in place, anticipation making her unable to stand still. "Not sure if I should be offended by that or proud of your good taste."

She responded with a sharp yip, and as soon as he had the door open, Mutt bolted toward the orange Renegade. A small puff of dust settled behind the now-parked vehicle, and Sophie appeared.

"Mutt, stay down." Lance grinned, though he spoke with a commanding tone. "She doesn't want you in her arms."

"Aw, why would you assume that?" Sophie bent to love on the obedient dog, who barely kept her exuberance from springing up all over. Instead, Mutt wiggled and danced as if the ground was hot and she couldn't keep one paw on the ground for longer than two seconds.

Lance strode toward them, hands pushed into his pockets. "Think you stole my dog's heart."

Sophie stood, a sassy joy lighting her eyes. "Hmm." She stretched to her toes, leaning into him as she moved, and caught his mouth with hers.

"Lucky dog." He dipped to meet her kiss. Unpocketing one hand, he folded her under his arm.

"Mutt or you?"

He nuzzled her scrunched nose. "Yes."

She giggled. "You're in a good mood today."

"Always." With a slight tug, he guided her across the driveway toward the vineyard. "You're extra peppy today yourself, sunshine."

"Hmm," she hummed again.

"There a reason?"

"Yes." She didn't turn up to look at him.

"Gonna share?"

"Maybe."

"Yes." Lance stopped and tugged her back when she kept moving, locking her lightly against him with both arms. "What makes my beautiful girl who smiles all the time extra smiley today?"

For a long, perfect moment, she simply stared at him. In the sweet silence, he thought he heard things he'd longed for, read things in her dancing eyes he wanted desperately to be true. The light playfulness between them simmered. "Sophie Joyanne." Slowly he closed the gap between them, lightly resting his forehead against hers. "Don't you look at a man like that unless you're serious."

"Serious about what, cowboy?"

"About wanting to be kissed."

"Oh." She slid back half a step, a teasing smirk making her lips more tempting. "Well then."

"That is very not nice, woman."

She tipped her head back and laughed, giving him full exposure to her neck. When he nuzzled the place below her ear, she sighed and wrapped both arms around him. He lifted her off her feet.

"You make me happy, Lance Carson."

While his heart did a roll that pushed a thrill through his veins, he pressed a gentle kiss onto her neck and then lowered her back to the ground. The longing to tell her, and to hear her return what he hoped was true, surged. He stepped back and framed her face. Searching her eyes and finding them soft, that longing turned to a sweet ache.

"How happy?" His tone sank low.

Her hands slid from his shoulders to his chest and then to his sides, where she gripped the fabric of his button-down shirt. "Perfectly, wildly, unbelievably happy."

The ache swept harder, becoming a force he could no longer hold back. Suddenly his pulse raced, and his fingers curved into the glossy curls of her hair. "What if—" The words cut short by a sudden lump he could barely swallow. He cleared his throat. "What if I told you I love you?"

Sophie held him in a gaze that felt like falling and flying all at once. Like a wild security that didn't make any sense.

"Do you?" she asked.

"Sophie." He groaned, finding her forehead with his again. "You're killing me here."

Grinning, she pressed her lips to his. A response almost as good as he'd hoped. As her lips lingered warm and soft, he indulged in a gentle exploration, feeling the flight of adrenaline all the way through.

The dog whimpered at their feet and then wound herself around their legs, pushing Sophie against Lance. She chuckled and then pulled back enough to find his eyes.

"I love you," he said.

Her eyes closed, as if she was savoring his declaration. And then she looked back at him with her response plainly written in her warm gaze.

"I love you too, Lance."

Beside the joy that burst within, there slipped a small draft that nearly made him shiver. He had no reason to doubt Sophie—she was as guileless as she was joyful. But even as he bent to kiss her again, that chilled breeze in his heart settled.

Fear. It seeped into the swell of love.

Lance held her tightly, fighting to reject that chilled presence, frantic to ignore the insidious voice that came with it. But the words slithered through his mind just the same, branding themselves into the places most vulnerable.

*It won't last.*

He squeezed his eyes shut, wishing he could believe in love enough to drown the doubt.

\*\*\*

"So she'd be on site all the time?" Sophie's question was merely inquisitive as she sat on Lance's desk.

His vineyard staff had all gone their way for the season, leaving the owner alone in his off-season work. But a ranch hand wasn't unusual, she'd figured. Most operations likely had more than one, and she knew keenly how hard Lance worked. Sure could use the help.

But a twenty-year-old girl—a southern belle at that?

"Hands usually stay in the barn loft, but Miss Jane said Daisy would live with her." A pause stretched, and in it Lance's brow furrowed. "You don't think it's a good idea."

Sophie sighed. "I think you should have help."

"But?"

She thought over the whole scenario again. Lance had said Miss Jane had called him right before Sophie had arrived. Her niece was looking for a job while she took a gap year from school. She'd started her sophomore year in college, but for whatever reason, she was dropping her classes and wanted to try something different while she reevaluated life.

The thought of a twenty-year-old woman out on the Carson land working with Lance all day every day didn't immediately settle with Sophie. But the fact that it was Miss Jane asking—and the girl was Miss Jane's niece—colored the situation.

Lance's hand covered her leg, and he stood from his desk chair. "I know. It's probably not the best plan. I just need to figure out how to tell Miss Jane no."

Unease upset Sophie's stomach. "I'm being..."

"Cautious."

"Jealous."

Lance's eyes softened. "You'll never have a reason to be jealous, Sophie." He leaned down and brushed a kiss over her forehead. Then one near her eye. Near her ear. Her jaw. Finally, her lips, where he lingered.

Sophie gripped his shirt at his shoulders and sighed. "I don't think you understand how handsome you are, cowboy."

"Looks have nothing to do with it. Didn't you hear me say that I'm in love with you?"

She gazed at him, a dreamy sensation floating through her. Ah, well then...

When she thought he'd kiss her again, and that would have been lovely, Lance stood straight. "I'll call Miss Jane and—"

"She said she rides well?"

Lance cut his look back to her, surprised. "Yeah. Rides real well—basically grew up in a saddle. And has an outstanding work ethic."

"Miss Jane isn't one to say things she doesn't mean."

He continued to watch her. "What are you saying?"

"You could offer her a trial period." A hesitancy still wove in her even as she said the words, but simply cutting off the idea because of the age and gender of the offered help didn't feel right. After all, Sophie wouldn't appreciate that sort of treatment.

Lance's brows lifted. "You'd be okay with that?"

Sophie drew in a brave breath. Honestly, the situation would require her to wrestle with some long-held insecurities. But that might not be a bad thing. She nodded.

"Might be a blessing. Maybe to all of us."

# Chapter Eleven

Sophie gripped the steering wheel as the car sped away from Big Prairie, leaving her comfortable new world at her back. She drew in a deep breath meant to steady her nerves and settle her racing heart.

"You okay?" Lance shifted in the passenger's seat beside her, and then his fingers burrowed into her hair to tickle the sensitive skin on the back of her neck.

She shrugged into his touch, suppressing a squeal. "Don't tickle me while I'm driving. It's not safe."

"Oh, we're ticklish here, are we?"

"Lance Albert, don't you do it."

"Or what, Sophie Joyanne?"

She shot him a glance and then reached to grip his leg. He intercepted her hand with his unoccupied palm. "Nope. That's definitely not safe. Drive, lady."

"You are an incorrigible flirt, sir."

"I'm not sure what that means, but I doubt it anyway. Especially since it involves the word *flirt*. I've not had enough practice to be a flirt of any sort."

She wrestled her hand free and replaced it on the steering wheel. Good thing Highway 20 was a lonely road that Tuesday before Thanksgiving. Not to mention clear of rain, snow, or ice. "Maybe you're a natural."

"That, my sweet Sophie, is not possible. Ask my brother." Lance moved his hand from the back of her neck and rested it on the small black console between them. "Or anyone else who knew me before you."

"Will I get to meet your brother soon?"

The space between them quieted, and something heavy but unidentifiable settled. When she glanced to gauge his thoughts, she found his face turned toward the fields flashing by his side of the road. Anxiety gnawed into the spot that was already chewed up by nerves. Why didn't he want her to meet his brother? Wasn't he going home with her for Thanksgiving? Coupled with the fact that he'd said he loved her every night for nearly a month, that was a pretty big deal. Right?

That raw place within began to scream warnings. This was a bad idea, all the way around. Old wounds, things that should have long since been scarred over and no longer tender, felt exposed and as sharp as the day they'd been cut nearly ten years before. Where she'd felt comfortable and confident with Lance and the man she'd believed him to be, she began to feel unstable. What if this was freshman color-day dance all over again?

*Come on, Sophie. Lance is not some fourteen-year-old boy who can't find a spine.*

There were moments though. She'd seen glimpses of Lance concealing something. Especially when they were in situations that involved other people. Times when Lance's discomfort was strong enough to make them both feel awkward, like if she stayed too long after church service to visit. He'd glance around like he hoped no one would recognize him, he could find some corner to hide in, or he could bury his face in his phone.

Ironically, she found herself feeling more insecure when they went out together in town than she was about his new ranch hand, Daisy. Daisy Jane Hopewell—or, *just Daisy, thank you*— turned out to be exactly what her aunt had said—a competent rider and an excellent worker, not to mention a super-sweet girl.

One both Sophie and Lance were thankful for, especially as this trip home for thanksgiving was made possible by her presence.

But those few moments in town, surely Lance was simply being the introvert that he was. Still, those insecurities reared.

"Sophie?"

She pulled in a startled breath. Had he answered her, and she hadn't even heard his voice?

"What's going on?" he asked.

Something sour stirred in her belly. Mom always said honesty was the best policy. Miss Jane would agree. Besides, she'd never feel confident in this if she didn't tell him why this trip was messing with her.

Lance leaned closer, poking at the corner of her mouth with a gentle finger. "Hey, sunshine girl, where'd your smile go?"

What happened to *smile, it'll help*?

Sophie nibbled on the edge of her bottom lip. "Lance, we're honest with each other, right?"

A weighted pause hung before he answered. "Yeah..."

"The thing is, going home with you is kind of making me a wreck."

"You don't want me to meet your parents?"

"More than anything, I want you to."

"Are they going to not like me?"

"No. I mean, I don't think that'll be a problem."

"Will your dad be sitting on the front porch with a shotgun on his lap?"

"In Omaha?" She snorted. "Definitely not."

"Are you afraid I won't pass inspection?"

"No." She cut her response with a serious tone, drew in a deep breath, and then met his curious stare with a glance. "The thing is, my dad is African American."

She could feel Lance's stare.

"He's black."

"You're kidding."

His deadpan response provoked a chuckle even as heat began to swirl in her cheeks. She cleared her throat. "This is serious, Lance."

"Are you serious, Sophie? Really? You think your skin color matters to me? That what your dad looks like is going to make a difference? Who have you been dating the last few months?"

The muscles in her shoulders tensed as Sophie fought to sort through what she actually meant to say. Did she think her mixed-race heritage mattered to Lance? No. When it was only them, no. But she'd lived through moments where she'd discovered, painfully—humiliatingly so—that in public people weren't always the same. And there was her boyfriend, who seemed uncomfortable out in public. Mostly, she believed that was his introverted personality. But the old hurts had a way of dragging up doubts. Especially when she was driving back to the place where she'd been convinced she'd never find a place to belong.

Lance covered her hand. "Pull over, Sophie."

She sighed as she pressed the brake. The car slid over the rumble bars with a vibrating *zzzt-zzzt* and rolled to a stop. Lance waited until she shifted the Renegade into Park before he nudged her chin with the crook of his index finger so that she'd look at him.

Those sincere green eyes, full of love and concern, demolished her building fears, leaving her with a need to explain.

"Things are different back home. I mean, not everywhere, with everyone, but, well, it's not like Big Prairie."

"Tell me," he said, all tenderness.

"Like, in Big Prairie, I know people will sometimes look at us, but it feels more like curiosity. Like either they're wondering where you've been because you're such a hermit."

He chuckled.

"Or they're caught a little off because I'm one of maybe five people in the whole town who isn't white. But it doesn't feel...condemning. Does that make sense?"

"Yeah. But it's different where you're from?"

"Sometimes. Not always, but... There's still a barrier there, Lance. There are still people who think it's wrong for a white woman to be married to a black man."

"Like your parents?"

"Yeah. Or for a white boy to date a girl who looks like me."

"Beautiful?"

She breathed a quiet laugh. "I'm being serious, Lance."

"Me too." He reached over the space separating them to run a feather touch over her ebony spirals. "You're beautiful, Sophie." His fingers turned to her face, and he traced a cheekbone with his thumb. "Here." With his other hand, he covered his heart. "And here. Don't ever think otherwise. Not because of what other people whisper or do."

She swallowed and suddenly needed to blink. This had been gnawing at her, but the extent of how much it mattered took her a bit by surprise. "I needed you to know before you get there about my dad. Because you already know that he's not my biological father, but..."

"Sophie." Lance framed her face with both palms. "It doesn't matter."

"Even if someone makes a horrible comment when we're out about my parents? Or about us? Because it happ—"

"It. Does. Not. Matter."

When he traced the trail of a single tear down the side of her nose, she broke. It *did* matter. To her it mattered, because she doubted Lance knew what he was in for. To her surprise, Big Prairie had been a bit of a sheltered existence. She'd been a novelty, yes, but for the most part, a welcome one. There were places back home though...

He wasn't prepared for it, and she knew it. Words still hurt, no matter what anyone ever claimed. Attitudes cut deep and sometimes divided. But it was a relief to hear him proclaim so firmly that he would not be swayed.

Not like that fourteen-year-old boy she'd thought had been a close friend.

Lance gathered her against him, one large hand cradling her head. "I love you, Sophie. Other people's issues aren't going to change that. I promise."

"You don't know what it's like," she whispered.

"I'm sure at some point I'll find out." He leaned back and peered down at her again. "And we'll get through it. I'm with you."

A wobbly smile moved her lips, and she reached toward him. They shared a gentle kiss, and he smudged the pools of her tears.

"No matter what, I'm with you."

***

"There's my baby!" Abi Shultz burst through the front door of the two-story home that sat among several groomed yards and houses on the mildly affluent cul-de-sac. "Finally come home to see your mother."

Lance stood at the bottom of the three steps while Sophie pounded up them and flung herself into her mom's embrace. The contrast between the pair was striking—in a way that made him grin. Abi was as fair skinned as the images he'd seen of Queen Victoria. She had crystal-blue eyes set in an oval face and long, straight blond hair gathered back into a ponytail. Even their heights were opposite. Sophie had a good three inches on her maybe five-foot-three-inch mother.

But their smiles...ah yes. There it was. Sophie had her mom's smile—not the same in looks, as Abi had thin lips where Sophie's were full—but the same in quality. Joyous.

Mrs. Shultz stepped back and gathered Sophie's hands in hers. With a grin that said *happy* and eyes that danced with delight, she studied her daughter. "You're all glowy, Soph." Abi's gaze slipped toward him, and then she winked. "Do you know anything about that?"

Sophie laughed the same moment the front door burst open again. This time a tall man of strong build strode through, his lips quirking as his attention found Sophie's. "There's my princess."

"Daddy!" With a quick pivot, Sophie literally jumped into the man's arms.

*Her own personal superhero.* A sudden onslaught of nerves crashed over Lance. Thinking about meeting her parents—particularly her dad, whom he'd known full well Sophie absolutely adored—had been a thing of mild tension in his mind. Actually standing there now, waiting for an introduction, was a full-on anxiety attack poised to sack his confidence.

While still holding his grown daughter off the ground in a tender-fierce hug, Mr. Shultz's attention clamped down on him. Lance's heart went stone-cold still, and he couldn't make his lungs work. Holding that stare and feeling like a paltry sixteen-year-old caught out after curfew—which had never happened—he barely managed to swallow.

The man lowered Sophie to the ground. "Who is this?" Each word was pronounced slowly, in a deep, interrogative voice.

Sophie rolled her eyes and pushed her dad's chest with playful force. "Oh, Daddy, stop it. You're not even scary."

Not true. Not one bit true. Lance was fairly certain he was literally shaking in his boots.

Gripping her dad's elbow, she nearly dragged him down the steps. "You knew Lance was coming, and I've sent you his picture."

"Lance?" The man frowned. "Lance who?"

Lance had to clear his throat, and the smile he tried for felt like a quavering mask. "Lance Carson, sir."

Abi bounced down the steps behind them. "Oh good grief, Derrick. Stop messing with him, you big meanie." She wedged herself in between the pair of Sophie and her dad—Derrick—and then moved toward Lance as if an ambassador of peace. "You're quite welcome here, Lance. Don't pay my husband any mind at all."

Lance fought to take a breath that wouldn't look like he felt nearly as intimidated as he did. Hard not to pay your girlfriend's father any mind. He went for a chuckle anyway. "Thank you, Mrs. Shultz."

Meeting the parents was a big deal—much bigger than he'd prepped himself for. Suddenly it became everything important in the world that they like him. With a palm that felt clammy, he reached toward Mr. Shultz. "Sophie talks about you both all the time." Thank heaven his voice didn't waver. "It's nice to meet you."

Derrick Shultz moved his stiff look from Lance's face to his offered hand and then back again.

"Daddy!" Sophie pried herself from her dad's side and replanted beside Lance, her playfulness being replaced by honest irritation.

Mr. Shultz looked at his daughter, and a fully amused smile overtook the sternness of his expression. He stepped forward and took Lance's hand with an enthusiastic shake and then pulled him into a man-hug.

"I'm messing with you, Lance." He patted Lance's back—a mite forcefully—and then stepped back. "Sophie's my princess. It's a father's duty to scare the wits out of men who want to date their daughter."

With a hard dip, Lance's heart finally restarted, forcing a throbbing pulse throughout his body. He had to remind himself not to sigh in relief, and found a touch of stability as Sophie slipped her hand in his. He shoved his other hand into his denim pocket, worried it might visibly shake dangling out there in the open.

"Sheesh, Dad. If I thought you wouldn't behave, maybe I wouldn't have brought him."

Mr. Shultz crossed his arms and rocked back on his heels. "He looks like he's sturdy enough to handle some fatherly interrogation." He winked at his daughter and then turned back to Lance with a grim expression. "A man worth his salt—and worthy of my princess—better be able to take it."

"Not on the front porch, and not at the first introduction." Though Abi looked like a wispy doll next to her husband—likely to be carried off by a stiff wind—she glared up at Derrick, not even a fraction of thinness in either her look or her voice. "Behave yourself."

"I always do."

"And remember what it was like to meet *my* dad."

"That's exactly what I had in mind."

Abi rolled her eyes and shook her head, though she grinned as she moved to Lance's empty side. Looping her arm through the crook of his elbow, she directed him up the steps. "He's all bark and no bite, I promise."

Looking at the man who had Lance's six-four height by two inches, Lance doubted the full truth of that. Pushed to real anger, he had no doubt whatsoever that Derrick Shultz could sink in a sharp bite.

They filed through the front door, and Mrs. Shultz turned with her arms spread, palms up. "Welcome to our home."

"Thank you for having me, Mrs. Shultz."

"Abi, Lance. Just Abi."

"You can call me Mr. Shultz." Derrick shut the front door behind them.

Abi again turned a reprimanding look up at her husband. "Derrick." She planted her hands on her hips, gaze unwavering from the big man behind them. "You can call him Derrick."

Derrick laughed. Lance had no idea what he'd end up calling the man. His thoughts drifted toward a particular item he'd retrieved from the firebox safe he kept in his office, and he pictured it nestled among his clothing in his travel bag. A slow burn crept up his neck as he made eye contact with the man he'd hoped to have an honest discussion with over the holiday.

Holy smokes, this was way harder than he'd thought.

# Chapter Twelve

Sophie finished setting out the pots and pans they would need at church the following day, inhaling the delicious aroma of her mom's apple crumble as she moved.

"I like him, Soph." Mom hip-checked her as she leaned over her shoulder to whisper. "Your dad does too."

Her smile started small and then bloomed full. "That's good. I told you you would."

"He seemed done tonight," Mom said, entirely concerned and not censorious. "Think he'll be okay tomorrow?"

Their Thanksgiving tradition was exhausting, even for people like Sophie and Abi, who both loved being in the middle of it all. It had crossed her mind that the following day might break her boyfriend. Then again, he owned and operated the River's Edge Vineyard, and she'd witnessed him brave through a crowd during the pickers' picnic. "He'll be fine, I'm sure. Tired, like the rest of us. But fine."

Mom filled a teapot with water and set it onto the stove to heat for citrus tea, seeming thoughtful. "Hey, Sophie?"

Sophie stopped at Mom's cautious tone and turned to look at her. Soft concern shone from her blue eyes as she leaned back against the counter. "Are things easier for you in Big Prairie?"

A mix of hope and something else—maybe a touch of sadness—flavored her mom's question, and Sophie's heart squeezed. *Honesty is the best policy.* That had always been Mom's advice. "Yes, they are."

"You don't ever plan on moving back here, do you?"

Quietly, Sophie shook her head.

Mom held her with a long look and then shook her head. "I was worried for you when you moved there. I was afraid you were going from one hard situation to another. Just another small town that wouldn't take you into its heart. But that's not what happened, is it?"

"No." Sophie couldn't explain why, exactly. Big Prairie was a lovely small town, but as with anywhere, people were people. There was ugliness there. Needles that stung—like a remark made in an aisle in the Big Prairie Market. *Did you hear the new band director is black? Don't know how she'll fit into a farming and ranching community.* It'd been hurtful. Especially when Sophie had struggled to fit into the community she'd been a part of. She'd feared that she would never find a place anywhere.

But those moments seemed more isolated in Big Prairie, though Sophie wasn't sure if that was the truth or merely a feeling. Life there simply felt easier. Maybe for a series of reasons. Finding such a good, close friend in Brenna—even if the past couple of months they'd drifted a bit apart. Discovering that she really loved teaching, and despite that thoughtless remark in the store, she fit in quite well with the school's staff. Then there was meeting and working with Craig Erikson, who though they hadn't worked out romantically, did a great deal to restore her faith in the decency of a good-looking white male. And then Lance...

"Maybe a few people make all the difference," Sophie mused, almost to herself.

"Hmm." Mom's hum came with a gentle smile. "That's very true. Maybe you needed to leave to find those few people." She touched her own heart. "Your people."

"Aw, Mom." Sophie stepped across the tiled space separating them. "You're my people. Always." She wrapped her petite mother in a long hug.

Mom chuckled a teary sort of laugh. "I'm glad to hear that. I'm also glad that you've found somewhere that feels like home." She squeezed tighter, and then Sophie stepped back. Mom cupped her face with one hand. "And the people there, with you and Lance? Are they..."

"We get a few curious looks." Sophie shrugged, and Mom's hand slipped away. "But nothing ugly yet. I'm sure there'll be something sometime—Big Prairie is not utopia—but those few people I mentioned? From them there's only happiness and approval. And Lance is...perfect." Knowing she wore a dreamy grin, she stopped and thought back to that Sunday after she'd gotten herself stuck in the mud. From that first moment, she'd thought that of him. Perfect green eyes. Perfect smile. And when he'd swept her up into his arms out of the mud, perfect gentleman.

But things didn't really get started there, did they? The real snowball had been pushed off the following Sunday, and the launch had a little help. Sophie chuckled. "Come to think of it, Miss Jane, who is like the town sage, sort of set us up."

"Well, if the town sage set you up, who's to argue?"

Sophie winked. "Exactly."

Mom's amusement faded into something more serious. "Actually, if it was *God* who set you up, then it doesn't matter who does argue—because more than likely, someone will, even if it's not someone in Big Prairie. But the thing is, God has always been more concerned with hearts than He ever was with appearances. It's so important that your *hearts* are the same— unified in Christ, walking with Him. On your own as individuals and together as a couple."

That was true. And reassuring as Sophie drew in a nervous breath thinking about how the following day could go. She'd tried to prepare Lance for the possibility of other people behaving in ways unbecoming a human, let alone a believer in Christ. But the truth was, she couldn't. It wasn't possible to know how deeply unkind words and attitudes could cut until you experienced them for yourself.

But there was healing too. Stability in that walk with Jesus. *He who did not spare his own Son, but gave him up for us all—how will he not also, along with him, graciously give us all things?* The portion of the passage she'd read only a week before came clearly to her mind. It'd been from Romans 8. Right along with *If God is for us, who can stand against us?*

Some pretty strong words. She had the gift of eternal life, given by the loving God who would sacrifice everything so she could live. Was it too much to think, then, that He who could love that big would also provide her with a life of joy?

Sophie lingered over those verses later that night and then thought about what Mom had said about Sophie and Lance walking in Christ together. She didn't doubt Lance's claim to salvation, and she loved that he was coming to church with her. But suddenly she had a craving for more. A deeper walk with Jesus that they shared.

As a couple.

*** 

Thanksgiving dinner had been a noisy affair as both Derrick's and Abi's families converged in a united effort to feed more than one hundred people at the Shultzs' church. People from all walks of life who trickled in from the church family and extended community attended the noon meal, filling the fellowship/gymnasium with the smells of turkey, gravy, dressing, and an assortment of pies.

As the constant hum of laughter and conversation filled the space with a rich atmosphere of community, Lance nudged against the familiar pang of sensing his own awkwardness. Typical for him, as he found gatherings overwhelming. Though he now had years of practice acting as host in a group, the feeling that he didn't fit in provoked a loneliness that made him wish for solitude. It was a contradiction, and he knew it, yet ever true. Even having grown up in a community generally more connected than most, it occurred to him that he really had no idea how to *be* part of one rather than just playing a part in it. Simply put, something in him seemed to be broken when it came to the social arena of life.

In contrast, there was Sophie. She thrived on the energetic hum of community. Her servant's heart and joyful spirit were on full display as she dished pie and delivered full plates to guests who could not make it up to the buffet table. Watching her easy sociability drew from Lance both a proud admiration and a sense of unworthiness.

He followed her lead, serving where he could and making conversation, though it felt clunky and awkward. She rewarded him with her smiles, and later—after the dishes had been washed and put away; the leftovers distributed and sent home with many guests; the tables and chairs wiped, folded, and replaced in storage; and the large gathering space cleaned—she slipped her arms around him in a warm hug.

"I'm proud of you." She rested her upturned chin on his chest, her eyes soft and lovely as she gazed at him.

"What on earth for? I'm awkward and stiff among so many, whereas you and your family are easy and comfortable." He curled an embrace around her and slowly released a long breath. "I don't know why you're with someone as socially inept as me."

"You gave," she said simply.

"No more than you, and not nearly as well."

She slid back from him enough to frame his face. "You gave yourself into something that cost you. Lance, that matters."

He stared at her as the glow of her kind love warmed him through. Sighing, he leaned his head against hers. "I wish I were different for you."

"Don't." Her lips pressed soft against his. "I love you as you are."

That memory stayed with him throughout the evening and into the next day, stirring tenderness and strengthening his determination to talk to Derrick.

As the girls left long before break of day for their insane Black Friday shopping plans, Lance found Derrick to be a relaxed housemate. They both slept late—eight being quite late for Lance—and the pair found a pot of hot coffee as well as a selection of doughnuts waiting for them on the kitchen bar counter.

"Ah, quiet." Derrick stretched his long arms toward the ceiling in a stretch. "A sweet change from yesterday, don't you think?"

Lance inhaled the nutty boldness of the strong coffee blend in his mug. "Your church is thoughtful, doing that for the neighborhood."

"It's more like trying to remember what the day is supposed to be about." Derrick settled onto the stool across from Lance. "Neighbors being neighbors, finding some kind of common bond in gratitude, even though we often have so many differences." He laughed, the sound deep and brief. "Funny thing. A few of those who came yesterday, they come every year. I can name at least two who have told me they'd have come to our church, except for me." He shook his head. "I am the Samaritan—mind you, I'm not trying to say that I'm the *Good* Samaritan. Just, the Samaritan—Abi and me, if you get my meaning."

Though he wasn't entirely sure, Lance guessed he meant that they were like the people looked down upon in the New Testament. A finger of disgust curled around his stomach. Nodding silently because he wasn't sure how else to respond, Lance bit into a plain glazed doughnut. Personally, he preferred Garrett's apple turnovers on the rare occasion he got to town and found something sweet. But there was nothing wrong with a Krispy Crème, that was for sure.

For several moments, quiet ebbed between them. Derrick bowed his head, and it took Lance a moment to realize the man was praying. His heart dipped as a wave of inadequacy rushed over him. He should be a more praying man. Especially given that he wanted to ask the guy across from him—not only Sophie's dad, which was intimidating enough all by itself, but the pastor of the church they'd served in the day before—if he could marry his daughter.

Come to that, a prayer would definitely be a good idea right about then. *God, if you're watching me now, could I ask you this one thing?*

Before he could finish that silent shot in the dark, Derrick cleared his throat. Lance looked at him, and the man leaned one arm onto the counter as a corner of his mouth quirked. "I'm a fairly bold man, Lance."

Okay? Lance's breath stilled.

"Here's what I'm thinking: you're in love with my daughter." Derrick's tone was as casual as you please, lacking even a trace of the disapproval he'd employed at their first meeting a few days back.

Even with the apparent approval he'd won, Lance's heart stalled. The perfect opening, if ever there was one, but still, this was Sophie's father. The man she nearly idolized. The one who could crush the future hopes that had emerged on Lance's horizon since that first day on the muddy road.

Lance swallowed and made a point to meet Derrick's eyes. "I am."

A subtle quirk moved Derrick's mouth before he nodded. He leaned back, coffee in hand, and took a sip. "Sophie ever tell you about the color-day dance her freshman year in high school?"

A strange turn in topics. "No, sir. I don't think so. She only said she really hasn't dated much. Something we have in common."

Derrick's slow nod seemed contemplative. "I wondered if she'd shared that bit with anyone."

A sour foreboding burned in Lance's stomach. With that kind of beginning, the story could not be good. Anger swept through him as he imagined the possibilities. "Did some boy hurt her?" He nearly growled the words.

Derrick reconnected their gazes, and there was a sense of approval there. "Yes, he did. It wasn't physical though. But, I believe he did enough damage to scare her off of dating all this time. At least—" He shook his head.

Lance's relief was minor. Physical injuries healed. It was the emotional damage—whether from a physical injury or otherwise—that often lingered for a lifetime.

"She asked a boy she'd been friends with since the third grade to go to the dance with her. He was a close friend—she called him one of her best friends. They were in band together and did track together. He would go with her to youth group, though his family went to a different church than ours. They'd grown up riding bikes through the neighborhood, and Sophie often helped him with his homework." Derrick paused, bracing his palms on the granite. "It all seemed good, you know? This boy picked Sophie up with his mom, and they went out for Italian and then to the dance. My princess's smile had been radiant. But somewhere in the evening, she found the moxie to tell him she had a crush on him—" The story cut off sharply there, and with a stiff jaw, Derrick shook his head.

Lance sat a bit bewildered, though a hunch cracked that he didn't want to acknowledge. Unrequited crushes were common in teenagers. Seemed a little much to believe that it would leave a deep emotional scar in someone as optimistic as Sophie.

"Know what that boy told her?" Steel chilled Derrick's gaze.

Brow furrowed, Lance gave a silent shake of his head even while that splintering suspicion widened.

"He said that he and Sophie could never be more than friends, because his dad would never approve of a girl like her."

That crack split wide open, and a gush of fury rushed through. *A girl like her? Godly? Kind? Smart? Happy? Industrious? What a dang fool!*

"He—like nearly everyone else in their school—was white."

Derrick's leaded words fueled the flood of Lance's anger. He rolled his fists as unbound rage roiled through him. His Sophie. His beautiful, amazing Sophie, demeaned *by a friend* because of genetics. Skin tone. How on earth was this ignorant attitude still a thing? Did stupidity know no bounds?

Derrick leaned forward again, laying both forearms on the counter. "I wanted to beat the fools—first that father, then his son." He grunted a dark chuckle. "How's that for a pastoral response? But Sophie's my princess, and he hurt her deep." Again he shook his head, and a dangerous heat sparked from his gaze. His lips pressed hard and his jaw hardened. "I had to admit to myself, though, that my rage wasn't only directed at that pair. This stuff, Lance. It still happens. Abi and me—we had some pretty big mountains to climb. Complicated is a mild way of putting our relationship. I was a single intern pastor at a new church, and she was a single mom. She'd already been through the interracial gauntlet when she'd dated Sophie's biological father, and unfortunately, the failure of that relationship only fueled those whose opinions went only skin deep.

"Thing is, I've studied God's Word a long time. Back in Samuel, when God told the prophet to go anoint the new king, He told him that man looks on the outward appearance, but God looks on the heart. That's still true on both accounts. When we see marriages blessed by God in Scripture, we see hearts that are the same. Rahab, who wasn't a Jewish woman—her heart aligned with God's, though, and she married a Jewish man. Her son, Boaz, he met a Moabitess woman who had also set her heart on the one true God, and he took her as his wife. They became the great-grandparents to that king Samuel went to anoint. Because it was never about matching skin or race. It was about aligning hearts. First with God's, then with each other. But here we are, still wrestling through these tensions and prejudices and assumptions today. Still giving and receiving wounds as if our own hearts refuse to align with God's."

Derrick looked to the counter, as if sorting what he really wanted to say. After several heartbeats, he nodded, his heart hearing a voice of guidance, and looked back at Lance. "I'm telling you this now, Lance, because I can see you love my princess. And I knew before you got here that she loves you. But you need to know, relationships are hard in general. Our world"—he motioned between them—"can be harder still. This stuff still happens, and I'll be blunt. As much as it wounds us and makes us want to take stupid men to the ground, it shreds our women's hearts. Sophie grew up in a neighborhood and went to a school that was predominately white. The girl spent her life caught between two worlds, and she never really felt like she could belong to either. She worked hard, was friendly and respectful, and usually was treated well. But there were some things that made her feel like she would never be able to fit in. And dating...after that one tepid attempt and being slammed so hard to the ground, she really didn't have the courage to try again."

Lance's pulse strummed with a mix of resentment and empathy, and he had to look toward the counter before he blinked.

"You seem surprised." Derrick said.

"I am, I guess. A little." Lance fixed his posture. "Maybe because I live in a fairly sheltered world. I've never witnessed racial prejudice, that I can recall. Perhaps that's lack of opportunity more than anything, I don't know. Big Prairie is rural, and the town is pretty close knit. And also, mostly white."

"No one's ever said anything when you and Sophie are out?"

He shook his head while thinking back on the few times they'd actually been out in public. He couldn't recall ever feeling looked down on. But that was hard telling, because he spent most of his life feeling like *he* couldn't fit in.

Derrick's shoulders eased. "I'm glad to hear it. Sophie says she loves it there—that it feels comfortable. But, Lance, if you stay with her, it *will* happen. Somewhere, someday, and probably not long down the road, it will happen."

Lance caught Derrick's gaze at *if you stay with her*. His chest expanded as he gathered every piece of courage he could find.

"I'd like to marry her, sir."

Wasn't quite the way he'd thought to ask. Actually, it wasn't a question at all. He gripped his hands together, hoping they wouldn't visibly tremble.

Derrick looked at him, his long study evaluative. Slowly, a lopsided grin poked into his cheek. "Was there a question somewhere in there, son?"

Lance's mind caught on the address. Son. It'd been years since he'd had anyone lay that endearment on him. Chuckling softly to himself, he nodded. "Yes, sir. I love your daughter. Will you give me permission to ask her to marry me?"

*** 

Sophie curled up against Lance as they snuggled on the couch.

Mom and Dad had gone out on their typical Saturday night date—which would end promptly at nine because Dad would go to bed early, as Sundays were a long day for him. Their day had been spent rather lazily. Dad had shut himself up in his office for several hours as he finished working on his sermon for the next day. Mom had spent that time baking and then cleaning. Sophie had started working with her, but Mom shooed her away, telling her to spend the time with Lance. She'd happily complied.

They'd packed a picnic, layered in warm fall clothing, and drove out to Standing Bear Lake. Hand in hand, they'd strolled the paths, and she could feel the man unwinding in nature's balm of quiet activity. Mom had left them her homemade lasagna, but Sophie's parents had already left by the time she and Lance returned home. After a yummy meal, they'd defaulted to her BBC series and cuddled on the couch.

"Are you anxious to get back home?" she asked.

He shifted to pull her under his arm and then pressed a kiss against her temple. "This has been nice."

"This trip? It's been a whirlwind. I was afraid if I put you through one more loaded day, you'd break."

"I seem that fragile?"

"Fragile? No. You hide your exhaustion well." She laid her palm over the place where his heart beat. "I just know you."

"Hmm." The sound rumbled softly from his throat. "And here you are anyway."

"Right where I want to be."

He squeezed her. "The week has been good. And though it was busy, it was nice to have a break from doing business stuff. Sometimes that overtakes all my thoughts, so this has been a good way to step back from that. And today"—he pressed another kiss to her forehead—"has been perfect. Almost."

She pushed away from him. "Almost?" Mocking a frown, she looked at him.

"Almost." His voice fell to a whisper, and the intensity of those green eyes glowed. He moved to sit straighter, clasping her hand as he did so. "Sophie."

Her breath caught as her heart launched into a gallop. She bit her bottom lip, pushing away the temptation to say something teasing as she waited for him to continue.

For a long moment, he watched her, seeming to hold his breath as he did so. Then he lifted his hand until the pads of his fingers traced her jaw. On a breath, he whispered, "I want to marry you."

His words, laced with a longing, a pleading, and a tenderness that tempted her to cry, drifted over her, surrounding her with warmth and the coveted sense of belonging and being wanted. Sophie's eyes slid shut as she savored the preciousness of it all.

"I mean"—the cushions next to her shifted as Lance moved again. And then he was on one knee on the shag rug spread in front of the couch—"will you marry me?"

In his upturned palm lay an antique ring with a dark iridescent stone set in white gold, with delicate scrollwork surrounding it. The setting was stunning, and the contrast of the white ring and dark gem absolutely beautiful.

Sophie's eyes found his—still so deeply green and filled with hope and love—and she laughed. "You planned this?"

He tipped his head. "Do you know me as an impulsive man?"

"Not one bit. Though, we've only dated for a couple of months."

"That is called decisive, not impulsive."

She giggled again, turning her attention back to the ring. Her fingers shook as she lifted it from his palm.

"I'm sorry it's not a diamond. If you want, we can get one and have it reset."

"Oh no," she whispered. "It's perfectly lovely."

"It was my grandmother's. Then my mom's."

"Now..." Emotion caught in her throat.

His hand closed around hers, the hold gentle, and then his other palm slid beneath her jaw. "Yours. If you want it."

She pressed her trembling lips.

After a long moment, Lance breathed out a breath that seemed half-laugh, half-anxiety. "Are you going to marry me, Sophie Joyanne?"

"Yes!" A thrilling delight flashed through her, making her believe that today she might be able to fly if she tried. She flung her arms around him. "Yes and yes and yes."

Though knocked a bit off kilter by her launch against him, Lance caught her up and held her close. He buried his head against her, the roughness of his evening shadow tickling her neck.

He'd been right. That had been the perfect day. No more *almost*.

It was simply perfect.

# Chapter Thirteen

Returning to life in Big Prairie held its mild disappointments. Lance rubbed the hair on the back of his head as he stared at the screen on his desk. Over the weeks since Thanksgiving, meetings had consumed his days. The week after Christmas, a snowstorm that had hit Big Prairie the day after he and Sophie had returned from another visit with her parents had prevented him from seeing her in the flesh.

Good heavens, he missed that woman. The warmth of her hand in his. The fresh smell of whatever lotion or fragrance she used that still provoked the lyrics of "Sweet Caroline" to scroll through his mind and made him feel remarkably content. And that smile. Heaven help him, he was addicted to her smile.

*She's going to marry me!*

His heart leapt in his chest with the thought. Sophie Joyanne. The sunshine in his world, the new point of stability in his life. Soon to be his wife. May could not come soon enough. In fact, sitting there alone, four days since the last time he'd wrapped her in his arms, tasted the sweet fullness of her lips, or felt the security of her leaning against his chest, he wished unashamedly that she'd gone for his teasing suggestion that they simply elope over the Christmas break.

Then again, he'd need to explain some of the things he'd not shared with her yet sooner rather than later. A far less happy thought.

His attention went back to the computer screen that only minutes before had been filled with the camera-fed images of the other men and women he'd met with on the video conference. It was all falling into place, this scheme of his.

*Scheme.*

Not a nice word. It was a plan. A legitimate business plan. Nothing illegal about it. Nothing especially unusual about it, actually. If he was good at anything, it was business, and he needed this. Lane needed this. They needed it to work if the rift between himself and his only brother was to ever heal.

Heart now heavy rather than giddy, Lance leaned back into his padded desk chair and shut his eyes. Waiting behind his lids was a burned-in memory of his dad's printed wishes.

*The land and all of my farm and ranch-related property are to go to my oldest son, Lance. As my son and I have discussed, he is to inherit all, with the understanding of his responsibilities therein. I have full trust in his ability to direct and to provide.*

*God bless your every endeavor, son. You have all my confidence.*

Both palms planted at his temples as an achy frustration gripped him. He'd always been the responsible brother. The industrious one. The one who studied and planned and found a way to make things work. Lane, however, did not see anything about what their father had willed as anything less than outright favoritism and unfairness. Forget that Lane had failed to prove himself responsible with even a small checking account, let alone an extensive ag property. The slight was equal to a disownment in Lane's eyes.

He hated Lance for it. And Lane's resentment ate at Lance's heart and conscience with an unrelenting and ravenous appetite.

*But.*

That was why Lance had come up with this plan. Scheme. If he could make his inheritance divide, and have both halves of that whole equally solvent, he and his brother might have a chance at resolution. It was his version of restitution for a decision he hadn't even made and a situation he'd had no authority in. This was his means of making things right.

*Surly those reasons measure up.*

He'd been doing that more lately, sending up silent...prayers?...longing to feel a sense of approval in place of the constant turmoil. Very likely, the increasing practice was an influence of Sophie's, and more recently, of her father's.

Lance liked the man very much. More importantly, he wanted almost desperately to earn his future father-in-law's respect.

Derrick Shultz's commanding presence and authoritative voice pushed into Lance's thoughts, and with them came a reflection of the sermon Derrick had delivered the Sunday morning before Lance and Sophie headed back to Big Prairie. Derrick had begun a study of the ancient kings of Israel as storied in the Old Testament, pulling from the narrative applications that were startlingly relevant. That Sunday, he'd started with Saul and had landed on two verses in 1 Samuel 8. *Nevertheless, the people refused to listen to the voice of Samuel and they said, "No, but there shall be a king over us, that we also may be like all the nations, that our king may judge us and go out before us and fight our battles."*

Derrick had taken them back several verses in the same chapter, showing them why this was so tragic. In verse 7, there was a conversation between God and Samuel: *The Lord said to Samuel, "Listen to the voice of the people in regard to all that they say to you, for they have not rejected you, but they have rejected Me from being king over them."*

There Derrick had paused. With his head bowed, hands clamped over the stand that held his Bible, and shoulders rolled in as if a weighted burden pressed upon him, he'd groaned. After a long moment that felt sharp and distinctly uncomfortable, he'd looked back at the congregation.

"Brothers and sisters." A tender plea ran a strong current in his voice. "Let us see this for what it is. When we decide we'd rather look like the people who are not of God, and have no inclination to be of Him, we are rejecting his Kingship over us. We are rejecting *Him*." He drew a long breath, and it seemed to Lance that his penetrating gaze focused on him. "Sometimes God gives us exactly what we want, even when He knows it will be our downfall. That is the permission he grants us—to choose our own will over His."

Lance couldn't say for sure why that moment—that leaded statement—had sunk into him so deeply. But it had, lodging itself into a place in his heart right alongside where this muddled matter of his inheritance, his brother, and his plans to reconcile the two resided.

The pairing of Derrick's words and Lance's intentions didn't make sense. Not on the surface, and Lance wasn't sure he wanted to go any further than that.

*God, I'm responsible for Lane. It was my father's final instruction. That's all I know.*

A vibration from his phone distracted him from listening for a response—not that he necessarily expected one—as well as thinking on any of it more. The chair clanged beneath him as he dropped forward to reach for his phone near the laptop.

At the name on the screen, a smile worked like magic against the growing angst in his body. *My girl*, he thought as he tapped open the text.

*Please tell me the roads are clear and dry.*

Shoulders relaxing, he eased back again. *Wouldn't matter. Five days without sunshine is unacceptable. I'll drive in tonight.*

A heart-eyed emoji popped onto his screen. Then, *How about we go out? I think Garrett's is doing a special pasta thing tonight.*

Ugh. Nothing made his stomach burn like the thought of going out somewhere in town. He'd always been uncomfortable with it—usually feeling like the uninvited guest everyone wished hadn't shown up, but ever since he'd submitted his application for approval to the Economic Development Committee, he'd felt like a leper whenever he'd encountered the restaurant owners in town. Surely by now they'd heard. Surely by now they hated him. And he wouldn't blame them any more than he was willing to change his plans.

*How about if I make Italian for you instead? I can make it before I head that way. Gourmet dinner delivered right to your door. I think I even have some of the lodge's very popular strawberry-lemon cheesecake in the freezer.*

Gourmet was over the top. He was decent in the kitchen—had learned to cook out of necessity when his mom had first fallen ill, and had been doing it for more than a decade. He'd also watched the lodge's chef at work a time or two during the midseason last year. He could do a decent homemade alfredo.

*Hmm... Brenna mentioned meeting us there.*

*Like, a double date?* The heat in his belly intensified.

*Yeah.*

Pressing his lips together, he tried to surrender himself to the idea. Sighing, he laid the phone on his desk and then pressed his forehead into his folded hands. People did things like that—went out with friends. Regular people. He was aware of how normal that behavior was. Just...not for him. Not even before. Especially not now.

*Lance? It's okay. We could do dinner at my house.*

Every decent gentleman inclination in him screamed to acquiesce to Sophie's wants. But the coward in him...

*Thanks, Sophie. I just want you to myself tonight.*

He typed the second half of that as an afterthought. An excuse—true though it may be—offered as a thin veil to his cowardice.

When she didn't respond, an emptiness knocked against his heart—oddly, in the exact spot where Derrick's sermon had stuck.

\*\*\*

Sophie had fought against irritation the entire day. Even before her text conversation she'd had with Lance over her lunch break. Moody wasn't really her style, so it frustrated her that she couldn't capture the childlike fitfulness that had been plaguing her and make it behave with some dignity.

Holding up her left hand, she wiggled the ring so that the oval-cut alexandrite stone caught the sunlight streaming onto her enclosed back porch. "I miss him," she murmured to herself.

She did. Intensely, which seemed a bit on the ridiculous side since they hadn't even been apart for a whole week. But knowing that she was going to marry that tall, shy cowboy had somehow bred in her an addiction for his presence.

That, however, was not the only reason she felt flustered.

Why hadn't he wanted to go out with her that evening? Come to think of it, how often did they go out together? Church on Sunday mornings, which still seemed to make Lance a touch antsy. Occasional coffees at Miss Jane's café. And, well, that was pretty much it. They did takeout. Occasionally walked the aisles of Big Prairie Market together if they needed groceries for whatever they'd decided to eat on a given evening. And stayed in. Their dates consisted of binge-watching shows, playing chess, which Lance had been surprised that Sophie was quite good at, and occasionally talking about work. That was it.

Perhaps their boring dating life would have given her a boost of confidence in them as a couple—clearly, they didn't need external entertainment to enjoy each other's company—except there was the niggling worry that had threaded itself through her mind. A worry that had been seeded when her mom asked weeks ago if anyone in Big Prairie seemed to have a problem with their interracial relationship. As Sophie had replayed that question later, a whisper seethed through her heart.

*He's hiding it.*

As much as she hated the ugliness of that small accusation, she couldn't silence it.

"But he's not," she insisted into the silence.

She stared at the depth of multiple colors in the gemstone of her engagement ring. Depending on the light and angle, it could appear purple, deep blue, or sea green. There had been no doubt in her mind when Lance had slipped the ring on her left hand, no hesitation in her answer to his proposal.

This fear was strangling and ugly. And wrong.

"Lance wouldn't do that." Most of her really believed that.

# Chapter Fourteen

Sophie slid into the booth across from Miss Jane as the March drizzle made the world beyond the window a gauzy white.

"Will that fine young man of yours be coming along soon?" Miss Jane asked.

Sophie busied herself with removing her winter coat, a distraction that allowed her not to make eye contact. "No. Not today."

"Oh. That's a shame. I was hoping to ask him about a rooting project I've been thinking on. Lavender is so hard to propagate by seed..."

"Yes, well." Settled, Sophie folded her hands, *smile, it'll help* whispering to her in the back of her mind. She did. "Maybe next time?"

She wasn't sure there'd be a next time. Not at The Grill, anyway. Perhaps not anywhere in public. Ever. After the last time she'd dragged Lance into The Grill, she wasn't about to try a repeat. She wasn't up for another long week of agonizing over why he'd acted so uncomfortable, battling the building sense that he was embarrassed about her. About them.

The sparkle of the iridescent gem on her left hand caught her eye. They were engaged. Engaged! She adored Lance and his kind, quiet ways. Wanted to marry him. And had felt certain after the weekend they'd spent with her family over Thanksgiving that he loved her and that the interracial issue she'd been worried about was no issue to him. Hadn't he said as much?

There had been that brief period right after when doubts had assailed her heart and mind. But when she'd asked Lance about it, having reached into the depths of herself to be bravely honest about her fears, he'd soothed every misplaced feather.

*"Ashamed of us?" His face had twisted painfully. "Never, Sophie. When you're with me, I'm dumbfounded, because I can't believe someone as beautiful and amazing as you are wants to hold my hand—not to mention take my name." He'd kissed the corner of one eye as she'd buried into him. "Being in public has never been my thing."*

It had seemed enough to her. But then she'd begun to feel stifled. She liked hanging out with friends. Going bowling occasionally. Seeing other people outside of the school environment.

Added to that, lately there had been an undefined distance expanding between them. He *was* hiding something. She felt it in the way he kept himself away from town, not even going to the basketball games with her, where she had overseen her pep band—a public appearance he'd been willing to make during the football season. More and more, the only time she actually had real face time with her fiancé was on his rural property. Granted, he'd had a few meetings with his business contacts in Omaha, Des Moines, Lincoln, and Kansas City. But...

But he was slipping from her, and she could only guess as to the reason.

The week before, they'd had an argument about how much time they spent at the vineyard and ranch rather than in town, and though he bent to her desires, she certainly hadn't won any ground. Their date had been a disaster.

Introverted, she got, and Lance was absolutely that. That was seriously okay. He could be himself, and she could be herself, and they'd figure out how to make their opposite personalities work. But last week at The Grill? Over the top. The way he'd fidgeted. Ducked when others passed. Looked almost sick until they were good and clear of the parking lot and out of public view. That wasn't simply being introverted.

It had been shame. And Sophie could only think of one reason he'd feel shame.

"You okay, honey?" Miss Jane reached a sinewy hand across the table to touch Sophie's.

Sophie blinked against the hot moisture in her eyes. "Yes, ma'am. I'm sorry."

"You look about to tears." Concern darkened Miss Jane's blue eyes.

Sophie looked at her arms, studied the creamy mocha skin that didn't match anyone else's in town. *I thought you were beautiful, and I wanted to know your name.* Heart aching at that sweet memory, now her stomach clenched. What if, after all, it did matter to him? Maybe someone had said something to him. Maybe in the reality of what would inevitably happen in their interracial relationship, Lance couldn't take it.

As much as she pushed against it, the devastating thoughts wouldn't budge from her mind. "I'm struggling with something that I'm not sure how to deal with. It's kind of—" Her voice caught, and she had to swallow back a sob. "Devastating."

That firm nod of Miss Jane's had a way of meaning exactly what was called for at any given moment. In this one, compassion. "If you need to talk about it—if it's appropriate— I'm here. If not, I'll pray. Actually, I'll pray either way. The Lord knows all about it, so I don't need details if you can't share them."

She wanted to lay her head down and weep. Instead, Sophie pinned her wobbling lips together and breathed in. Letting her lungs empty slowly, she leaned forward to whisper, "Lance is a good man, don't you think?"

"Honey, I know it." Miss Jane's brows wrinkled inward. "And you do too. If there's something amiss between you two, you need to talk to him about it."

Sniffing, she could only shake her head. When Wes approached with two orders of waffle fries and a pair of cherry-chocolate shakes, she looked out the window opposite.

"Here we are, ladies." Wes slid the tray in front of them. When Sophie thought he'd brush his hands together, as he often did, and leave them with an *Enjoy the goods!*, he remained rooted in place. Unable to resist the draw of curiosity, Sophie looked up at him.

"Will Lance be joining you?" Wes's words were clipped.

Sophie nearly drew back. Wes was a jovial, boisterous man who usually said what he thought, but wasn't ever...this. What was this sharpness he was wielding?

"Now Wes." Miss Jane turned a stern look on the man.

"Just a question." He folded his thick arms, his tone still harsh. "I have a few more for him, if he's gonna show up."

Discomfort spiraled through Sophie as she moved her bewildered gaze to Miss Jane.

Miss Jane did not look confused. Upset, yes. Not one bit perplexed though.

"What's going on?" Sophie asked.

Wearing a grim frown Sophie wasn't sure she'd ever seen on the man, Wes slid his attention to her. "You don't know? Not sure I can believe that. You're marrying the man."

A sickish feeling swirled in her stomach while defensiveness rose up hard and strong in her chest. "Yes. I'm engaged to Lance. And I'd appreciate it if you'd state the problem with that plainly." It was a dare. She was daring him to say something about her skin not matching Lance's. Flat out daring him to be a racist to her face.

Seemed almost bizarre. She'd never have imagined this of Wes. He'd always been kind. Friendly. Never once did she feel like he looked at her and saw only a woman with skin a darker tone than his own pale color. The absurdity of it sliced clean through her—a wound she hadn't prepared herself for.

Was this why Lance had acted the way he had the week before? Had Wes confronted him about—

"Fair's fair, I'll say." Wes unfolded his arms, snagged a chair from a nearby table, dropped onto it in a straddle, and lowered his voice. "Here's the deal, if you really don't know, Ms. Shultz."

"Hold on now, Wes." Miss Jane cut him off.

Miss Jane knew about this? Did she think the same way? Sophie wanted to stomp and scream. Why now? After she'd let her guard down. After she'd thought she'd found people who saw the beauty in diversity and the unity in love. Who looked at all people as the beloved creation, made in the image of God. People who saw *her*.

*God, this is a mean trick.*

"No, Miss Jane. I know you want to protect him—protect them both." Wes's tone softened. "But if Sophie really doesn't know, then someone ought to tell her. Clearly Lance hasn't buckled on his man pants tight enough to do it himself."

"Look." Sophie let anger rise as she sat straight. "The pair of you better put whatever this is on the table, because I'm jumping to some conclusions here, and they don't put either of you in a very godly light."

"What?" Wes scowled. "Godly light? *Your* fiancé is fixing to put us out of business with this franchise deal he's set on bringing into Big Prairie."

Her breath escaped with a gush. "Franchise?" She barely had enough time to get the word out before Wes launched into his rant full steam ahead.

"You want to talk about a godly light?" Anger blazed in his eyes. "That bulb don't shine, young lady. It's the most selfish thing I've ever heard of, and seems he don't care if he's harming his neighbors to build his empire. And the cherry on the sundae? He's not man enough to face us while he's working out our demise. Won't even hardly step a foot in here, and when he did, wouldn't even look me in the eye like a man."

The following silence stung, and Sophie wasn't sure if she could even pull in another draw of air through the tension.

Wes's glare softened, and then pity took over. "You really didn't know?"

Her lips parted, but she couldn't find words. She shook her head.

"Honey, Lance is a good man. We both know that." Miss Jane covered Sophie's arm with her hand and then looked at Wes. "We *all* know that."

"Sure thought I did." Wes said. His shoulders sagged. "His dad would have a fit if he knew. Honest and as hard a worker as they come. Wouldn't have allowed this. Wouldn't have even dreamt it."

"Lance is just like his daddy, Wes. Last year you would have said so yourself," Miss Jane said.

"Last year the boy hadn't been consumed by greed."

"Maybe he has a good reason. We don't know."

"If he had one of those, he would have stood up in front of everyone and said so. Instead, he's sneaking around doing everything in the dark like a raccoon robbing the sweet corn."

"How do you know about it?" Sophie finally found her voice. "What if this is all rumor, and you're spreading lies?"

Wes held her with a long gaze. She refused to back down, warming to her theory.

"Lance *is* a good man, and he cares about this town. He might not be the social guy you are, Wes, but that doesn't mean he's calloused. He wouldn't—"

"The EDC has the final approval for it on the agenda this week," Wes said gravely.

"The EDC?" Sophie looked to Miss Jane, silently begging the woman to say something that would clear all this up. Lance wouldn't do something like this. He just couldn't. Any more than he would be ashamed of their relationship...

A gush of sour shame flooded through her. How could she have supposed that of him? It seemed old wounds had a way of triggering bad assumptions.

"The Economic Development Committee." Miss Jane looked at the table. "He needs their approval to bring in this business."

They were serious. The small bit of relief that she'd relished in discovering that her theories about Lance's behavior last week had been wrong quickly vanished—though they left behind the rotten stench of her own failing. Sophie felt dizzy as she slipped under the weight of what was going on.

"Miss Jane?"

Miss Jane wouldn't look up.

"How long have you known?" Sophie whispered.

"Long as Wes." Miss Jane's whisper wobbled. "We caught wind of it in August. Hoped when word of it died down over the fall that it wasn't going to happen. But..."

"You didn't say anything."

She shook her head and then finally looked at Sophie. Tears sheened her blue eyes. "I kept hoping he'd open up about it. At least tell me what he was doing, if not why. I thought...hoped that if he knew I was *for* him, he'd confide in me. Bless his soul, he's been alone so much in his life. I really wanted him to know there are people around here who care about him. Maybe then he'd feel as though he could be honest."

"That's what the Sunday afternoons have been about?"

Her mouth twisted, and she looked to her hands as she nodded. "Maybe it seems wrong to you." She sighed. "Maybe it was. I don't know. But I wanted to know him and to give him the opportunity to explain. That time I said you have to know someone to really understand what they do? I meant it. And I can say I know Lance now. Much better than I did a few months back."

Wes smacked the table. "Then tell me why he's doing this."

Sadness cloaked Miss Jane as she met Wes's demand. "I can't." She looked back at Sophie, this time with the typical conviction she usually wore. "But I can still say that he's a good man. He must have reasons—legitimate ones. Lance keeps himself closed up, but he isn't selfish, and he's not mean. The way he opens the lodge to the town every year for the pickers' picnic, the way he donates produce for the schools—it's not all a marketing gimmick. Those things cost him, and more than just in the bank."

*You gave...and it cost you.* It had been a moment when the love in Sophie's heart had swelled to near bursting. Lance did love like that—quietly, yes. But certainly.

But this? Wes was right. Bringing in a large franchise restaurant was selfish. Big Prairie simply didn't have the population to support such a thing alongside the smaller home-grown businesses. It would ruin them. Lance would ruin his neighbors.

Everything she'd believed about the man she'd said she'd marry became hazy, and Sophie felt her very soul quake.

A long pause rested between them before Miss Jane drew her shoulders straight and jutted her chin up. "He's a *good* man, Sophie." Her grip on Sophie's hand seemed as though one given in a rescue attempt. Firm and unyielding, as if whispering *I will not let you go.*

Sophie met those bright-blue eyes, desperate for hope.

"I choose to believe that of him." Miss Jane nodded in that resolved way that, this time, lent hope. "Even with this."

***

Lance knew she was upset before she stepped out of her Renegade. Hard to miss, with the way that she'd sat in her car long after she'd cut the engine and had simply stared out her windshield. Not to mention that deep frown. Not normal for his always-pleasant fiancée.

He could guess why. She'd been distant all week—ever since their date at The Grill, and he knew he needed to explain some things. Should have a while back, actually. Now he was caught between a rock and a hard place, so to speak, because the last thing he wanted her to think was that he wasn't willing to do the things she liked. Hanging out in public had never been his favorite thing, and Sophie knew that. But she'd been right; occasionally he needed to think about the things she liked to do. More than occasionally, actually. And he thought he could handle it.

But why did she have to pick The Grill? Of all the people he knew would be upset with him, Wes's anger was the hardest to take. He'd been one of Dad's closest friends. And he'd been one of the biggest reasons the EDC had invested in Lance's vineyard with a start-up grant several years back.

Lance was a traitor. He would never be seen as anything but, not after next week's final approval and the public unveiling of his investment plan.

The truth made him feel sick.

But now he had another problem. After his obvious discomfort at The Grill—driven by that nauseating guilt—Sophie had clearly formed some wrong ideas. Assumptions he should have been more careful to avoid, especially after what her dad had shared with him about her experiences in high school.

*But she knows better.* His defenses sparked yet again. *I love her, and she knows that.*

When she finally left her car, the sound of the door smacking the frame cracked through the silent winter evening, Lance closed his eyes and prepared himself. He'd have to explain, and in doing so, he was risking her respect. Either way, he could lose her.

Her knock rapped against the back door. Yeah, she was more than a little upset, knocking that way instead of breezing through with a *Hey, cowboy, did you miss me?*

He'd much prefer that routine. The one where he'd wrap one arm around her, smile into those gorgeous brown eyes, and answer, *You know I did.* Then she'd wrap a set of her long fingers around his neck, pulling his mouth to hers.

Yes, that'd be much better than her standing stiffly on the other side of the door as if they were distant strangers. Lance's heart jabbed hard against his chest as he turned the knob to face whatever was to come.

"Hi, beautiful. I missed you." Opting for a casual, innocent tone, Lance braced himself for a storm.

"Hi." Sophie's greeting fell flat, and she didn't turn her face up to him as she stepped into the house.

He shut the door and turned to her, then pressed a kiss into her hair. She stiffened, and he felt her pull in a long drink of air. Wanting to breeze past this upset as they'd done before with other things, Lance pressed a palm to her back to pull her against him. She went pliable as a fence post.

"Sophie." He sighed her name as she stepped back. Dark, angry eyes shot up at him. Madder than he'd ever seen. Honestly, more than he'd guessed she'd have been. This was not merely upset. Sophie was steaming toward livid. She stepped around him, and he brushed a palm over his face, turning to follow her. "This about last week at The Grill?"

Hands on her hips, she spun around and pinned him with a glare. "No, Lance. This is about you."

"Me?" If she'd been this upset, why hadn't they talked about it sooner? The spring snowstorm during the early week had kept them apart, but they'd spoken on the phone. Couldn't she have brought it up then, before she'd gotten herself all worked up?

He rolled his shoulders and employed his calm business voice. "Look, last week at The Grill, I was uncomfortable. But that wasn't about you, so I don't think you need to be so fired up—"

"No. It *wasn't* about me. Never mind that I've been plagued with doubt and worry all week about that detail, because we can't even cover that right now. Not when I found out today what it *was* about when I met Miss Jane at The Grill. But, by the way, if you knew I'd felt upset about how you behaved last week, why did you wait until I was good and mad before you thought to apologize about it?"

"Because I thought you'd know better. Jeez, Sophie. I love you. I think you're beautiful and amazing and the best thing in my life. I'm going to marry you. Why would you think for a moment that I was anything like that boy your sophomore year? I'm not that guy. I will *never* be that guy."

Sophie blinked, and the fury in her expression wavered. Softened a bit as her lips trembled. Lance stepped toward her, hand lifted to cradle her face. She ducked away, catching his palm and lowering it.

"Don't distract me by being all sweet," she mumbled.

"Come on, Soph. I'm sorry that I made you feel that way—it wasn't intentional. And it *wasn't* about you."

"I know." She lifted her eyes back to him, traces of her anger rekindling, though now it mixed with a keen disappointment that knifed into his gut. "I know what it was about. Wes told me." Tears sheened her stare. "Lance." Her voice broke and dropped to a strangled whisper. "What are you doing?"

Pain lodged in his chest, and he struggled to breathe. *Did* she know already? Wes told her...yes, then. She knew. And as he'd feared, she did not understand. Her disapproval was as plain as the anger she'd shown up with, and though he'd expected it, the weight of her disappointment in him nearly crushed him.

Sophie Shultz was no wispy woman. She drew up to her full five-seven height, stepped into his space, and held a challenging gaze right on his face. "Lance, this is your hometown. These people, they've watched you grow up. They're *your* people. Your community. How could you bring in a business that will likely wipe out several local restaurants in town?"

Defense roiled within. She was his fiancée. Shouldn't she be loyal to him? Why was she so quick to defend others without even considering his position? Fists rolling at his side, he simply stared at her in silence.

"You are not this man." Her low tone cut with hurt and anger. "You're not selfish. Not a bully. Why—"

"I haven't seen my brother in five years." Answering in a low voice he fought desperately to control, he stepped backward, needing space as he shook with mixed emotion.

"Your brother?" Confusion folded her brow. "Lane? What does he—"

"He left. Refuses to come home. Won't answer my calls. Barely responds to my texts."

"What does that have to do with the franchise?"

Lance turned toward the window over his kitchen sink, jabbing a hand toward the field beyond. "This. Everything."

"I don't understand."

"My dad left all of it to me. I *inherited*. But while he told me what he was planning, he failed to mention his intentions to my brother. Lane didn't find out until Dad's will was read. After hearing it, he shot me one long glare, turned around, and walked out."

"Lance..."

He stepped backward toward the counter and gripped the edge of it. "Do you understand how much responsibility that is? Dad left it to me with the expectation that I would provide. I'd take care of the land and my brother. I was twenty-one years old. How could he expect me to know how to do that?" The words rolled out like steam from a release stack, and as he surrendered to it, he was no longer clear about who he was speaking to. Sophie? Obviously. Lane. Yes. Wes, Miss Jane, his dad...

All of them.

"Lane won't come home. I've lost both my parents and my brother, and I can't stand it." Lance tipped his head back and shouted upward. "How am I supposed to carry all of this alone?"

Silence crackled through the kitchen. Lance shut his eyes, rolled away from Sophie, and gripped the edge of the sink fiercely. Yes, he'd lost his family. And now...Sophie too.

A sniff sounded softly behind him, and then the warmth of her palm touched his back, sliding around his side to his chest. "You're not alone, Lance."

He opened his eyes and lowered his gaze to find her at his shoulder, tears leaking onto her face. The sight cut into his bundle of unshed tears he'd kept packaged and stuffed away deep. Barely aware of the tears until she caught one with her thumb, Lance struggled against the need to surrender.

"I can't lose you too, Soph. You're everything to me."

She winced. Shook her head. "I can't be your everything, Lance."

With an urgent move, he pulled her into a fierce hold. "But you are."

Pressing her forehead into his chest, she leaned against him, slowly wrapping her arms around him. He buried his face into the mass of glossy black curls that smelled of coconut, regaining control over the emotions that had shaken free. As she pressed against him, the moments long and intense, his heart resettled, and he relaxed his hold on her.

Slowly she pulled away and looked up at him. "How will this bring Lane home?"

*She'll listen.* The thought breathed in him a new hope.

"If I can make the property split and still able to support a household, then I can give him the farm and ranch land. All of the fields for soybean and wheat. All the cattle pasture, as well as the livestock. But I have to make the vineyard solvent."

Her brows pulled together. "Seems like the vineyard is doing well. How much more do you need?"

Her tone sounded disapproving. Like she thought he was being greedy. Lance worked to smother a rise of irritation. "The vineyard is almost entirely in debt, Sophie. I can't live off it, and I certainly can't support a family from it yet. If I want to be able to give Lane the farm and ranch—which I do, because I know he wants it—then I have to find a way to make all of the ends meet. For him and for me."

Lips parted, Sophie stared at him, her expression equal parts shock and concern. "Lance, you're not responsible for your brother's—"

"Yes I am." Though spoken low, his tone was harsh. Loaded with frustration and the pressure he felt to make it all work. He jammed a hand into his hair and pressed his mouth closed, fighting again for composure. "I am, Sophie. That's what it means to inherit. At least for me—from my dad. He gave it all to me so that I would provide for my family. For my brother."

Sophie hadn't flinched, even in the face of his wavering control. "Have you prayed about this?"

He couldn't answer.

She waited. Still, he offered her nothing—because he didn't have an answer that would satisfy her. After she visibly swallowed, she lay a warm hand against his chest. "I doubt your dad meant for any of this."

Again, Lance found himself blinking. After a shakily drawn breath, he covered that hand. "Who ever means to die? This is what I have to live with."

"Can you?" Now her lips quivered again. "Can you live with this, Lance? Putting your neighbors, your friends, out of business to bring home a brother who has shut you out for things that were beyond your control?"

Friends? At the moment, didn't seem like he had any, save perhaps Miss Jane. He wasn't sure he'd ever had any—not any true friends. *Alone* had been his whole existence from the moment his dad had died. Until Sophie.

Lance read the ache in her gaze. The disappointment, the pulling away. He couldn't answer, and when the sheen in her eyes produced giant drops of tears, his own lips trembled.

"Sophie…" His whisper was all pleading and need as he remembered that voice of warning so many months before. *It won't last.* His heart cracked.

She shut her eyes while her fingers curled into his shirtfront. "I'm not sure that *I* can."

# Chapter Fifteen

A heaviness had cloaked Sophie for more than a week. She and Lance hadn't come to a resolution. Though they hadn't argued in anger, they weren't in agreement either. How could they? This thing he was doing was huge.

Truth was, she could see his point of view. Lane was the only family Lance had left. His only connection to the parents they'd both lost. And one of the things she loved about Lance was that he carried responsibility responsibly. He was not a man who shirked the weight of it, no matter how heavy. No matter the cost.

In this case, the cost was steep. Reputation. Friendships.

Maybe them.

Because as true as all of that was, Sophie still could not reconcile to Lance bringing in a big-name restaurant that would stamp out the long-held businesses in Big Prairie. She couldn't do it. Which left her and the man she truly did love on opposite sides of a dividing issue.

It made her physically ache. Robbed her appetite, instigated a headache that wouldn't let go. Provoked night after night of silent tears, most of which followed their evening texts.

*Say you still love me. I need you.*

Lance's nightly plea would blur on her screen as her throat would swell. *I still love you.*

*But* he would respond.

Yes. There was a *but* in there. One she wouldn't deny. *I still don't know that I can stand by you in this. These people... Lance, how can we face them if you do this?*

To which, usually, there would be a long pause of heartbreaking silence. And then: *I love you, Sophie.*

Last night, however, he wrote instead: *I can't see past any of this. I know you don't see it, but I am responsible for Lane. I inherited, and there is this huge responsibility in the blessing. But I know what you are saying—I can hardly face anyone in town.*

She hadn't known what to say. He said nothing more.

Dressed in her baggy sweatpants and wrapped in a hoodie she'd borrowed from him several weeks back for an evening walk in the vineyard, she huddled into the soft hold of her overstuffed chair. They had yet to say anything more. Her fingers tightened around the mug of warm peach-ginger tea—a gift from Miss Jane several days back when the kind woman stopped in at the school to check on her. *It's a soothing blend*, she'd said, gripping Sophie's hands. Then she'd tugged Sophie down and placed a motherly kiss on her cheek. *These are hard times. I'm praying for you, my dear girl. And for Lance.*

Miss Jane hadn't even asked for an explanation. All that mattered to her was that there were people she cared about who were hurting. Even if the cost to herself would be great, Miss Jane chose to love. At the memory, a lump swelled in Sophie's throat. Miss Jane's prayers—and her own—they seemed to go unanswered. Sophie and Lance couldn't find a way to meet on this. But the example she set could not go unrecognized by Sophie.

*When it hurts, love.* The new mantra superseded Sophie's typical *smile, it'll help*. A much less rosy phrase, but one that she repeated nonetheless.

As she did often when emotions grew too much to be held in, Sophie reached for the notebook and pen waiting on the side table. As the words poured forth, first stuttering and dry, then as if a flood, her tears seeped and then poured.

*Bless the Lord, oh my soul...*

*A darkness has fallen, the way forward shadowed and unclear. How do you love someone this much when you cannot agree with the choices he's making? I can't stand beside him in something I feel is wrong. But I can't unwrap my heart from his either. Maybe I am not supposed to. Oh, God, what would you have me do?*

*Bless the Lord, oh my soul...*

*Redeem this pit. Mine. And his. Old hurts, past mistrusts taint our emotions and decisions. But You can heal those wounds.*

*Bless the Lord, oh my soul...*

*Show us a different way. Make something else known.*

*Bless the Lord, oh my soul...*

*In this fallen darkness, even in this place of ache.*

*Bless the Lord. Oh my soul, bless the Lord.*

A surrender wove through her, one of will and of knowledge. Daddy had told her many times that when the shadowed valley loomed large, the sheep needed to trust the goodness of their Shepherd. Such conversations had bonded her and her dad, especially when they came up because Sophie had been excluded. Times when she'd felt the sting of loneliness that came from knowing she was different than her peers. Moments of rejection that were petty and mean.

*Press into the kind heart of your Shepherd, princess, and do not surrender to the easy path of resentment.*

So much easier said than done. Then. And now. With the thought of resentment, her mind quickly turned toward Lane. A faceless man who would make an easy target for that tempting bitterness. Did he know what his anger was doing to his brother? Did he realize the lengths that Lance would go to build a bridge between them?

No. Certainly that answer would be no. Lance said Lane hardly acknowledged him. Tucked away in some remote part of Wyoming, living as a wild man who earned his living as some kind of backcountry and river guide, Lane had cut his brother out. A snub if there ever was one.

Sophie closed her journal, securing her pen on the cover, and slid it back onto its place on the side table. Her phone lay there, whispering to her the idea that had ribboned through her mind for several nights in a row.

She'd found Lane's number in Lance's kitchen on a faded Post-it stuck under a magnet clinging to the side of his fridge. That had been last week, and she hadn't mentioned it to Lance. Not when they were already in turmoil with each other. But she had snapped a photo of it. And hadn't forgotten.

After lifting the phone, she cradled it in her palm and shut her eyes. *I don't want to make things worse...*

Still, after a week of asking the Lord for wisdom, this idea kept surfacing.

"Don't let me do something stupid," she whispered as she looked back down at the phone. Then she tapped open the apps she needed—the photo file and then texting—and proceeded.

*Hi Lane. You don't know me, but you probably should. My name is Sophie Shultz, and I'm engaged to your brother. Maybe we should talk?*

***

Sophie walked the quiet dirt road that wound through the barren ash and birch trees. It'd been a while since she'd been down this way—since she and Craig had agreed that they were friends but not more.

A footpath cut from the road at her left, and she turned onto it. With a few gentle curves and a couple of spots where she had to high-step her way over fallen logs or low points of half-frozen mud, the trail opened to a half-moon beach. Craig had called this the swimming hole, and it was where he'd brought her for a Saturday morning coffee date thing.

Life had changed so much since that day six months before. She and Craig were both engaged now—but not to each other. Sophie only knew that Brenna and Craig were blissfully happy at this point—and she was enormously happy for them. Only heaven knew all that they'd had to struggle through to get to that point.

*Thank You that You are good, even when we are at our worst.*

Truthfully, Sophie didn't know the storms Brenna and Craig had faced. She only knew that there was a long, hard history between them, and that something had changed—beautifully so—between the two.

As she neared the large piece of driftwood that had been placed on the edge of the beach, Sophie turned her thoughts back toward her and Lance. Lowering onto nature's seat, she sighed. She had fallen fast and hard for that tall vineyard cowboy. So much so that it still made her head swim a bit.

But now...this. Wasn't romance supposed to be all hearts and smiles and easy rides into the sunset? Sophie chuckled at her own simplicity. Of course, there was life, right? The reality of life said plainly there were going to be hard places. Storms. She hadn't expected one to brew so soon—and so fierce.

*God, what do I do with this?*

With her head bowed, her eyes squeezed shut, she squeezed the phone she carried between both palms. Sitting there with only the quiet symphony of nature stirring around her—the gentle lap of the river as the current met the beach, the call of early spring robins as they flitted through the leafless branches above, and the occasional rustling of small animals as they scurried about their lives—Sophie let this moment of struggle press in. For the first time since she'd confronted Lance with what she'd heard in town, she stopped fighting against the disappointment and anger. Instead, she surrendered to the reality of it.

Goodness it hurt. How could one love another so much and yet feel so deeply upset with them? As she surrendered to the emotions that had been brewing for days—emotions she'd worked to suppress throughout the week—hot tears ran along her nose and then dripped to the already damp ground at her feet.

She couldn't smile her way through this.

She wanted to shake Lance, to tell him to *stop this*, until he behaved himself. How could he think this course was justified? How could he live with himself after he ruined Wes and Jaycee, Miss Jane, and the Garretts? He was a smart man—surely he knew how his actions would affect his neighbors. He was a compassionate man—deeply so. How could he act in such a selfish way?

*He's my brother, Soph. How can I just let him go?*

There had been no denying Lance's agony when he'd responded to her confrontation. Yes, this step was tearing him apart, and he understood the consequences. But he was willing to move forward with it for a brother who, by all appearances, didn't care nearly as much for Lance as Lance did for him.

The unfairness of it split her heart. The pain burned—an ache for Lance at the complicated, impossible position his dad's decision had put him in, and the careless rejection he suffered from his own brother. And a heartache all her own—so fresh and unexpected that she felt her world crumbling in instability.

With vision blurred, Sophie turned her phone over in her hand and reread the last text from Lance.

*Say you still love me.*

She did. But last night she couldn't bring herself to say it.

Even now, in the new morning that had dawned in an irony of sunshine and clear skies, she didn't know what to say to him. Part of that could be that now she was wrestling with insecurity and perhaps a touch of guilt because she'd gone behind Lance's back in reaching out to Lane. How would Lance feel about that? She wasn't sure. So instead of tapping his name in her text menu, she scrolled a few names down.

*Daddy. I need to talk.*

Her plea sent off, Sophie leaned in to her hand as a fresh wave of tears washed over her. When her phone vibrated, she wiped the streams of tears with the back of her hand before she accepted the call.

"Good morning, princess."

Hearing his voice made her lips tremble. "Hi, Daddy."

"Uh-oh. Why are you crying, baby?"

She had to sniff and swallow before she launched into the story, ending with, "I don't know what to do."

For many moments, the connection remained quiet. Daddy was like that—careful with his advice. Thoughtful and prayerful. Sophie waited, her heart calming.

"Sophie, do you love this man?"

"You know I do, Daddy. But I don't agree with this decision. And I hate that he hid it from me."

"Yeah, that's no good. Not good at all, princess. So where does that leave you?"

Sophie gripped the phone harder. "Lost. Confused. I told you— I don't know what to do."

"He knows you are not in favor of this business move?"

"Yes."

"And?"

"He loves his brother and can't see any other way to bring Lane home."

"Hmm." Daddy's deep, wordless response let her know he did understand the hard place she was in. "So what are your options, as you see them?"

"What do you mean?"

"Are you going to call things off?"

"I don't want to—I love him. That's what makes this so hard. This isn't normal for Lance. He's tenderhearted and kind. This callousness isn't who he is at all."

Another long pause. Then, "Princess, the thing of it is, the people we love will disappoint us. That's just human fact. That's when it's hardest to love. So this is your moment, kid. Will you choose to love when it's hard, when this man you've built up to be so much has shown you his humanity and it's disappointing—will you still choose love?"

The streams of tears ran again. "Yes. But, Daddy, I *don't* want him to do this."

"You can't make people behave as you want, Soph. Even the people you love—and who love you in return."

"But what can I do?"

"Pray, princess. You can pray."

"But—but *just* pray?"

Dad grunted, a sound of mild chiding. "*Just* pray? Is that what you think, Sophie? That prayer is a *just* sort of thing? My daughter, you need to ask yourself what it is you believe about God."

Sophie sucked in a startled breath. This conversation suddenly felt like a gut punch. "What?"

"Do you think that anything you say or do is going to be more effective, more powerful, than what God can do?"

Heat filtered into her face. "Well...no. I mean...uh, no."

"Sophie Joyanne, hear the Word of God: 'Is anyone among you suffering? Then you must pray. The effective prayer of a righteous man can accomplish much.' Those words are in James five. Find them and ask yourself if you believe them. While you're in James, look in chapter one and see what it says about asking for and receiving wisdom. And then go over to Philippians four and read about what to do with this anxiety. Finally, find yourself in Ephesians and hear what Paul says: 'Now to Him who is able to do exceedingly abundantly more than you can ask or imagine.' Ask yourself, child—who is your God?"

Daddy drew a breath, and his next words came more gently. "*Just* pray, Sophie? That's not the kind of praying I'm talking about at all. We are not talking about some kind of incantation you found in a fairy tale that you know doesn't have a flea's bit of chance of reaching heaven, let alone changing anything on earth. You want God in this? Then you *pray*. You pray like a warrior, dressing herself for battle, ready to fight for that man you love. You pray like you believe the God of all of creation is sitting up on His throne hearing you. Pray like you know He is absolutely able to do more than you can think or imagine—including this. This problem you can't solve, sweet baby, this might be God's way of showing you how mighty He really is. He's asking you to pray with your faith firmly set on Him. It might feel simple, but girl, *prayer* is the most potent gift our heavenly Father has given us. Don't you dare treat it as a *just* kind of thing. Do not underestimate the power of the God who *hears*."

That was her Daddy. The preacher. The man of God.

Sophie breathed in, feeling her lungs expand with air that felt clean and fresh, and her spirit climbing out of the mire of helpless defeat. Her eyes raised skyward, she bathed in the warming light that covered her face. The story of her life to this moment had assured her of something she grabbed hold of now—when the preacher reached into the Word of God and delivered her a sermon, she'd best listen.

And when the Spirit of God stirred direction into her soul, she'd best obey.

# *Chapter Sixteen*

Stress ran through Lance's body like a slow-release toxin. His stomach seemed to be ever on fire, and the tension he carried in his neck and shoulders created an unrelenting headache. Both symptoms sparked with fresh strength as he leaned back against his office chair. The phone call should have been one of confirmation. The EDC had approved his petition for a zoning reconfiguration as well as a recommendation to the city council to approve the pending business permit.

As far as the restaurant went, all things were moving forward. His next business plan was a go. All he could think about, though, was the deep disappointment and hurt in Sophie's face.

*Can you live with this, Lance?*

Her question pressed painfully into his heart. Honestly, even before her—before them—he'd wrestled with the idea. The idea of endangering Miss Jane's, Garrett's, and The Grill brought him no pleasure at all. If it weren't for the driving need to mend what he'd lost with Lane, to reconcile with and provide for his brother, he never would have considered bringing in a big outside business. But what he'd told Sophie was the hard truth—the vineyard wasn't solvent yet, and despite all appearances, it wouldn't be able to support him for many years.

He'd worked his mind mushy trying to figure out how to make the living feasible. All the external contracts with wineries in Lincoln, Iowa, and Missouri, and with a juice company up north, didn't make the numbers black. Building the lodge was supposed to drive the ink out of the red, but the debt he'd taken on, as well as the extra staff and utilities that move had required, barely budged the numbers north. Lance understood math and business. He understood this was a long-term deal. Eventually it would all come right.

But he didn't have eventually. Lane had been gone for years—and had slipped into a lifestyle that was brazenly dangerous, for several reasons. Living as a river rat was one thing—Lance couldn't fault him for taking on the challenges of white water, because Lane always had loved a thrill. But the lifestyle that came with it...

He'd read an article about the river guide slums. Had made some investigative phone calls of his own to see if the printed word had exaggerated to sell a story. Turns out, the information had been censored, not overblown. No one could live that way and not come out unscathed. No one.

This rift between the brothers had gone unmended for much too long. It'd gone beyond hurtful and now lived squarely in the line of real danger.

Bringing a franchise into Big Prairie might look like robbing Peter to pay Paul, as Sophie had said last week. But the truth was, the big name was known to people outside of their small town, which meant that not only would it add drawing power to the River's Edge Vineyard, but it was a much more stable investment with a shorter payout timeline than anything else Lance could think of.

People were drawn to the familiar. They were much more willing to risk traveling to something unfamiliar if they knew there was something they were acquainted with waiting nearby. With the two combined—the familiarity of a known brand alongside the novelty of his vineyard—it seemed certain that he'd be able to hand over the rest of the property and business to Lane before he was thirty years old and the years between them neared a decade. Hopefully, before it was too late for his little brother to escape the consequences of his chosen life.

All the reasons were valid. But inside, Lance felt rotten. Literally, like his heart and spirit were rotting.

*There is a way that seems right to a man...*

Man. That didn't help. How on earth had that verse from Proverbs lodged into his mind with such clarity? He'd started reading his Bible more—not really consistently, but more—since meeting Derrick, something in him telling him that if he really wished for Derrick's respect, he'd better get more familiar with the Bible. He hadn't thought that what he took in from those readings would stick.

Usually, he'd not be bothered by that. Probably would even think it was a good thing. He did believe in the Bible. Believed it was God's Word every bit as much as he believed Jesus was God's son and the Savior of sinners. That hadn't been the question or the issue. He'd simply assumed that everyday life and the ancient Word of God didn't really intertwine.

At the moment, this was much more than an intertwining. This was a twisted-up knot, the likes of which he wasn't appreciating much.

*Can you live with this?*

Another pang flashed through his gut, and frustration followed closely behind.

"I can't live with any of it," he growled, face tipped up to the beams of the ceiling. His voice rose to a near shout. "No matter what I do, I lose people I love. How am I supposed to live with that?"

Silence descended in response. Which didn't surprise him as he sat alone in his office.

This was how life had always been.

***

*Engaged? You're lying. My brother can't hardly talk to a woman, let alone propose to her.*

Sophie stared at the text that had come in sometime during one of her afternoon classes. She hadn't known when it arrived, as her phone lived in her backpack during working hours. With one strap of the bag slung over her shoulder, she'd passed through her classroom door, only to stop short when those words had crossed her vision.

What on earth? Was this guy teasing? Or was this a completely serious reply?

"There's my long-lost friend." Brenna's voice dragged Sophie back into the present, in which Sophie stood like an ice sculpture in the middle of a deserted hallway gaping at her phone. "I had a meeting with—"

Looking up, Sophie found Brenna's smile fading.

"Hey. Everything okay?" Brenna asked.

"Uh…" Sophie bit the bottom corner of her lip. She certainly wasn't going to share the details of her current issues with Lance, but this part about Lane…

Brenna stopped in front of Sophie, wearing an expression of concern. "Sophie?"

"Umm, how well did you know Lane Carson? And be honest this time."

The concern on Brenna's face morphed toward injury.

Yeah, that was a cheap shot. Everything between Sophie, Brenna, and Craig had worked out, and they were all friends. Sophie hadn't needed to put in that jab. "Sorry," she whispered, lowering her phone.

Brenna bobbed her head like she was debating, and then grinned with a shrug. "Forgiven." She winked. "What about Lane?"

"He's Lance's brother."

With an eye roll, Brenna looped her arm through Sophie's. "I did know that much."

"They haven't really spoken much in the years since Lane left."

"I didn't know that. But I guess that's not really surprising." On a small tug, Brenna began down the hallway toward the door. "They were never really close, as far as I could tell. Complete opposites, actually, and while Lance seemed kind of indifferent to that fact, Lane resented it."

"What do you mean?"

They pushed through the front doors together, and a chilled breath of air met Sophie's cheeks. The late winter and early spring had been frosty and wet, and by the clouds hovering in the northwestern horizon, Big Prairie was in for more of the same. Which meant the roads would be muddy, and likely as not, she wouldn't be seeing much of Lance.

Her mood felt about like that storm cloud she'd eyed. Gray and heavy and ready to burst.

"Lance was an overachiever," Brenna said. "But not one who did so to show off. He's driven, as I'm sure you know."

Indeed, she did.

"Lane was a bit of a troublemaker. Not anything of real trouble, but he was a show-off—the kind of guy you know craves attention and is willing to do anything to get it. It was like he felt overshadowed by things—by his mother's death and by Lance. Mostly, it seemed like, by Lance."

"Why?"

Brenna stared off at something across the parking lot. Sophie followed the trail of her gaze and found Grant Hillman walking toward his car. "Should I ask Grant?"

That provoked a bit of a chuckle. "I'm sure Grant could probably tell you a professional analysis—except for he wouldn't do that. He hates that people think he's always evaluating them."

Sophie squared her look back on Brenna. "Was that an issue with you two?"

"It was." Brenna's expression pinched. "And I wasn't very fair to him about it."

"Does he resent you?"

"Not a bit, it seems. Nor does he resent Craig. He has let it go so we can all move forward. Which is nothing less than who Grant Hillman is."

"Quite a good man." Sophie whispered.

"He is that." Brenna leaned in to Sophie's shoulder. "I keep hoping some woman will show up who deserves him."

"Is that guilt?"

"Maybe a little."

Sophie leaned her head against Brenna's. "Some things don't work out."

"Yeah. And other things do. Don't get me wrong—I'm happy." Brenna lifted her left hand, the glitter of the diamond Craig had given her catching the weak bits of the smothered sunlight. "Craig and I are really happy. But all of us still have to live with the choices we made, you know? We all still live here, work together, and see each other at church. There are things that will simply take some time."

"Yeah, I get it." Sophie sighed. She wanted badly to unload her own burdens on Brenna. On one hand, it seemed like it would help to have a friend's point of view. On the other, it also seemed that it would be a betrayal to talk about her and Lance's issues without his knowledge or permission. Especially considering that Lance was a very private person.

Brenna moved forward again, and they descended the front steps in unison. "Back to Lane. What brought him up?"

This part of the story, surely that would be okay to tell Brenna. Especially since Lance knew nothing about it. A thread of guilt wove into that thought. Had her contacting Lane equated to going behind her fiancé's back? Unsettled about that, she lifted her phone anyway and tapped the screen until Lane's text reappeared. "I sent Lane a text introducing myself. He sent me this in response." She moved the phone so Brenna could read it.

After a silent moment, Brenna hummed. "That sounds like Lane."

"Is he joking?"

"Yes, but in a serious way." Brenna stopped at her car and turned to Sophie. "I don't know what exactly happened between the Carson brothers, but Lane took off a while ago, and Lance has buried himself in his work. Like I said, I'm not surprised to hear that they haven't really talked much since then. It thrills us to know that Lance has found a new snippet of life in you, and when you're together, I'm pretty sure he glows. All of us want that for him—for Lance to be happy, because his life hasn't been easy. Lane..." She sighed, looking as though she were searching for a tactful way to say the truth. "Lane will look out for Lane. He always has. So be careful with that, okay?"

Sophie slipped her phone into her back pocket, slowly blowing out a breath.

"Hey, Sophie?" Brenna grabbed her left hand and held it up between them. A fresh smile smoothed the concerned wrinkles from her expression. "I'm really, really happy for you."

Sophie looked down at their clasped hands, her own ring a mellow beauty on her finger. "Thanks," she whispered.

That shared delight was a tender gift of joy in the middle of her anguish. A reminder of the good she had, even in the midst of the hard. Because even in all of this turmoil, she loved Lance and was loved in return.

That was a gift worth treasuring.

After Brenna gave her a quick hug and strode away toward her own car, Sophie retrieved her phone again. With quick typing, she sent off the text she should have days ago, hoping the man at the other end would know her words were true.

*I still love you.*

And then she prayed. Like a warrior.

# Chapter Seventeen

Lance stared at the man standing in the doorway. He looked like a hobo—trucker's hat covering a wild tangle of long, unkempt dark hair; army-surplus backpack slung over his shoulder, packed to near bursting, like he lugged everything he owned within the heavy canvas panels; and baggy denim jeans that gave the impression they'd be better off burned than washed.

Lane.

His brother, nearly unrecognizable as he slumped one shoulder against the doorjamb, stood across from him in their home for the first time in years.

"You haven't changed a bit. All clean shaven and buttoned up." Lane grinned beneath the shade of his cap, the white of his teeth splitting the dark scraggly hair of his long beard, betraying the truth of the man. He was not some unkempt vagrant stumbling in off the highway. Teeth that white came by drugstore, at least. And that bottle of Fat Tire he lifted to smirking lips wasn't the kind of drink a desperate man of no means toted around.

"Lane." Lance shook the sudsy dishwater from his hands and snatched a towel. "Are you in there somewhere?"

A grunted chuckle shook his brother's chest—a sound of derision, not amusement. "This is me. Me in all my rebellious glory. And don't think that I'm that prodigal son come back to beg for forgiveness. I'm not that desperate or humble, my pious older brother. Just came back to see if it was true."

Humble? No. Humble was not something Lane had ever been. Not since his first wail at birth. Mom said her second born had screamed as though he'd been insulted from the first breath. Back then the comment had been made with an adoring laugh, a loving mother's joyful memory as she'd reminisced about life.

"See if what was true, exactly?" Lance finished wiping dishwater from his hands and tossed the towel back to the counter.

Lane took a drag from the bottle. "You clubbed a woman over the head."

"Come again?"

"Heard you were engaged."

Had he? Where had Lane heard that? Far as Lance knew, Lane had cut every tie from Big Prairie, including the one between them. "You've kept spies in the land?"

"Nope. Don't need to. News worth knowing finds me."

"How did this news find you?"

Lane dug his phone from his back pocket, tapped a few times, and then nodded. "Sophie Shultz."

At her name, Lance's heart clenched. Sophie? How? Why would she go behind his back to—

Ah. It made sense. Lance tempered the rise of irritation building in his chest and stuck to the task at hand. Choosing to cling to cool indifference in front of Lane, because Lane thrived on pulling a rise out of anyone—most of all his older brother— Lance crossed his arms and leaned against the counter. He even summoned a grin. "So you've met my fiancée?"

"That's bizarre." Lane threw back another swallow of beer and then wiped his face with the sleeve of his ratty flannel. "She used that word too. Like she liked it. One would assume, of course, that a clubbing victim wouldn't."

"Funny, Lane." Lance stepped toward the kitchen table and hooked the toe of his boot on the leg of a chair. With a calculated shove, he pushed the chair free of the table and nodded to it. "Come in and shut the door. Sky's working on a storm out there."

"Bossy as ever."

"Or stand out on the porch, if you'd prefer. Either way, shut the door. Heat's not free in March."

Lane held a cool stare, took another drawn-out swig, and then pushed off the doorframe. He sauntered the seven steps it took to go from the doorway to the table and dropped his pack. Without bothering to shut the door.

Lance held a disapproving stare on him and then moved to close it himself. Silence threaded through the room while he returned to the sink, washed the last two dishes that remained in the suds, and then redried his hands. When he turned back to Lane, he found his brother slouched on the chair, watching him with a look of contempt.

"She a mail-order bride?"

"Nope. Clever of you to think so though."

Lane tapped the wood table with the butt of his beer bottle. "Inflatable?"

"Brilliant, brother. Didn't you say she contacted you?"

"You have me there." Lane lifted his drink, only to pause near his mouth and swirl the bottle around. Finding it empty he raised it toward Lance. "Don't s'pose you keep a stock?"

"I'm not a beer guy, Lane. Bet you remember that though."

"I remember you were not a *fun* guy. Maybe you should try the beer. Might help with the fun."

"Are you drunk?"

Lane's head lolled back, and the laugh he shouted felt like a whip.

Lance had no idea why he should feel surprised. He'd spent most of high school and all of his tech-school college years dragging Lane's drunk butt out of trouble all over the county. Covering his younger brother's foolishness so that their dad wouldn't know.

"Of course you are."

"Of course I am!" Another laugh that pierced. "But not near enough for me to stomach being back. We need a drink, brother. You've got wine somewhere, right? Drag out a bottle so we can toast to your good fortune." Lane bent forward and slapped his palms on the table. "My straight-as-an-arrow brother found himself a woman. No one would have believed it!"

Unable to suppress a sigh, Lance gripped the back of his neck. "You didn't drive all the way home drunk, did you?"

"From Wyoming?" With a breath, Lane made his lips vibrate. "Nah. But from that spot on the river—you know the one? Yes. About half-drunk from there. Finished two bottles in the Rover, and this"—he held up the empty bottle—"was the last of my supply."

"Shocking." Lance padded across the wood floor to the back door so he could peek out the window. Parked at a reckless angle that epitomized his brother's life and attitude was the 1980s Land Rover that Lane had taken when he'd packed up and moved out.

"Am I blocking you?" There was little effort to hide Lane's mocking tone.

"Not for the moment. But you need to move it anyway. Sophie's heading this way."

"She living here?"

"No." Lance pushed away from the door and turned back toward the table. "Doesn't stay here either. Anything else you'd like to know?"

"Does she know you're impossible to live with?"

"You can let her in on that." He held a hard look on Lane while he lowered onto the chair across from him. "Like I said, she'll be here in a while."

"Huh." Lane ran a hand over his face, dragging his fingers over the heavy, wild beard covering his cheeks and jaw. "Might be I'll scare her off."

"Doubt it."

"Think she loves you that much?"

Lance made a point to sit in stoic silence. As much as he'd thought about having Lane return home, he hadn't thought about how obnoxious his brother could be. Perhaps because he'd assumed growing up would have worn away the punk kid Lane had been really good at pretending to be. Never would have thought it'd make it worse.

Yet worse sat there, in the hairy, unwashed flesh.

Lance thought back to the text Sophie had sent him earlier that afternoon, and he gripped on to the relief he'd found there. She loved him. Still.

Lane's crack of laughter split the silence that had settled between them. With a long, searching look, he leaned forward, stretching his forearm onto the table. "I'll be nice, big brother. Promise."

Lance arched an eyebrow. "Is that any good these days?"

"What? My promise?" A smirk moved onto the seam of Lane's lips. "As good as it ever was."

"That's what I thought."

Lane tossed his head, leaned back, looked at the ceiling, and then stretched his arms upward. With a growlish yawn, he unfolded his long body from the chair and stood. "Guess I better wash the homeless off me before your lady gets here. There any hot water?"

"Should be." Lance stood. "Towels in the closet, where Mom kept them."

"And my room?" He bent to snag his backpack.

"Just like you left it—except clean."

Lane nodded, flung a wilting salute, and meandered toward the doorway that would lead him to the back part of the house.

"Lane." Lance swallowed, a turn of emotions brewing within.

"Yep?"

"Welcome home."

The pause in Lane's step and the subtle jerk in his posture hinted at a sore spot. He ran a hand over his face, then turned an easy-boy grin back to Lance. "Thanks." His tone said anything but.

As Lane disappeared from view, a text alert drew Lance's attention.

*Radar looks bad. Mind if I bow out tonight?*

He felt flattened, missing her as much as he did. Then again, there was Lane. Sophie not coming out just then was likely for the best.

***

He looked destroyed.

Sophie moved to weave her arms around Lance's shoulders, her hand cupping the back of his neck. He wrapped an arm around her waist and pulled her in as he sighed.

"Was he always like that?" Sophie whispered.

"He can be charming when he wants to be." His shoulders sagged as he leaned the side of his head against hers. "Actually, to be honest, I think he works hard at being a jerk. Charm is more his nature."

Guilt weighed heavy in her heart. She'd done this—brought Lane back. Apparently the night before—though Lance hadn't said anything about it when she'd texted about not going to the ranch because of the predicted rain.

That had made for a long night and day, and having now met Lane, she could only imagine. Made her wish she'd made the trip last night, especially since what had been warned as a downpour had produced not much more than a few sprinkles. "Why is he determined to be a jerk?"

A low sound rumbled from Lance's throat, something like a painful groan. "Because he doesn't want to be anything like me. He resents being my little brother and wants to make sure everyone under heaven knows that we are *not* the same."

Sophie dragged the tips of her fingers through the back of his hair. "He doesn't want to be smart and responsible and kind and honorable?"

"I wasn't fishing for compliments, Sophie. And you know I'm not all of that."

The ache that had been throbbing in her middle concerning this man had intensified from the moment she'd walked through his back door. He'd looked exhausted, and a mite bit betrayed, and when she'd asked him what was going on, he'd simply said, "My brother came home."

She'd sucked in a breath as an alarm fired through her mind. One connection with those wearied green eyes, and she'd known her interference had been a mistake. It was hard to comprehend that the men were brothers. Except their size and build, Lance and Lane Carson were absolutely nothing alike. And Lane apparently intended to keep it that way.

Added to all of that, sitting next to that fireball in Sophie's stomach was the continuing turmoil that stretched between her and Lance—the very thing he'd insinuated.

"Lance..." She sighed his name as she leaned back to look at him. His furrowed brow, the sadness shading those eyes a stormy sort of green, and the downward pull of his mouth all made her heart ache more. "You are a good man."

"Seems not many agree. Including, on occasion, my fiancée."

She shut her eyes against the liquid burn that threatened to spill and pulled his head back toward hers until their cheeks met. "Please, let's not go there tonight." Especially not when she found herself despising this younger brother Lance was risking so much for. That kind of discussion at this point in the evening would spiral badly, and quickly.

His breath released with a slow, warm tickle beneath her ear. "Okay. Let's not." He nuzzled her, then pressed a series of kisses along her neck, causing her breath to catch. There, he stopped and then pulled her back into a hug. His hold felt both desperate and drained, and when he spoke again, he sounded resigned. "You contacted him."

"I did. Are you mad?"

"No. Wish you'd said something. But he's here."

"And that's what you wanted?"

"It was."

"Is it now?"

For many moments, Lance simply held her. The only bit of anything between them was the prickling sensation that reached her scalp as he fingered the ends of her curls. She moved her hand up his shoulder and again burrowed her fingers into the hair at his neck. Slowly the muscles that had been hard and tense in his shoulders began to give.

"Lance?"

"He's my responsibility. I'm glad he's here. Safe. Alive."

Again, she stepped back, and his hold loosened until only his hands rested at her waist.

"He's all grown up, you know?" She cupped his jaw, ran a thumb along his cheekbone. "You're not able to make his choices for him, and you can't save him from himself."

Lance wouldn't meet her gaze. "If I don't try, Soph, no one will. He doesn't have anyone."

"That's not your fault."

There, his eyes flashed. "What if it is?"

"How would that be possible?"

"I don't know, but what if I'd figured out how to be a better brother? How to keep him out of trouble and make him want to live up to the potential he has? He's smart, Sophie. He really is, and there is a gentleness in him that I think he's actually ashamed of—that he's working really hard to suffocate. Maybe I could have encouraged him more instead of telling him he was acting stupid all the time. I could have told Dad to stop comparing him to me, telling him to be more like me..."

As she feathered the pad of her thumb over his lips, her heart shook with ache for him. "Such a burden, Lance." She covered his chest with a palm, then leaned in to kiss the place where the beat beneath her fingers throbbed. "So much in here that isn't yours to carry."

"He's my brother, Soph." His voice broke. "My baby brother. Only brother—only family now."

To that, she found herself once again without words. In that moment she understood a truth that she'd never really grasped before. One she'd heard and believed but hadn't known in experience.

Love hurt. Whether it be between a man and a woman or between siblings. It could really, really hurt. Especially when it was as stubborn as Lance's.

# Chapter Eighteen

*God, please reveal to Lance Your constant goodness. Let him know that You hear and care.*

Sophie stared out the window of the bus, peering into the star-studded night while her students dozed in the seats behind her. They'd done well at district music. Every one of them, whether they'd played solo or in an ensemble or duet. She'd seen several achieve superior marks and had two top placers. It'd been a good day, but Lance hadn't left her thoughts.

The unsettledness between them nagged, and it was so tempting to pray daily for God to change Lance's mind. Seemed like a fair prayer—except who was she to boss the King of heaven around? But in fairness, she was praying. After her talk with her daddy, conviction had settled deep, and she was approaching prayer like a warrior when it came to the love of her life.

Maybe what she was praying now wasn't much different than her trying to boss God. But it seemed that the plea lifting from her heart aligned with Scripture. So much of what she read—especially in Psalms—was a continual reminder that God was good and faithful. That He was trustworthy, even in the hard places.

*Bless the Lord, oh my soul, and all that is within me, bless His holy name...*

The passage that was as familiar to her as any friend eased through her mind, and in it she found that current of peace that was ever available, no matter what the circumstances.

*He redeems. He heals. He crowns. He satisfies.*

She closed her eyes, settling deeper into her seat on the bus, and moved the reminder into praise.

*You redeem. You heal. You crown. You satisfy.*

In her heart she lifted a hallelujah and paired the praise with a *hosanna!*, which meant *save now*, as she turned her thoughts back toward Lance. And then Lane. The two men now in her life, settling deep into her heart. So much there to redeem, to heal.

*You are the God who sees. The God who restores. So here I am now, asking for You to do that for them—for Lance and for Lane, in the things I can't understand. Do what only You can.*

A single tear seeped from the corner of her eye as Sophie prayed, allowing that deep, painful love for Lance to move without restraint even as a touch of healing hope trailed in its wake. In all her life—the loneliest moments when she'd felt rejected—even then, her God had never abandoned her. Never left her alone. Not once.

What if those experiences of rejection and loneliness had been a gift?

The thought was as startling as it was revealing and commanded her consideration. If she had never known what it felt like to be on the outside—not really accepted—would she have understood Lance's heart as she did now? More importantly, if she'd never known the complete need for God's faithful care in the cold loneliness, would she be able to trust Him for it now?

*Young David trusted the faithfulness of his God because God had proven himself faithful before. In times of real danger, and in moments of felt rejection, God had shown Himself to be solid.*

Sophie pondered the portion of one of her dad's sermons.

*Faithfulness is one of those things that is proven, and children, God intends to do it. Over and again, through His Word and in our daily lives, He will prove who He is. The faithful God. Leaving us with the choice—will you trust Him?*

There on that bus, with miles to go before she reached home, and the ache of loving a man who found himself in a struggle, Sophie asked her heart that question. *Will I trust You?*

Her answer was a surrender and a release. She really didn't know for sure what would come after Lance signed those contracts in the morning. Guesses, assumptions—yes, she had those, and they weren't good.

But her hope wasn't in Lance. Wasn't in the home she'd finally found in Big Prairie. Her hope was in Yahweh—the only I AM.

And even in the moments of silence and uncertainty, she could trust Him.

\*\*\*

Lance sat in the corner office, the massive glass panes overlooking the congestion and activity that was Kansas City. The task he'd driven the more than four hours to be there in person for was relatively simple: sign the final contracts. Everything else had been discussed, renegotiated, approved, and written up in official form. This was the last step.

"Mr. Carson, sorry about the delay. It'll be about five more minutes. Can I get you a water while you wait?"

The heat that had been coursing through Lance's body could have used a dousing, but he waved the young assistant off. "I'm good. Thanks."

The young man, dressed in a gray suit and pink tie, and sporting a cut that looked like Jeremy Renner's in the last *Bourne* movie, nodded. "Let me know if you need anything."

"Sure."

He needed this to be done. Needed out of the madness of the city, needed the lava in his stomach to meet an end, and needed to see Sophie. He sucked in a painful breath and found that it provoked a sting in his eyes.

*How will I face her once this is done?*

She hadn't begged him not to do this. He'd expected her to. Had all his rational arguments laid out in his mind, though they'd gone over them several times without finding mutual ground in any of it. In the week since Lane had arrived, Sophie had come out to the ranch as much as she could, but that time had been limited. She'd had district music to prepare for and then attend—a full day-into-the-night event for her and her students. On top of that, because of their performance at State Band and at Harvest of Harmony, her groups had earned an invitation to march in Disney. They would be leaving mid-April and were working like mad musicians to prepare. That left her little time for drama—either between himself and her or him and his brother.

In the meantime, Lane had kicked around the house and property, moaning about Lance's lack of beer—but too pathetically lazy to go get his own stock from Big Prairie Market—and had found a weird new hobby in interrogating Lance's ranch hand, Daisy.

"Why'd you hire some southern beauty queen as a ranch hand?" Lane had wanted to know the morning after he'd bumped into Daisy.

Lance had looked up at him from his paperwork. "She wanted a job, and she's a good worker."

"Sophie know you have that fox on the property all the time?"

With a piercing scowl anchored on Lane, Lance had sighed. "Sophie and Daisy get along perfectly. As Daisy is Miss Jane's niece, and Sophie and Miss Jane are very close. Sophie was all for me hiring the girl last fall."

"She living in the barn loft?"

"Who, Sophie?"

"No, Daisy."

"No. I offered it to her, but she opted to live in town with her aunt for now."

"Huh." Lane eyed him with a gleam that made Lance's stomach turn. "But you offered..."

"Always do with the full-time ranch hands. You know that."

At that, Lane chuckled. "Ever the gentleman."

Ignoring the backhanded comment, Lance had looked back at the papers he'd been sorting through—one of which had been a draft of the contract he was at that moment in Kansas City waiting to sign.

"She's fair game then, right?"

By that point, entirely annoyed, Lance had dropped the slim stack of papers in his hand and had given his full, not-impressed attention to his trouble-seeking little brother. "Not for you, she isn't."

"Come on."

"Not kidding, Lane. Daisy's a good kid, a hard worker. One of the best hands I've had, if you want to know the truth. Don't even think about messing with her."

Lane lifted his eyebrows. "Or what?"

Lance had glared at him. Just like that, Lane's challenging posture went back to that of the devil-may-care attitude he'd perfected somewhere in grade ten. He'd snorted, crossed his arms, and pressed a shoulder against the doorjamb. "You'll take away my inheritance? Already have, brother."

His teeth had mashed together painfully. Moments pounded by in a silence that felt as cold as death and as threatening as war. Lane was the first to fold. With another scoffing laugh, he stood up, his light-brown eyes somehow mocking and resentful at once. "No worries, Lance."

Lane turned to go.

"Lane." Lance caught him before he pounded down the steps.

Though twenty-four and should have been able to behave like a grown man, Lane stopped, tossing his face upward like a petulant child, and growled. "What?"

"I'm not kidding. Leave Daisy alone."

His answer had been a pounding down the steps and a door slam at the back of the lodge.

As the scene replayed in his mind, Lance rolled his fists in his lap. *That* was the brother he was doing this for. The kid who'd somehow become a spoiled, entitled man-child. Who didn't bother to apply any of his God-given brains or talent into anything other than his own whims and pleasures.

*You're not able to make his choices for him, and you can't save him from himself.*

Sophie's tone had been so gentle, full of understanding and anguish for Lance. The memory of it caused a squeeze of painful love to shiver through him. She *did* understand. Still didn't agree, but she felt the impossibility of what he was dealing with.

And she loved him. Man, that woman loved him, even when he was sure she'd turn and walk.

Lance stared out the window, not really seeing the hazy gray sky or the sun trying to pierce through the dreary day. He sat absorbed in his thoughts, not really registering the constant noise of sirens and traffic and horns that reminded him with certainty that he never wanted to leave his rural life. He only saw Sophie: her beautiful smile, her love for life. And in that, he remembered the stories her dad had shared with him. Of the boy who'd rejected her because of the color of her skin. The way she'd felt like an outsider in the affluent white suburb where they lived. And then the way she'd told him that she felt like she'd finally found a home—a place that welcomed her, for the most part—in Big Prairie.

He would destroy that. Right there, that day, with a few strokes of a pen, Lance would take that belonging Sophie had finally found and mark it off indefinitely. As his fiancée, then his wife, she would carry his cross of exclusion, of resentment and rejection. She would bear this choice every bit as much as she bore the subtle racism of her youth.

How could he do that to her?

Something in his heart crumbled, tumbling piece by piece until the resolve he'd retained the past several weeks now lay in shambles. He leaned forward in the leather office chair, placing elbows to knees, and cupped his head in both hands. "God, I can't do this," he whispered.

At that, it seemed a shaft of light touched his soul.

*Then don't.*

The words weren't comforting, but they were compelling.

"I won't," he whispered more forcefully this time. Drawing his shoulders back, he looked around the office. Voices in the hallway drifted nearer as a new resolve locked into his mind. Standing, he turned to the door to meet the company delegates who were to orchestrate and witness the contract signing.

Before the woman who stood at the helm of the group could speak, Lance cleared his throat. "I'm sorry. I've wasted your time."

The woman, dressed in a dark business jacket, pencil skirt, and spiked heels, scowled at him. "Excuse me?"

Lance drew in a deep breath, his mind wavering. As he shut his eyes, hunting for clarity, a sweet voice from years past—all the way into his childhood—whispered into his heart. *Trust in the Lord and do good.* Shocked yet strengthened, he blinked, and the businesswoman came back into focus. "I can't sign. I mean I won't—I've changed my mind."

"This is rather late in the game for that." She pointed to a packet her assistant—the young man who had spoken to Lance earlier—held. "All the documents have been drawn."

"I understand, and I'm sorry. I can't do this."

Irritation morphed into anger on her face. "You've had months to consider all this, Mr. Carson. This is grossly unprofessional."

"I know. Really, I don't think you'd understand if I tried to explain, so all I can say is, I'm sorry. Very, very sorry for wasting your time." He stepped forward, and the group surrounding her parted, giving him access to the door.

"You cannot rethink this," she snipped.

He paused, looking at her.

With a sharp glare, and her hands perched on her hips, she continued. "Walk away now, and that's it. You will not get a second chance."

A slight sense of freedom unrolled within, and he nodded. "I understand."

With that, Lance walked away.

\*\*\*

Lance had texted, saying he'd be back sometime mid-Saturday morning. He'd wondered if Sophie would check on the vineyard and ranch. Reading between the lines, she'd guessed that meant *keep an eye on Lane.* Trepidation rocked through her as she pulled up to the small farmhouse and parked. Sitting at an angle she was certain would drive Lance insane, Lane's old Land Rover proclaimed that yes, the prodigal brother was still there.

If only he'd *actually* come home like he meant it. Puffing her cheeks, she blew out a breath. "You heal, right? You mend? Redeem? Lord, these boys need exactly that, you know?" The corner of her mouth pushed up. Yeah, God knew—He saw. She gripped the steering wheel, though she'd already shut off the engine, and leaned so that she could look up through the windshield. "Okay. Whatever You want from me here, I'm Yours. Help me see things Your way."

Though still uneasy about hanging out with Lane the Lost, she chose to grip the building thread of boldness weaving within as she left the car. Before she reached the kitchen door, Lane called to her from the lodge. Redirecting her attention, she found the hairy-beary man standing on the wraparound deck of the vineyard's lodge, a mug of something steamy lifted, as if in a toast toward her.

"Morning, future sister-in-law." His voice was clear, tone sincere.

Sophie smiled, not even needing to reach for her old *smile, it'll help* mantra. "Good morning, Lane. Good to see you out and about."

"Yeah." He grinned as if he were a long-lost friend and they were easy companions. "The old house is a bit stuffy. Thought for sure Lance would have built something new for himself."

As she strode closer, she waved a hand over the lodge. "He did. He built this."

Lane sipped his hot drink. "This is business. Not the same."

"That's true." She climbed the two steps up to the deck and met him by the rail.

"That's my brother though."

"How's that?"

"Determined."

Sophie tipped her chin to find Lane's eyes. They were the color of polished amber, and that morning they were clear and bright and not one bit combative. "Yes. Lance is quite determined."

"And you love him for it."

"I love him for lots of reasons. Mostly, though, I just love him for him."

Lane studied her with a curiosity that was neither censorious nor doubtful. Where had this version of the brother come from? Sophie found herself hoping he'd stay.

"You a coffee drinker?" He lifted his mug as he asked.

"Every single day." She winked.

With a relaxed stride and a beckoning nod, he moved toward the lodge. "I have a fresh pot on."

Sophie followed him willingly, wondering what had happened that Lane had suddenly turned pleasant. He led her through the big front room and into the kitchen and poured her a fresh mug before she decided to ask.

She accepted the mug he passed to her and looked up at him again. "Which version is real?"

His dark eyebrows lifted, as if he was ready to launch into some kind of banter—which she wouldn't have minded—but as he studied her back, a small smile eased the expression. "I'm not sure."

"I think I'm not going to accept that."

At that, he laughed and then backed toward the door they'd come through. "And here I thought you were nothing like my brother."

She followed along, and they settled on a picnic table washed in the morning sunshine, which seemed determined to erase the frosty chill that had descended the night before.

"On some things, we're very different," she said, leaning her arms against the wood of the table.

"Like, you know how to smile."

Sophie rolled her eyes. "Lance's smile is one of the first things I noticed about him. It's shy, a little serious, but quite kind."

"Hmm." He took another swallow of coffee. "Glad to hear he's got one. What was the first thing you noticed?"

"Those green eyes."

"A sucker for green?"

"No. For intelligence."

"Touché." Lane chuckled. "How did you get him to talk?"

"Didn't have to try. He rescued me from a bad decision involving a muddy road. Conversation came easily as we spent the afternoon together."

"We're talking about Lance, right?"

"Yes. The tall guy you sort of resemble, except he's much better looking."

Lane gripped his chest. "Ouch. Another dart."

She laughed with him, and then a lull settled on a cool breeze. In the distance, down by the river, a chorus of birds sang, nearly convincing Sophie that it really was spring at last. Thank goodness. The snow accumulation had been more than usual that winter, and she was ready for the coming thaw.

The touch of spring felt like hope—the clean air, the sense that under the surface of the soil, and on the tips of the trees, there was brand-new life ready to burst forth. So much promise sitting out there. Surrounding her—them. Her attention wandered back to Lane, finding his focus had drifted toward the northeast, where the pastures lay on the other side of the river.

"Do you miss it at all?"

His head jerked, as if she'd startled him. "What's that?"

"The ranch. Do you miss it?"

An unexpected seriousness fell into his expression as he looked back to the land. "Yeah, a little. I used to ride fence with my dad. Or we'd take the four-wheelers to check the pivot out in the southeast field."

"So you don't hate farming?"

"Nah. I like working with the cattle better than farming, but our operation depended on both."

"Then?"

He shook his head, cutting her off. "It's Lance's. Dad left it all to him." His focus fell to the table, lips together.

Ache and tension throbbed into the moment, usurping the promise of hope that had filled her heart. Sophie bit the inside of her lip.

"He wants you to come back." Her voice was soft, words barely passing through the tightness of her throat. "To come home to stay."

Lane's shoulders curled inward, and as his gaze wandered back out to the land beyond the vineyard, she saw pain pass through his eyes. The same kind of pain that she'd seen in Lance.

*He wants to come home. Lord, why doesn't he just—*

"Don't think so." Lane's voice was like lead. Heavy and chilled and final. When he brought his attention back to her, the softer, nicer version of Lane Carson had been eclipsed. Back was the man of distance and hardness. "Nope, Sophie. That's not gonna work."

The grin that split his dark beard was that of the cocky jerk she'd met his first night back. A mask. One Lane wore intentionally.

Sophie had no idea why.

# Chapter Nineteen

Lance found a great measure of relief in seeing Sophie's orange Renegade parked near the house—equal to the amount of trepidation edging through him, sparked by Lane's vehicle sitting catawampus nearby.

His brother had remained. He was glad, but concerned. Especially after Lane's interest in young Daisy. Not only was Miss Jane's niece important because of her special aunt and the place Miss Jane had carved into Lance's life, but Daisy had earned high regard from him as an extremely intelligent and hard worker. Not to mention pleasant. He'd yet to see a bad attitude out of the young woman. Lance had not been exaggerating when he'd told Lane she was the best hand he'd ever had on the ranch. And he had a strong sense of brotherly affection toward his young employee, which translated into protectiveness when it came to gaming men.

Gaming men...it was tragic that his own brother numbered among such. Lane didn't have to. He had the capacity for depth and real human connection—the latter much more so than Lance himself ever owned. Lane simply chose to deny the world knowing it. Because, for all the adventuring, devil-may-care swagger Lane put out, the truth was, the man was a coward.

Loss made such out of tender young men.

But Sophie was there—and by her text earlier that day, she had been so since midmorning. Lance's fun yet responsible fiancée would see that Lane behaved himself at least moderately, even if she had to employ her classroom discipline skills to see the job done.

Lance walked around the nose of his truck to the passenger door so that he could retrieve his pack containing his laptop and documents. By the time he had the strap of the bag hung over his shoulder and the door closed, Sophie had made her way onto the deck of the lodge. When he turned that way, she stood at the top of the steps, her long legs in skinny jeans that disappeared into the midcalf Muk boots he'd bought for her, and his zip-up hoodie swallowing the rest of her frame.

Lance paused, soaking in the view while his heart throbbed with some kind of addictive ache, and wondered what she would do. Scowl, maybe? At least frown with worry about what came next?

Sophie didn't know he'd walked away from the deal—he hadn't told her. Standing there now, she likely wavered between loyalty and disappointment. Yet her head tipped to one side, a shadow of a smile edging those lips. Likely at command—what was it she'd shared with him, the thing she said to herself when things seemed hard?

*Smile, it'll help.*

He didn't want her to have to tell herself to smile. Not at him. Wanting to eliminate the need for her to force an unfelt expression, he strode toward the lodge and up the steps. She stepped into his one-armed embrace without hesitation, running a hand along his jaw.

"You made it home."

The warmth in her eyes melted him, confirming the longings of his heart. To have this woman as his wife and to find every possible way to make her happy. Genuinely happy.

He touched his forehead to hers and then sought her lips. She kissed him softly, and he found himself washed in a sense of unworthy gratitude. Even knowing what he'd gone to Kansas City to do—and understanding the cost—she stood there loving him. Sophie owned a stubborn sort of devotion that he felt certain he didn't deserve. The power of it shook his core, and he gripped her tighter to steady himself.

Sophie leaned back to search his face. "How did it go?"

"It didn't," he whispered.

Rather than relief—as should have been—concern darkened her eyes. Lance let the strap of his pack slide from his shoulder and then bent to lay it on the deck. When he stood to hold her, he found her still staring at him with worry. He traced a coil of her hair, then feathered the pad of his thumb along her cheek.

"I couldn't live with it," he said lowly. "You were right, and I don't *want* to live with it."

Sophie's eyes slid shut, and a single tear leaked onto the side of her nose. "Lance." His name was barely a breath from her lips. Where he thought he'd hear relief, there was only compassion, and when she tangled her arms around him, it seemed that she held him more than he held her.

He did not deserve this woman's love. Yet she gave it, even when it was hard. It was unnatural, not normal. Entirely selfless, and, he suddenly realized, a mark of her faith in a God that she knew to be both personal and compassionate. Standing there, being held by such a love, Lance felt a fresh and powerful pull in his soul.

He needed to know—to *really* know, the way Sophie did, her God.

***

Sophie leaned against Lance's shoulder, the chill of the March ground seeping through the blanket he'd spread at their spot near the river. Mutt wandered in and out of the still-dormant brush, sniffing out what was likely some kind of rodent.

As Lance looked out over the river, past the trees tipped with new green and toward the lowering sun, he seemed at peace—and had since the moment he'd told her he didn't go through with the contract.

Relief had surged through her at his words back at the lodge. He wasn't going to do it, wasn't going to risk suffocating the small local businesses with a well-known restaurant. How could she not feel relieved? But alongside that place of comfort, there was and still lived a sting of concern. Now what would Lance do? What would *they* do?

He wanted almost more than anything for Lane to come home, and she'd seen exactly why. The younger Carson was a time bomb, set to self-destruct at any moment. The swagger, the carelessness, the me-against-the-whole-world attitude, it was all warning bells and caution flags. Lane needed stability. He needed to come home.

Lance inhaled a long breath and wrapped his arm around her. As the wind played a gentle game of chase the prairie, he pressed a kiss to her temple.

"Did you pray for me to change my mind?" he murmured, head still near hers.

"No." She tipped her face toward his. "No, Lance, I did not pray for that."

Curiosity made his green eyes seem darker. "You didn't? I felt sure you would."

"It was tempting."

"But?"

"But I'm not God."

The angle of his head, and his long study, begged for more.

"I know you to have a kind heart. You *are* a good man, Lance—I haven't doubted that, even in this—and I think maybe you should know Miss Jane hasn't either. And your brother...Lane *does* need you. Needs to come home."

"But you said you didn't think you could live with it."

She shut her eyes, heart filled with the miserable sense of being mixed up, as it had the night she'd spoken those words. "I know. But—"

"I thought you were going to break up with me that night." Strain tugged on his low voice.

Sophie found his eyes again. "I'm sorry for that."

He shook his head. "I would have understood."

The world around them seemed to hold its breath, and Sophie clung to the moment, holding those beautiful eyes while he held all of her heart. When he blinked, a stray tear flicked from his dark lashes, the sight of it clenching pain in her chest.

"I'm with you, Lance." She wove her fingers into his hair near his ear and ran them down to his neck, and he leaned into her. "I'm always with you," she whispered.

A renewal wrapped around them as they held each other. While clouds gathered in the north, and the chilly breeze worked toward a cold wind, Sophie and Lance remained side by side, strengthening what had seemed for a time to be weakening and shaky.

"Why did you walk away?" she asked, resettling against him as he opened back toward the sunset.

"I kept thinking about how Big Prairie has felt like home to you."

For many beats, she waited, wondering if that was all he would say.

"I couldn't take that away," he finally whispered. "And the more I thought about that—how much you would shoulder for my choices—the worse I felt and the more I resented Lane for it. All around, it suddenly seemed like a really bad solution to a situation that wasn't good to begin with. Then there's Miss Jane—have you ever known anyone like her? And Wes—he was one of my dad's best friends. How many people should I injure in my attempts to lure Lane home?" He swallowed and then breathed a small chuckle. "But the part that seems craziest was that I was sitting alone in that office, waiting for all the suits to bring in the official contract, and I suddenly said *I can't do it.* And I heard—" He cut off, as if emotional. Or unsure.

"You heard?"

His brow furrowed. "I think I heard God. In here." He tapped his chest. "Is that crazy?"

Sophie chuckled. "No, that's not crazy. What did He say?"

Lance blinked again. "He said, *Then don't.*"

His gaze drifted from her, off into some faraway place. "Soph, I don't think that's ever happened before."

"What?"

"God. Speaking to me. Like I...like He's there. Here. With me."

Sophie reached for him, cupping his face as emotion swelled within her. "He is though, Lance. Always."

His face contorted with a mix of emotions, he nodded. "I think maybe I know that now. Why haven't I heard Him before?"

"I don't know." Tears clogged her throat, beckoned by the deep emotion she watched shudder through him. She pulled him close again, and he buried his face into her neck. "I did pray for that, Lance."

"What?"

"I prayed that you would know God's presence. That you would know that He hears you and that He cares about you."

Lance didn't respond with words. But by the shuddering of his breath and the tightening of his hold, she knew.

Something had changed in him. A silent miracle that would build in him new hope.

***

He looked up the reference for the words that had pressed into his heart and mind during that brief meeting in Kansas City. His search took him to Psalm 37.

*Trust in the LORD and do good; dwell in the land and cultivate faithfulness. Delight yourself in the LORD, and he will give you the desires of your heart. Commit your way to the LORD, trust also in Him, and He will do it. He will bring forth your righteousness as the light and your judgement as the noonday.*

The verses flowed like easy poetry, and yet the depth and current of the words slipped through his grasp. There were a lot of promises in there. Rosy ones, if he were going to be honest. Lance's life had been too hard for him to swallow it all. But the strength and peace he'd known in that office two days before, and several times since that decision to walk away from a deal he'd spent nearly a year working out, was too powerful to deny.

What did it mean to cultivate faithfulness, anyway? And what about the part of judgment and noon?

Lance hunched over his desk, his forearms pressed against the surface while he studied the words in his Bible. At his feet, under the desk, Mutt whined for attention. Absently, he reached down to stroke her head.

*How does this deal work, God? I kind of think Sophie talks to You all the time. Like You're in a conversation or something. Is that even real?*

Maybe he had gone a touch crazy. Who talked to Someone in their head and expected to hear an answer?

Sophie did. And he adored her. Respected her. Kind of hoped he'd become a little more like her. Was she still praying that he'd know God's presence? He sure hoped so.

A clomp of boots on the steps outside robbed his attention from both his thoughts and Bible, and Lance sat back. Mutt yipped as a pair of voices drifted from the deck up to his office, and though muffled, he knew to whom they belonged.

"It's all right, girl," he muttered to Mutt. "Well, no. It's probably not all right. My brother is trouble, isn't he?"

Lane was out pestering Lance's ranch hand. Again. Pushing away from the desk and up to a stand, Lance sighed. Man, it was so much like their old high school days—half his time was spent being on guard, hoping to keep his younger brother out of real trouble—for Lane's sake and for those who Lane interacted with.

Didn't help that to Lane, Daisy's easygoing sass was like honey to a bear. His hairy younger brother being that bear—and a foolish cub at that. Lance had been tempted to frustration with Daisy—for the first time in the months she'd worked for him—and had more than once had to have a conversation with himself about it not being fair for him to be irritated with her about something he knew to be entirely innocent on her part. Daisy had a bright personality, which was part of the reason she was downright pleasant to have around. Wasn't her fault Lane took that as a *gaming men welcome* sign.

That was entirely on Lane.

"Come on now." Lane's easy banter drifted from downstairs. "We'll play with M&Ms. No money involved, so it'll be perfectly legal and even Christian." The sound of the back door smacking closed accompanied Lane's now-clear voice.

"I only know how to play Uno, mountain man. I won't be suckered into your traps."

"No trap." Lane had perfected the innocent-boy routine, and Lance's irritation as he listened to the exchange shifted completely toward his brother. "I'm offering to teach you how to play. Never know when hold'em will come in handy."

"For some of us, that would be never."

"Lane." Lance stepped down from the loft office with a measured gait, Mutt at his heels. "Are you irritating my employee?"

"Yes."

"No."

The pair answered in chorus. Lane's grin was all cheeky boy working his game. Daisy's was innocent and good natured. Both made Lance want to groan. He didn't have time to play chaperone. He laid a none-to-impressed frown on Lane and then addressed Daisy. "Did you get those bales moved from the lower shelter?"

"Next on the list." She passed a good-natured but irritated look at his brother. "Someone moved the skid steer and then lost the key. Spent the past hour playing trace the trail until he remembered he left it on his dresser."

Lance leveled his brother with a death-warning glare. "If you're not going to be useful, just go to town. I'm sure there's something for you to do there."

A touch of pink brushed over the place above Lane's beard line, and his eyes flashed with something like indignation. But after a long-held look, his grin broke against his wild beard. "I'm going to show my young apprentice here how to properly stack the bales."

"She's reached expert level on that particular chore," Lance responded dryly.

"Can't hurt to have some guidance."

"That would be like the blind leading the one with perfect vision." He reached the floor of the ground level and stopped in front of Lane. "And as I've said, Daisy knows what she's doing. You've wasted enough of her time—and mine—for the morning." With the shift of his eyes, Lance looked at Daisy. Her expression had morphed into discomfort.

"Sorry, Lance. I'll get it done." With a small droop in her shoulders, Daisy pivoted and made for the door she and Lane had come through.

Lane scowled at Lance and then turned. "Hey. Don't you want that water we came in here for?"

Daisy kept moving, tossing a half-lifted wave as she went. "I'm good." And then she was gone.

"Nice." With arms crossed over his chest, Lane returned his glare to Lance. "She's worked all morning. Can't even take a ten-minute water break?"

"I don't have a problem with that. In fact, I don't have a problem with Daisy at all." Lance met Lane's frown with a speaking look.

"Of course." Lane's arms dropped to his sides. "It's always the same, isn't it, Lance?"

"Seems so." Lance shook his head, and Mutt whined from her seat near his feet. "Here I'd hoped that five years out doing whatever it was you've been doing would have helped grow you up."

"I'm a river guide. People trust me to get them safely down the Snake—that's not grown up enough for you?"

"See, this is the problem. Right there, Lane. I *know* you're capable. I *know* you're smart and have more than a thread of responsibility in you. This is why I get so frustrated with you—you *choose* to act like a reckless idiot. If you weren't able to be better, I could accept it. But you're more. You could be so much more."

Lane barked a derisive laugh. "Why should I bother? You'll never see anything than what you've already decided is true."

"I see exactly what is, Lane."

"Yeah, what is that?"

"You quit trying a long time ago. Decided life was too hard and unfair. And more, you've blamed Dad, and then me, for all of it."

"It is your fault!" Red splashed Lane's face and the tips of his ears as fury unleashed. "All of this is your fault. Spent your whole life proving you were more, which means that I'll never be enough. Because of you, I don't even have a home."

"You have a home, you stubborn fool." Lance braced his stance like they were about to dive into a physical fight. Mutt dropped to the ground and eyed the brothers like she expected a brawl to erupt at any moment. "You've always had a home. You left by your own stupid pride. All of this"—he motioned over the acres of fields and pastures beyond the large windows of the lodge—"Dad left for *us*."

"No. He left it to *you*."

"For me to manage. Don't you know what it means to inherit? Didn't you ever listen to Dad when he talked about the responsibility of—"

Lane held up his hand. "I can't stand living in your shadow, and I sure as hell don't want your help. You can take your inheritance, and all your pious crap about responsibility, and keep it to yourself. Go parade it out in town where everyone will pat your back and tell you what a fine man you are. Take it all, Lance. Keep it—I don't care."

"Yeah?" The sting of Lane's words buried deep, especially in the contrast of what was really happening between Lance and the people in town. His fists shook as the surge of blended anger and hurt pulsed through him. "Is that why you're still so mad about it? Clearly you don't care. Not about Dad or the ranch or this town. That's why you've stayed away—ignored every attempt I've made to reach you. Why you live in that stupid old vehicle like a homeless man and drift from job to job, season to season, like you're too afraid to attach yourself to anyone or anything. All of that because obviously you don't care."

"Shut up!" The hard rise of Lane's chest and his stiffly pinned lips punctuated his glare. "Just shut up!"

Mutt launched back to her feet and barked toward Lane. Lance reached down with a calm hand to quiet her with a pat on her head.

Heat swirled between the brothers as they continued in a deadlocked stare, both men stubborn, angry, and at least for Lance, drowning in a strong current of loss. How much more could he take? For Lance, the answer wasn't much. He'd done everything he could think of over the years to show Lane he cared. Maybe it had all come across as pious and overbearing.

Lance didn't know and couldn't think straight enough to give it a fair evaluation. All he could really know in that moment was that Lane had great potential, and Lance hated watching him continue to send his life down a river of total destruction. Because he loved him. He also was sick to death of his younger brother blaming him for all his problems.

*You can't save him, Lance.*

Sophie's admonishment repeated in his mind. No. No, he could not save his brother, and right there, in the wake of yet another failed attempt, Lance saw the truth: the more he tried, the further Lane slipped.

Perhaps it was time to simply let him go.

The thought was a blade in his chest. Lance had spent a lifetime letting the people he'd loved go—none of it by his choice. Even still, it settled firmly in his mind.

"You win, Lane," he said, his tone low and resigned. "Whatever this war between us is, I surrender. What do you want?"

"For you to leave me alone."

Lance nodded, his gaze drifting to the ground, where he didn't have to see Lane's contorted expression of rage. Maybe hatred.

"Let me be and quit trying to interfere with the stuff I do." Pure outrage still rang in Lane's voice. "Like Daisy."

Lance looked back at him. "You can do whatever you want, Lane. Leave. Stay. Live whatever kind of life you see fit. But not with Daisy. She's a good girl, and she's innocent. I won't stand by silently and watch you wreck her life."

"How do you know I'll wreck it?"

Lance let a silent beat between them suffice as his answer.

Wasn't good enough for Lane. "How do you know I don't actually, genuinely like her?"

Lance had answers, many of them. Things like he'd watched Lane flirt, take things as far as he wanted with other girls, and then leave them brokenhearted. He also had heard about the river guide camps and the lifestyle associated with them. Perhaps it wasn't fair to assume that Lane lived out that reputedly debauched lifestyle, but honestly, it fit with the pattern Lane had already established. Carefree and careless. Selfish and self-indulgent. Lane fit the mold.

Still, he was Lance's brother, and Daisy was a nice, likable young woman. Hadn't Lance said that he knew Lane *could* be more?

After several long, painful moments of silence, Lance narrowed his gaze on his brother. "Do you?"

Lane looked away, gripping the back of his neck. After squirming like a junior high boy who'd landed himself in trouble for the very first time, he shrugged.

Mutt yipped again and turned toward the kitchen. The sound of feet pounding up the steps on the deck preceded the squeak of the back door, cutting off any further response. Lane jabbed one more angry glance at Lance and then moved for the opposite door.

"Hey, boys." Sophie's voice held a smile, but when Lance moved his attention toward her, he saw the expression fade. She bent down to welcome his dog's enthusiastic greeting—all wagging tail and licking tongue. "Everything okay?"

"Dandy." Lane pushed through the exit and then flung the door shut in his wake.

Rising slowly, Sophie's eyes shifted from the door Lane had stormed through back to Lance. Sympathy drew on her mouth. "So I'll take that as a no."

"Situation normal." Lance sighed. "Except one thing. I'm done."

"Done?"

"I'm done trying to save my brother."

# Chapter Twenty

"He didn't do it, Miss Jane." Warm tears lined Sophie's eyelids, and the need to let them fall made her throat swell.

They sat together in the near-back row they had often shared with Lance during Sunday services. Lance hadn't come in that morning. The latest rains made the roads slick, but more, the predicted storm in the next several hours kept him at home to move cattle with Daisy and Lane.

Miss Jane covered Sophie's hand. "Lance?"

"Yes. He didn't sign the contract." Sophie kept her voice hushed. "The deal is over."

When one would have expected victory and relief to have passed on Miss Jane's face, maybe even a whispered *Praise the Lord!*, there was only surprise. And a small furrow of concern.

"So you managed to talk him out of it?"

"I didn't." Sophie shook her head and leaned toward Miss Jane's place on the seat next to hers. "I wanted to so much at first—and we did fight about it. But there was this feeling in me—strong as anything I've ever known—that I needed to surrender this situation and find a way to live well through whatever happened. To be able to stand beside him and love him even when I didn't agree with him. It was confirmed by my dad, who told me to pray hard."

Miss Jane nodded, her clear blue eyes a careful study on Sophie. "And you prayed about it?"

"I did, but not for God to make him change his mind."

"No? What for then?"

"That Lance would know that God hears Him, and that He is with him. And to give him wisdom." At that, a few tears ran free. "Miss Jane, God did that." She had to pause, swallow, and blink away the blur. "He did exactly that. Lance said that while he was in that meeting, he felt like he couldn't do it—and he heard in his heart very clearly *Then don't.*"

Wonder entered Miss Jane's gentle smile, and then she drew Sophie into a motherly hug. "That is quite beautiful, my friend. So much more important than whether he went through with the deal or not."

Sophie pressed into the woman's bony shoulder and nodded. For a moment, she rested there, her eyes shut as she drew in a moment of peace. "It sort of feels like a miracle."

Miss Jane's soft chuckle felt like spring rain and sweet music. "Is all well now?"

"No. I mean, Lance and I are good, and I feel so much that he has taken a giant move closer to God, which is the best thing ever. But, well..." She sat up, biting her bottom lip. "Did you know Lane came home?"

"Daisy Jane mentioned something about it. When?"

"About a week before Lance went to Kansas City."

"Because you texted him?"

"Yes."

"And that is not going well, I take it."

"It is so very complicated. Lane is like one of the lost boys in *Peter Pan.*"

Miss Jane hummed softly. "Yes. That is the perfect way to describe Lane Carson. He needs a mother."

Sophie sighed as frustration welled up inside. "Or the Father, I think, would be better."

"Indeed. So much better. The very best, in fact."

"Wish with all my heart that he'd realize he had a brother—one who cares very much about him—and was willing to show a costly kind of love for him."

"Hmm." Miss Jane rocked back, retaking Sophie's hand, as the wizened expression Sophie had come to know well contoured her face. "I believe Lane knows. He knows his brother loves him, and I'm quite certain he knows the Father does too. He is simply mad, and he needs a target for his anger. Unfortunately for Lane, a big target is God. Unfortunately for both Lance and Lane, the other target is his brother."

"They fought the other day. Again." Sophie slumped against the back of her chair. "Lance told me he was done."

"Done?"

"Done trying to save his brother."

"And you're worried that's a bad thing?"

"It feels bad. But in my head, I know it isn't." Sophie sighed. "It makes me wonder about the father in Jesus's parable—you know, the one whose son took his money and left home?"

"I know the one."

"How much that father loved his boy, even in the pain of the son's hatred." Sophie lifted her gaze and let it drift across the nearly empty worship center. "I think about how much would that hurt, you know? Not only to know your son basically wished you were dead, but then to hear and know that boy kept going deeper and deeper into a dark pit. I think that'd be really hard. It'd be so tempting to swoop in and rescue him."

Miss Jane squeezed her hand. "That's what I would want to do for the people I love."

"But then he'd never have come to the end of himself, would he?" Sophie's attention fixed on the cross at the front of the room. "He would have never known how badly he needed forgiven. How much he really needed his father."

A long silence settled between them, one of comfortable reflection.

"Sophie, I think God has given you a rich and beautiful gift."

Sophie turned back to Miss Jane to find admiration in her eyes. "What's that?"

"Empathy."

She blinked. "Why would you say that?"

"Because many young women would resent a man like Lane for making things difficult. I think...in fact, I'm sure, as I sit here watching you process this, that you do not. In fact, I'm willing to bet that you are begging the Father for his restoration, aren't you?"

Again, tears rimmed her eyes, making them sting. "I am, because he is simply lost in resentment. Miss Jane, I've spent some time with Lane over the past few days, and I've seen glimpses of a tender heart. We had a conversation, a real one, where he wasn't putting up a jerky front. You know what I saw?"

"What's that, lovie?"

"A boy longing for home." Sophie let the memory of Lane's eyes—the way they softened as he spoke about working the property with his dad—replay. "He really loved it. Did you know that? He loved working with his dad. And he loved the ranch."

"Perhaps that's why Lance was trying to see that he got it?"

"Yes," Sophie whispered. "Yes, I think that's exactly so."

"Will he give the ranch portion to Lane anyway?"

Sophie shook her head. Honestly, she'd never thought to ask Lance that. It simply didn't seem possible, especially after he'd explained to her the real situation with the vineyard. "I don't know. I don't know that he can afford to split it—that dividing the property would do either of them any good. The vineyard isn't independent yet, and Lance is afraid that the ranch won't support two households."

"Well, it's a good thing, then, that we pray to the God of healing, provision, and redemption, isn't it?"

Her heart lifting at Miss Jane's encouragement, Sophie sniffed and nodded. *You redeem, You heal, You satisfy, and You renew.*

"And we'll keep on praying." Miss Jane's pronouncement was like a final verdict. "You and me, we'll pray for them both."

***

Lance read through the weather alert that had flashed on his phone. More rain. Flash-flood warning.

"Did you get that alert?" Lane asked.

Nodding, Lance looked over the river ground. "How long has it been since the water's reached the old homestead?"

Lane rode over to Lance's side. "Never, that I know of."

"They should be okay, right?" Wasn't often Lance checked with Lane about anything. Truth was, his younger brother was more intuitive with the ranch—a big reason Lance really wanted to give that part of the inheritance to his younger brother.

"It'd have be some kind of flood to put them in danger. Even if the waters did creep up to the old place, there's a bit of room for the cattle on the rise." He nodded toward the northern fence line that bordered the soybean field. "I think they'll be fine. Never been a problem before."

Lance nodded again, turning back to the cattle. An achy exhaustion rolled over his chilled body. They'd been working cattle for three days, most of that on horseback because the pastures had a top layer of soggy ground covering the still-thawing subsoil, thanks to the recent rains. Last thing they needed was to tear up the land with four-wheelers.

What that had meant was long days in the saddle, pushing cattle over the old narrow bridge that spanned the river a half mile downstream from the vineyard where the original family homestead had been built. No one had lived there in three generations, but it served as the best place for working cattle.

He was thankful for Daisy—her work ethic and her experience in the saddle. On top of that, he was quite thankful that Lane had not only come home but had stuck around. Even after their confrontation.

Seemed like a minor miracle. Lane was more prone to run or to sulk than to pick himself up and make himself useful. But for whatever reason, Lane had put himself in the middle of the work, thrown all of his know-how and experience into it, proving again to Lance that his brother was, in fact, quite capable. More than that, proving that Lane did care about the ranch. Very much so.

Made Lance question his decision to walk away from the restaurant deal.

*God, he's homesick. Can't you just bring him home?* Frustration was the undercurrent of his prayers. But he was praying. Maybe that would count for something?

In his shirt pocket, Lance's phone buzzed again. Fairly certain it was another weather alert, he was tempted to ignore it. How many rain and flood warnings did they need? Truth be told, he hardly ever paid attention to them anymore anyway. They were almost always overblown. But then the jingle vibrated again, and he reached to check it.

Ah. A text from Sophie. In spite of the wet, the chill, and the tiredness, he grinned. The tune to "Sweet Caroline" meandered through his mind, as it often did since the first time he'd met her, and his grumpy mood sloughed away.

*Gonna bring dinner out tonight. Will you be at the house or down at the homestead?*

Lance tugged his horse to a stand and texted her back. *Supposed to be wet again tonight. Maybe you should stay in town.*

He'd rather see her. Hadn't in five days, because he'd not gone in on Sunday. Impatience snarled within at that thought. Man, he wished they were married already. Then he wouldn't have to worry about her getting stuck out at his place when the roads weren't dry. Wouldn't have to kiss her goodbye on the seemingly rare evenings they actually got to spend together, only to lay awake at night wishing she was tangled in his arms. The end of May could not come soon enough.

Her reply made his phone dance against his palm. *Missing you too much. I'll risk it. Lane and Daisy are both there, right?*

He should argue. Tell her to stay home. But he couldn't find the self-discipline to do it. *They're here.*

*You've all been working like crazy. I'm bringing a feast. See you in a couple of hours.*

Lance didn't have the fortitude to argue. Not with that kind of a promise dangling in the very near future. He'd have to get her home—even if it did take him near an hour to navigate the muddy road should it dump on them as the weather prediction claimed.

It'd be worth it.

***

The rains came in swift and fierce as Sophie pulled up to the lodge. Maybe she should have listened when Lance had told her to stay in town. Already, the road had been squishy. With the sheets of moisture pouring on them right now, they might become impassable.

A gnawing of guilt chewed in her gut. That was a surefire way to trigger some rumors in town. Wouldn't matter if she and Lance remained innocent despite appearances. People would talk. More fuel to the fire—as they were already upset with the business situation Lance had been pursuing.

The back door to the farmhouse screeched open, and Lance jogged out in his mud boots, a pair of sweats, and a hoodie—with the hood drawn over his head. "I was worried you'd get caught in this," he called as he came toward her.

She smiled, watching him. Her own hood on her Big Prairie Marching Band rain jacket barely protected her from the sheets of water, but at the moment, she didn't care. This man. Good heavens, she loved this man. The sight of him made her heart balloon with joy, and when he stopped in front of her, she gripped his shoulders and moved to her toes. With a deep chuckle, he bent to meet her kiss.

"Worth it," she whispered.

His lips pressed against hers again, his agreement a soft rumble. "I missed you too."

"We should have married over Christmas."

He chuckled, his breath a warm tickle on her lips. "That's what I said."

"You were right."

"Hey!" Lane's call drifted through the rain. "It's raining."

"You're kidding me," Sophie called back, spotting not only Lane but Mutt waiting at the door.

"People only make out in the rain in movies."

"Is that so?" Lance pulled Sophie closer.

"Daisy is too innocent to witness this," Lane said.

Sophie tipped her head back and laughed as the rain washed over her face.

"Come on," Lane called amid Mutt's barking. "I'm starving in here."

Lance stepped to Sophie's side. "You could come out here and help bring in the food."

"Three's a crowd," Lane returned.

With a grin, Sophie looked up at Lance. "He's in a good mood tonight."

"Apparently." Lance met her look with a wink. "Working cows seems to make him happy."

The truth in that playful statement nudged against her heart. Lane did belong there, and Lance had known it all along. She saw even more now why Lance had been so determined to do what he'd almost done, and she felt a prick of disappointment that her fiancé hadn't followed through.

*God, please make another way for them.* Her prayer lifted silently as she opened the back of her car and began handing foil tins to Lance, stacking them as he waited. By the time they had the lasagna, Greek salad, garlic bread, and chocolate brownies inside, she and Lance were soaked through.

Daisy and Lane worked shoulder to shoulder, laying out the food Sophie had brought, commenting with enthusiasm about how good it smelled, and moving in sync, as if nature had paired them perfectly. Clearly the pair got along just fine.

Lance tugged on Sophie's hood until it fell back as they stood dripping on the linoleum in front of the door. He gathered the thickness of her natural curls, and grabbing a towel from the nearby counter, he moved to wring it out. Sophie pushed the cloth away. "You'll make it frizz. How about a clean T-shirt?"

"You're literally dripping wet." He turned toward the small laundry cove and snagged a dark-blue shirt from the dryer. "I should have insisted you stay in town. It's pretty bad out there."

"Think I would have listened?" Accepting the shirt, she squeezed her fresh-from-a-shower wet hair. "Plus, I got more practice on a slippery road. Before too long, I'll need to be able to navigate it every day."

"I like the implications of that."

"Y'all are so cute." Daisy's comment caught them as Lance leaned in for another kiss.

"They're disgusting," Lane responded flatly. "Like a couple of high schoolers making out in the hallway."

"This *is* Lance's house," Daisy argued.

"Yeah, and we're stuck here." Lane tossed a hot pad toward the couple. "So no PDA."

Sophie laughed as she coiled her arms around Lance. "What are you going to do about it?"

Lane stared at her for a moment, and then a grin broke through, splitting his dark beard as he shook his head. "Man, I never would have thought..."

"Thought what?" Daisy started serving up lasagna on the plates she'd pulled down.

"My brother. The guy too shy to even look at a girl. Now he's standing over there all tangled up with a woman. Not even blushing. What on earth has happened since I've been gone?"

"Awww..." Daisy elbowed him. "He grew up on you, didn't he? Someone jealous, maybe?"

Lane grunted like he was annoyed. The look he settled on Daisy said anything but. Lance stepped back, and Sophie let her hands slide away from him, looking up to find a mildly suspicious/annoyed scowl furrowing his brow. His focus trained on her, rather than watching the two at the counter continue their playful banter, and she reached up to peck his cheek, hoping he wouldn't push the issue.

Just one night they could all be together and enjoy it, couldn't they? One evening they could hang out and let the drama of everything between the two brothers rest. That wasn't asking too much, was it?

She sure hoped not, because by the drumming on the tin roof above them, they were going to be stuck there together.

"I'll find you some dry sweats." Lance spoke low and then lifted a half smile, as if he understood her thoughts.

Boots kicked off and placed in the mud tray by the laundry room, he strode off, and Sophie wiggled out of her drenched jacket.

"Think you're both gonna be stuck here." Lane finished piling up his salad. "In all seriousness, Sophie, is that going to be a problem?"

"I've got to get to school tomorrow."

"What about rumors?"

"You'll not do anything to provoke those, will you?"

"Like talk?"

"Like misbehave."

Lane barked a laugh. "You assume the worst of me? What has my brother told you?"

"Not much." Sophie raised her brows and then shifted her look to Daisy. "But I do have eyes."

Daisy looked up at Lane with an independent sass. "No need to worry there, Sophie. I can handle myself."

"That right?"

"You know it is, Lane Carson."

"Might be so, but know what I think?"

"What's that?"

"You give as good as you get."

Sophie couldn't help but chuckle. The pair was amusing with their lighthearted banter, and she liked seeing the brooding, sour version of Lane disappear in favor of this playful but not offensive version of the man.

Lance reappeared, his soaked hoodie replaced with a dry sweatshirt. "I laid out a few options. Hope something will work for you."

Still scrunching her hair with the T-shirt, Sophie nodded and walked toward the doorway Lance had passed through. His room was down the hall, second door on the left—known only to her because she'd toured the house with him the third or fourth time she'd come out last fall. Finding the promised dry clothes on his bed, she shut the door behind her. Once the wet clothes had been replaced, she took a moment to take in the space, a surreal sense of life ahead enveloping her.

"Soon," she whispered. A nervous sense of hope and excitement rushed through her. Only a couple more months, and this would no longer be simply his room, but theirs. No longer Lance's place, but his and hers. She was all open arms and delight about that future.

But then there was Lane. Her heart lurched on that. He seemed to be in no hurry to leave, which wasn't a problem. She wanted him to stay, because she knew how much Lance wanted his brother to come back. The problem was that with that, there were a lot of complications.

The boys, they didn't see eye to eye. And Lane seemed to have perfected how to get under Lance's skin. Separating the family ranch seemed like the best way to keep whatever was left of their relationship intact. But now, that wasn't possible.

*God, please make another way for them.*

Sophie shut her eyes as she sat on the bed, praying. And the rain continued to drum overhead.

***

Ticket to Ride was spread out on the table, the pieces blurring in Lance's view. He was not used to late nights like this. Ten p.m. was his standard shut-down time, and his body functioned like it had its own internal clock. Now near midnight, his head was heavy and he could barely keep his eyes open. Still, the rain continued. Hadn't let up one bit.

The most recent weather alert was a flood warning. The area under closest watch included most of the Carson land.

"Might have been a mistake, leaving the cattle at the homestead." He leaned into his hand, his fingers squeezing his temples.

"Think it'll breach the banks this time?"

"Never has." He looked at his brother. "Still."

Lane took his phone, scrolled for a second, then frowned. "They're saying the dam's still holding. Should be okay."

"I don't remember them ever even bringing up the dam during one of these. Makes me nervous that it's even being talked about, you know?"

"Yeah." Lane laid his phone back on the table. "I can  move the herd to the high ground."

Lance considered it. He'd been thinking about doing the same thing, but there was the problem of getting Sophie back home. She couldn't go before morning—they'd already known that pretty much from the moment she'd arrived. The roads would be impassible in the dark, with the amount of rain that had fallen since sunset. But if the rain stopped before daybreak and the winds continued, then there was a possibility that he could get her through in time for school. He wasn't about to let her test her newly practiced mud-driving skills on her own.

"Sophie needs to work tomorrow," he said, more to himself than anything.

"I can call in, Lance." Sophie laid a hand on his leg. "The ranch needs to come first on this."

He looked over his shoulder at her, and a mix of gratitude and regret stirred within at the fact that she was there. What were people going to say in town, at church? Sophie had already taken a bit of the cold shoulder—he was sure of it—because of his business pursuits. This was a bad call, her coming to the lodge, and he'd known it before she'd even left town. Selfishness had overridden good sense.

"I can head out now." Lane stood from his place on the floor.

"I'll come too," Daisy said.

"No." Lance shook his head, trying to sort through what was best for this situation. What good would it do to go try and move them in the dark, anyway? There was no sense in it. "No, we'll wait it out. Gotta stop raining at some point—these things don't usually last all night. We can sort it out when the sun's up." He looked to Daisy, whose reputation he'd also put in jeopardy by not sending her home earlier in the day, and then to the beauty at his side. "We'd best figure out where you girls are going to sleep. I'd say you should take our rooms, but I haven't washed bedding in way too long and am scared to know what Lane's room looks like, let alone smells like."

Sophie leaned in and pecked his cheek. "Not to worry. Daisy and I can bunk out here. It'll be like a girls' slumber party." She winked. "No boys allowed."

"Right." He shot a pointed look at Lane.

"Don't look at me." His brother held up his hands. "I have no interest in chick flicks and nail polish."

Daisy snorted. "Yeah. That's how all females roll." She shook her head. "This slumber party will involve me with my eyes closed and not a whole lot more."

"Exactly." Sophie stood and gathered plates that were still scattered about the room.

Lance muffled a sigh and moved off the couch. "I'll find a couple of sleeping bags and extra pillows."

The group dismantled, to pick up and then set up. As tired as he was, Lance felt the night ahead was bound to be long. He'd worry about tomorrow—about Sophie and Daisy and how this innocent setup was going to play out in the long haul. Worried about getting his fiancée back to town, because he really didn't want her to miss work on account of his bad judgment. Worried about the feed they'd stacked down by the old homestead getting wet and ruined.

Never once, however, did he think to worry about that dam. Not that it would have helped.

# Chapter Twenty-One

The whisper of feet against the floor drifted into Sophie's consciousness. Seemed weird. Whose footsteps could be intruding on her sleep? No matter...

She settled against her bed, tugging her thick comforter up to her chin. Strange that—felt slick and smelled a bit of earth and musk.

What?

"Lane?"

A soft whisper now interrupted her confused sleep. Still, Sophie remained in the foggy grip of not-quite conscious.

"Lane, where are you going?"

"Shh."

The sound of something crumpling—fabric maybe?—preceded a man's low voice.

"Go back to sleep."

"Not until you tell me what you're up to."

The man sighed. "It's still raining."

"Yeah?"

"I got another alert on my phone. I don't think the cattle are safe."

There was a space of stillness. Then, "I'm coming too."

"Not a chance."

"I'm a better rider than you are."

"Lance will kill me. More, I don't want you hurt."

"I'm not some frail sorority sister who can't get her boots dirty." The sound of shuffling increased. "I'm coming."

"No, you're not..."

The voices trailed into the distance. Sophie covered her head with her arm and drifted back into the quieter place of sleep.

She rolled to her back. Except she couldn't. There was something solid there.

What on earth was happening? She reached for her phone, which she always kept plugged in on her nightstand. Her extended hand hit nothing but dead air. For goodness' sake, what was wrong with—

The memory of those whispered voices and then the faint impression of the door clicking in the distance, jolted her heart rate. Had that been real?

Sophie bolted upright, and the pieces fell into place. The shadowy room was not her bedroom, but the Carson living room, the cushions beneath her not a mattress, but Lance's couch.

And that conversation? Lane and Daisy's—all too real, she realized, as she squinted into the dimness to make out Daisy's sleeping bag in an empty, crumpled pile on the floor. The young woman was not there.

They'd left. Gone out into the storm to work cattle.

***

"Lance."

Lance rolled toward the voice hissing his name. He heard her often in his dreams, but she didn't usually sound upset. Inhaling, he wiped his face with his hand and pushed sleep away from his brain.

"Sophie?"

"Yeah."

"What are you doing in here?"

"Your brother and Daisy left."

"What?"

"Lane and Daisy."

Lane and Daisy left...for where? *Oh good heavens, Lane!* Really? His brother couldn't behave himself for one night?

He sat up and swung his feet to the floor. "How long ago?"

"I'm not sure. I was asleep—pretty out of it, apparently. Took me a while to figure out what was going on."

"I'm gonna kill him." Lance stood and snatched a flannel hanging on the back of his door.

Sophie slunk back into the doorway. "He said something about an alert."

"An alert?"

"Yeah, said it was still raining, and he got another alert on his phone."

Arms pushed into the sleeves, but his flannel shirt not yet buttoned, Lance swung around to his dresser and grabbed his cell phone. There was a stack of notifications when the screen lit up. Scanning them, his attention narrowed in on one near the top, put out at near 4:00 a.m.

*County dam breach likely. Flood warning for all areas down river. All residents within the one-hundred-year floodplain advised to evacuate. Warning level critical. Repeat, county dam breach imminent. Evacuate now.*

"Oh no." Lance squeezed his eyes shut. That had been over an hour ago.

"What?" Sophie stepped back into his room until she was at his back, her hand on his shoulder.

"The dam. They think it might not hold."

He felt her gaze freeze on him for several breaths. "Might not hold? Like the water will overflow, or like it's going to break?"

"I'm not sure."

"Will we be okay here? I mean, how far will the banks overflow?"

"The house isn't in the floodplain. But then again, this has never..." The hard throb of his pulse surged with fear and adrenaline.

"What about the lodge?"

He shook his head. "Should be out of it. But the old homestead—"

She met him with a wide, wild look. "Lane and Daisy."

"Yeah. They went to move the cows. I'd bet on it." Lance jerked back into action, jamming his phone into a shirt pocket and snatching his jeans to replace his sweats. "You don't know how long ago they left?"

"No." She blinked as if she was about to tears. "No, I'm sorry. I was so out of it. I'm a pretty hard sleeper."

Lance kept moving, gathering his clothes.

Sophie jumped out of his path. "What can I do?"

"Stay here. Watch your phone for alerts—"

The vibrating buzz of his interrupted him, and when he looked, the words that filled his screen registered in his understanding with a furious alarm. He trembled as he continued to stare at the warning.

"Lance?"

His fists clenched while his heart hammered. Didn't seem possible. This had never happened—never even come close to happening. It couldn't be possible...

Sophie tugged on his elbow. "Lance, what is it?"

He wiped his hand over his face as she took his phone. Only a breath passed before hers was a rush into the silent room.

"Oh no." Her voice wavered. "Oh God, help."

The dam was failing. Not too far up the river that cut through the Carson farm and ranch, the county dam was failing. If it collapsed completely, a wall of water would charge straight for them.

Lane and Daisy...they were somewhere out there in the middle of the flood zone. And there was nothing Lance could do.

*** 

Sophie had never known such helplessness. After a minute of standing in utter shock, immobilized by the gravity of what was happening, Lance charged into action, changing into his work clothes almost before she could remove herself from his room, then silently grabbing boots, coat and hat, a headlamp, and a handheld floodlight.

"What's the plan?"

"We'll take the F350 toward the old bridge. I'm guessing that's the way Lane went. You text Daisy and Lane while I drive. Keep texting and calling until you get an answer."

Grabbing her jacket, Sophie nodded, noting silently Lance's change of mind and glad of it. It was better than him leaving her there in the house. Better than doing nothing.

"Will we cross the bridge?" she asked.

Lance stilled, his look agony as he settled on her. Mouth pressed gravely, his eyes sheened as he shook his head. "No," he whispered. "If they're not there, I think it will be too late."

Pain rolled through her belly, and her throat nearly closed over. "God, help," she whispered again.

Lance's jaw clenched, and then he shoved his hat over his sleep-disheveled hair. With nothing more than a prayer, she followed him out the door, Mutt right at her side.

The rain continued to fall.

***

Lane still wasn't answering.

*God, where is he?*

What on earth had possessed him to take Daisy with him? As much as Lane was carefree, he wasn't stupid. And typically, he didn't intentionally put others in danger—especially when he had cared about those others. So many of the heated arguments Lance and Lane had as early teens had been about Lane doing something dangerous and telling Lance to stay back and watch.

*You've got too many brains to risk.*

It'd been a long time since Lance had thought about the response Lane had given back when Lance had tried to join in Lane's antics. Truthfully, Lance had figured that Lane was simply shedding his brother because he knew Lance would try to keep him out of trouble, which was true. It occurred to Lance, though, that Lane might have been protecting him.

Just like Lance would have expected Lane would have protected Daisy. More than a few times over the past week, Lance had observed his brother's interactions with his pretty little ranch hand. Yeah, there was flirtatious Lane. Boldly mischievous Lane. But there was also something honest beneath Lane's attentions.

Like the other day, when Daisy had accidentally stepped between a cow and her calf. Mama cows could turn to mama bears if they felt their young were in danger. Having a one-hundred-and ten-pound southern belle unintentionally back in between mama and baby had triggered that instinct. Lane had seen the rage in the brahma's eyes, and in less than ten steps he'd sailed over the working pen, had Daisy bundled in a hold that would handle a calf, and had hauled her out of danger. When she'd turned on him with the spitfire that didn't at all match her petite stature or generally soft face, he'd stood there shaking. Taking her lip. Staring at her like he needed to be sure she was standing all on her own, unharmed. Instead of giving her spice right back, he simply swallowed, pulled in a deep breath, and asked, "You okay?"

Not a typical Lane response.

What had he been thinking this morning?

*God, please let that dam hold—don't let it fail completely. Please keep my brother and Daisy safe...*

The prayers continued to roll through his mind, one behind the other, as he navigated the big truck through the deep muck. The mess of the road was unparalleled—he'd never seen the mud so deep. He couldn't guess how much it'd dumped, and with the rain being warmer than a winter blizzard, that meant the frozen sub earth was likely thawing. Quickly. With the ground saturated, the rain continuing, and the amount of snowfall that had blanketed the northwest of the state, the situation appeared grim. A disaster on the brink.

The back of the pickup fishtailed again, and Lance corrected course as the old bridge came into view. The sun ahead had cast the faintest light upward from the horizon, chasing the blackness of night with a dreary gray that seemed more ominous than promising. The gray of new day lightened enough to contrast against the darker, angry rush of the river. Large white chunks of broken ice rode the surging current, eating at the banks and catching on the base of the old bridge. Water built behind the ice blocks and heaved against both the ice and the bridge, demanding passage. The river, typically a good six feet below the bottom rail of the crossing, edged nearer to the top lip.

They were too late.

Lance braked, and the truck slid sideways. Without real thought, he corrected until the tires aligned straight with the road again, and when their movement ceased, he simply stared at the waiting destruction.

The first wave of overflow ran over the thick wooden slats.

"Lance?"

"We can't cross that." Defeat and fear made his voice quiver. Even as he said it, the near side of the crossing heaved upward. The ice blocks that had been caught between the incredible pressure of the raging, swelling river and the final stand of the bridge broke free. With a wicked ripping and crashing that made him shiver, the bridge rolled and then surrendered to the flood.

Silence encased them. A cold recognition. A surreal, disbelieving chill. Lance's phone vibrated against his chest, still tucked into his shirt pocket. He didn't need to check it.

The dam had failed. He knew by the skyrocketing pulse of the raging water in front of him, by the unreal gray current that moved massive ice blocks and full-sized bridges with the ease of a child tossing a whiffle ball.

Beside him, Sophie's phone beeped. Another alert, likely. One they no longer needed—they were staring at the unfolding disaster.

"It's Lane!" Sophie bounced on the seat beside him. "They're at the homestead."

Her words jarred Lance out of his stalled horror. "Daisy with him?"

"Yes."

"Tell them to move. Head north toward the highest ground possible."

"He says they're driving the cattle toward the northern soybean field."

"No." Ice ran through his veins as his heart restarted with a painful new jolt. "Tell him to leave the cows. They don't have time—the dam has failed."

Sophie didn't respond, and when he looked at her, he found her staring at him with an expression of near terror.

"Tell him, Soph." Driven into new action, he shifted the truck into reverse and began to slip-slide backward while Sophie sent a call rather than a text.

The urgency of her voice made the race of his pulse increase, and once he'd reached the fork in the dirt road that would lead them south—away from the riverbank, he jammed the gear back into Drive.

"No," she barked into the phone. "Lance says you don't have time."

"Move, Lane!" Lance shouted, leaning forward as his tires spun, struggling for a grip to climb the slight incline ahead.

Silence met him.

"Sophie?"

At his side, she sniffed. "The call dropped."

Reality sank as the day broke full. He couldn't save his brother.

# Chapter Twenty-Two

Sophie slipped her hand into Lance's. The feel of it was large and chapped—familiar. But so cold. She closed her eyes as she wove her fingers with his lying against the table in front of them. The Grill had a few patrons that early in the morning—the regular coffee club of old ranchers and farmers and local businessmen. A group that had met in that very spot every morning for longer than Sophie had been alive.

She'd been surprised—shocked actually—when Lance had pulled up in front of The Grill. It was the last place she would have guessed he'd stop at in the middle of this crisis. But she hadn't said anything. When he'd sat in drawn silence after shutting off the engine, staring out the windshield, she'd stayed silent. When he'd slowly opened his door and lowered himself to the ground, she'd followed him wordlessly.

Sitting in a booth beside him, she lay her cheek on his arm and looked out the window. The rain had let up but not stopped. The new day didn't feel like promise. There was instead an atmosphere of sadness and foreboding.

Lance's truck had been baptized in mud. From the hood, to the top, to the bed, to the tailgate, not a smidge of paint poked through the thick layer of pale-colored mud. The sludge hung off the wheel wells in thick clumps, plopped from the running boards in huge drops. Only the windshield remained somewhat free— though the glass was streaked with brown.

"Hear things are bad on the river." The gruff voice sounded from across the dining room, all matter of fact and disconnected.

Her shoulder against his, she felt Lance tremble.

"Hush, George," Wes barked from the swinging door that connected the dining to the kitchen. He scowled at the table of five across the room. "We all know what we've all heard. Just drink your coffee. And pray." When his attention turned toward herself and Lance, Wes's frown eased. He met her look with sympathy, and carrying a pair of steaming mugs, he strode forward.

Sophie squeezed Lance's unresponsive hand in the quiet space before Wes reached them, and she felt a fervent plea for God's peace to intercede. As far as she knew, the two men hadn't spoken in months. Wes didn't know what Lance had done—or hadn't done—in Kansas City. For all she could guess, the owner of The Grill was about to unload on her fiancé.

Sitting up straight, she stiffened. She wouldn't have it.

With a pair of clunks, Wes set the mugs onto the table in front of them. He stood, silently appraising the pair, and then sighed. With a grunt, he fit himself onto the bench across the table.

"You okay, son?"

The man beside her tensed and then squeezed her hand. Sophie looked up to find his jaw quivering.

"No, then." Wes's response was heartbreakingly quiet and gentle. "What needs done?"

"Lane's out there." Lance nearly choked on the words, and the agony in his voice brought the sting of tears to Sophie's eyes.

Surprise flashed in Wes's eyes. "Lane's home?"

"Yes. Near on two weeks." The weight of Lance's gaze hung in the air, full of pain. "He took young Daisy—Miss Jane's niece and my ranch hand—over to the old homestead to move cows before the sun was up. I didn't know."

Wes's low groan was pain and sympathy. "Oh, son." He leaned forward, and then one large, meaty hand pushed across the table to cover hers and Lance's tangled together. The pressure of his strong hold wrapped over her hand in Lance's. "Lord, we know You to be a big, big God. And that's sure a good thing, because we've got ourselves a big, big problem."

Lance trembled, and the proof of his emotion provoked a sob from Sophie. She sniffed as she pushed into the man at her side, wanting so much to lend whatever measure of her strength, small though it was, to him.

Wes's low, rumbling prayer continued. "Up there on Your throne, we know You see Lane and Daisy Jane. Looking at them right now, I expect. God, we beg for Your mighty compassion right now, for your rock-solid protection. Bring 'em home, Lord. Please, bring 'em both home."

The chime of the patron door broke into the end of Wes's prayer, and Sophie opened her tear-filled eyes to see Brian Tuck, the county sheriff, pass through the door. His focus lasered on Lance.

"I was heading out your way," the uniformed man said. "Thought that mud-monster out there was your truck though. Glad to see you're safe. There's an evacuation order."

Lance nodded, his expression distant. "Lane's still out there. And Daisy Elderson. They went to move cows to higher ground."

Tuck frowned, gripping the sidearm secured at his waist, as if habit. "How long ago?"

Sophie met Lance's glance. She hated that she couldn't give a definite answer. Hated more that she hadn't been able to sort reality from sleep in any kind of timely matter so that she could have prevented this part of the disaster.

"There was a flood alert on my phone about four a.m.—one that came before the evacuation order because of the failing dam. I'm guessing he went then."

Sheriff Tuck nodded. "They're on the north side of the river?"
"Yes."

"And you're sure that's where they went?"

"Sophie got a call through to him right before the water took out our private crossing. They were moving cattle north, away from the river. I told them to stop, to get themselves to safety. But the call dropped before we got a response."

Tuck nodded and then reached for his phone. With a few quick punches and a brief pause, he was talking. "I need someone in the air."

Sophie searched Wes for answers.

"Big Prairie aviation, I suspect." Wes tried for a reassuring nod. "A couple of the dusters are trained for search and rescue."

Sheriff Tuck continued to give instructions. "North of River's Edge, to the old Carson homestead. That's your starting point. Lance said they were pushing cattle away from the river. But he told them to leave the herd." Tuck paused his conversation, moved the phone from his mouth, and addressed Lance. "They on horseback?"

"Likely. We left five saddle horses up at the homestead. Lane wouldn't want to rip up the pasture with a four-wheeler."

Tuck nodded and continued with his phone conversation.

Sophie's heart lifted. "Where would they land?"

"They won't. Not with the ground completely saturated the way it is." A slim thread of hope wove in Lance's voice. "But maybe they could spot them."

\*\*\*

The complete failure of the dam sent a ravaging swell of ice block–strewn water downstream, flooding fields, pastures, and homes indiscriminatingly. The flood not only covered bridges but dislodged several. The strength of raging water picked up full-size storage containers, Quonsets, and ill-parked vehicles, adding them to the litter of unintended river vessels. Long-established bank boundaries were breached, and the powerful currents ate away paved highways as if they were nothing more than soft sand.

Along with much of the town that turned out as if on instinct to stand together in equal amounts of horrified astonishment and desperate prayer, Sophie watched video reports as they flashed on a computer screen that had been opened and displayed in the middle of a booth at The Grill. Unimagined destruction played out in front of them—there on the screen and only a few miles up the highway, in the town's backyard.

Big Prairie had been built up off the depression of the riverbed, so the waters didn't pass through the middle of town. But other populated areas were not so lucky. As they continued to pray for the safety of those they knew—Lane and Daisy, the people braving the continuing bad weather to search for them, and those who had been called upon to see to the needs and safety of others—they also were keenly aware of the massive impact this flood was having and would continue to have on Big Prairie's downstream neighbors.

Whole towns had been evacuated. No one knew what to expect or how exactly to respond. For a semiarid climate that typically saw an average of fifteen inches of rain a year, a flood of this magnitude was unprecedented in their lifetime.

Tears leaked from Sophie's eyes as the prayer that had been her staple since the beginning of this awful day repeated through her mind yet again. *God, help.*

In the midst of the stunned silence surrounding her, she took notice of the gathering. A host surrounded them—her and Lance. Miss Jane sat on his other side, her strong, slim hand gripping his, refusing to let go. Craig and Brenna stood behind them, Brenna's warm palm on Sophie's shoulder and Craig's anchored on Lance's. So many others standing shoulder to shoulder around them.

Wes came and went, seeing to his business in the kitchen and updating Jaycee, but stopping often to see what played out on the screen, and perhaps more to his intention, now and then laying a thick hand on Lance's head, mumbling a low but fervent prayer. "Lord, You still see us. We don't know what to do, but we're looking to You…"

Whether they knew of Lance's previous business plans or not, every individual there stood in solidarity with him. Praying. Hoping. Grieving.

Sophie's chest quivered as she surrendered to another wave of emotion. In the midst of the fear and the heartbreak, a steadiness solidified. It was a presence, a hope anchoring deep within that would not be moved. In fact, every time Wes, or Miss Jane, or Craig voiced another prayer, that anchor dug in deeper and became more known.

*You redeem. You heal. You give new strength...*

The prayer seeded by the psalm she'd long since tucked deep in her heart, grew in the midst of this crisis and became not only a plea to God, but a praise. He *did* see. Not only that, He was *right there* in the midst of the storm. Present and known.

*Oh, let Lance know it too. Please, God...*

The chime of the diner's door cracked through the eerie quiet.

"Archie saw them!" Tuck's announcement boomed from the doorway. "They're out there—up on Prairie lookout. Lance!" He waited until Lance stood. "They're okay, buddy. Archie saw them both, and they're okay!"

Sophie stood, and within a breath Lance had her gripped in a hold that nearly crushed the breath from her lungs as he inhaled like a man who had been drowning.

"Thank You, Lord. Thank You..." His mumbled words drifted over her as his body shook.

Sophie clung to him, crying.

***

No one could get to them, but the aerial watch kept Lane and Daisy in view. Washed-out bridges and the continuing flood made for one barrier. The other, just as significant, were the mud-sopped, minimum-maintenance roads. Impassible, likely for days.

For the moment, though, knowing they were safe, and having them know that they'd been found, was enough. Tuck assured Lance they were working on an extraction plan.

"Can we find a way to communicate with them?" Lance and Sheriff Tuck talked between themselves, both with fists wrapped around a fresh-brewed mug of coffee.

"Working on it. Keep trying his cell. I'm not sure why you'd not be getting through, unless his phone was lost or damaged, but keep trying. Daisy's too."

Lance nodded. "That area is riddled with dead zones. Never understood why, but working pastures, we'd often have problems. Never considered it a big issue until now."

Tuck nodded, and a lull dropped between them. Lance's attention moved over the crowd still gathered around the computer screen and then to the pair of women huddled in a booth, likely praying. Lance's emotions had been wrung out more times than he could count that day, but when he followed Tuck's look and it landed on Sophie, a painful squeeze resonated in his chest.

She hadn't signed up for any of this. Not the earlier drama he'd put her through with his personal business plans putting himself at odds with most of Big Prairie. Not his brother's unpredictable antics. And certainly not this. *God, I don't deserve her.* The heavenward thought made his eyes and nose sting. He honestly believed it to be true—he didn't deserve the lovely, happy, steady Sophie Shultz. And yet in the middle of this chaos that sent his world careening upside down, there she was—as she had been all day—being his constant.

What could he possibly offer her in return? Now...now, it appeared not much. He couldn't imagine the flooding river hadn't covered his vineyard, drowning the dormant vines, dumping massive amounts of mud and sand overtop the carefully cultivated rows. No, the vineyard would be ruined. Possibly forever.

The cattle likely gone. Drowned in the torrent of icy waters.

The fields and pastures devastated. Just like the vineyard.

All of everything he had to offer had been swept away within hours, leaving him empty handed and uncertain.

How could he possibly ask Sophie to step into such a bleak future with him?

# Chapter Twenty-Three

It was late evening, the cold light of the long day fading in the west, before a helicopter was able to land near enough for Lane and Daisy to be lifted and delivered to town. They'd been sent to Big Prairie Community Hospital, but other than being chilled straight to the bone, and a little dehydrated, not to mention hungry, they were determined healthy enough to be released.

The question was, to where? Daisy went home with her aunt Jane. The Carson brothers had been rendered homeless for the time being.

Wes wandered through the self-opening doors to the ER, his gait a pronounced limp born of a lifetime of constant work and a bad back. He aimed straight for Lance and Lane, standing near the ER desk.

"Come on." He clapped a hand on Lance's shoulder. "You'll both stay with Jaycee and me."

"We can't do that." Rancid guilt churned in Lance's gut, another flavor of emotion that washed through during the course of that day.

"Yes, you can." Wes met him with a commanding look. "And you will. Both of you."

Lance looked at Lane, who wore clean clothes donated by the local secondhand store and a heavy coat one of the firemen had lent him. Exhaustion pulled on his brother's face, and perhaps an etching of brokenness. Lane had arrived in the ER sheet white, eyes bright with high alert, and insistent that Daisy be seen to first. All traces of the arrogant and obnoxious brother Lance often saw was gone. It was actually a bit concerning. As was Lane's lack of response or opinion to Wes's offer.

"We can get a room at the Six." Lance barely looked away from Lane while he refused Wes's offer again.

"No." Wes tugged on his arm. "No, you won't. You'll stay with us, for as long as you need."

Lane, looking more to the ground than at either Wes or Lance, gave a small nod. "Thanks," he mumbled.

Which closed all doors on arguments. Lance was at once thankful he'd sent Sophie, along with Mutt, home so she could go to sleep after such a long, horrible day, and a bit regretful that she wasn't there to hold his hand. How could he go to Wes and Jaycee's home after what he'd nearly done? How could he stomach staying with them, accepting their hospitality as if...

As if he deserved it?

Numb and lost in his head, Lance followed Wes out the doors and toward his crossover still running in the parking lot.

"My truck's over—" Lance stopped midsentence, his hand frozen in the air where he'd begun to gesture toward the other side of the lot. His mud-monster pickup was not there.

"Craig and his boys picked it up. They'll take it through the spray-n-suds in the morning. Hopefully we'll have sun by then. Anyway, they'll take care of it." Now beside his car, Wes patted the top of the white vehicle. "You're with me."

No way out, then. Lance opened the front door and gestured for his brother to slide in. After, he climbed into the backseat, folding his long legs up tight to fit.

The drive was quiet. Wes didn't feel the need to chatter needlessly. Lane tipped his head and leaned against the door, his shoulders drooping. The wind that had gusted throughout the day continued to blow, causing tree limbs to sway against the cold gray sky. Lance shivered as he shut his eyes.

*Lane's alive. Safe.* He focused on that, allowing the thought to wrest a prayer of gratitude. *Thank You for Lane and Daisy, for keeping them safe and bringing them home.*

Defeat threatened to nip at the gratitude. Lance pushed it away.

***

*Are you safe?*

Curled up on her bed with Mutt curled up against her, Sophie read her dad's text, and tears blurred her vision. *All are safe. Lane and Daisy have been recovered.*

*How is Lance?*

*Shaken. Pray for him, Daddy. He is at a breaking point, and I am afraid.*

Several moments passed before her father responded, and when his text lit up her screen, it was with Scripture. So very much her daddy. Slowly, and with the leaking of several tears, she read through the entirety of Psalm 23, which she was certain came from her dad's memory.

*The LORD is my shepherd, I shall not want.*
*He makes me lie down in green pastures;*
*He leads me beside quiet waters.*
*He restores my soul;*
*He guides me in paths of righteousness*
*For His name's sake.*
*Even though I walk through the valley of the shadow of death,*
*I fear no evil, for You are with me;*
*Your rod and Your staff, they comfort me.*
*You prepare a table before me in the presence of my enemies;*
*You have anointed my head with oil;*
*My cup overflows.*
*Surly goodness and lovingkindness will follow me all the days of my life,*
*And I will dwell in the house of the LORD forever.*

Sophie gripped the phone as she trembled. "Be with me," she whispered in prayer. "And with Lance. Be with him in this dark valley. For Your name's sake."

A new text from her dad flashed on her phone. *Amen.*

She snuggled in close to Mutt and slept.

\*\*\*

The bed he'd been given had been warm and comfortable.
Even so, Lance hadn't slept much. Not for lack of desire, nor for
lack of need. Every muscle ached with fatigue. Images had
replayed throughout the long hours of the night—pictures of the
water swelling before his eyes, heavy, jagged chunks of ice
crashing against the banks and then dislodging the bridge he'd
intended to cross.

Then, more scenes that had come over the internet. The dam
failing as massive blocks of ice pushed against the structure and
the buildup of water piling behind them, until finally the initial
breach cut a new channel of rushing water to the side of the dam.
As the current sped, pulled along by the new channel, the blocks
of ice—some the size of small pickups—heaved against the dam,
surpassing its capacity to hold. Catastrophic failure had followed,
releasing an eleven-foot wall of water.

Lance couldn't unsee those replays. He couldn't shut them out,
nor could he turn off the tortuous thoughts that piled up on top
of them. The dam failing had happened in mere moments. The
consequences would stretch into his life with a reach he couldn't
yet calculate. The ranch had been his inheritance—given not
only by his father but bestowed by the generations of Carsons
who had settled and worked the land. Generations of work now
washed out or buried under an untold amount of sand and mud.

He had no idea what to do. But he'd spent the long, agonizing
night fruitlessly trying to figure it out.

When the slightest hint of light slipped through the blinds at
the window, Lance sat up. Dressed in a pair of sweats Jaycee had
produced, Lance released himself from the room he'd been
provided and wandered toward the kitchen. As restaurant owners,
Lance suspected Wes and Jaycee would be up soon, if they weren't
already.

The hot pot of coffee waiting on the counter confirmed the
second. Somehow they'd been soundless as they'd started their
day.

Lance reached for a clean mug sitting upside down on the counter near the maker, then poured himself the coffee. As habit, he wrapped both hands around the warmth and lifted the mug so he could inhale the bitter nuttiness of the brew.

A shuffling of a page jolted into his awareness, and he jerked his attention toward the kitchen table.

"I'm sorry," Jaycee whispered. "I didn't mean to startle you."

"That's okay." His spiked heart rate eased back to normal. "I'm sorry to interrupt you. I figured you and Wes were already at The Grill."

Her gentle, motherly smile invited him to sit with her. "Wes is. I take my time."

Lance chuckled. "It's like five a.m. and you're up. Taking your time might be relative."

"Closer to six." Jaycee grinned. "And Wes gets to the kitchen by four thirty. He's always been that way though. Early at it. The man has endless energy. Used to make for quite a conflict between us. I'm not built that way."

Planting his elbows onto the table, Lance nodded. A span of uneasy quiet extended.

"Lance?" Jaycee's quiet intrusion sounded uncertain.

"Yes, ma'am?"

"I want to apologize."

He shook his head, looking away. "Not your fault, Jaycee. You didn't bring the blizzard that dumped over a foot of snow last week. Didn't ask for the rain and runoff. Didn't cause the dam to fail." A hint of bitterness threatened as he spoke. No, Jaycee hadn't done any of it. But God could have prevented any part of it. One change, and all of this would be different. None of it would have happened.

*Why, God?*

"I'm not talking about the flood, Lance. Though I am sorry for it—for you and Lane. I'm sorry—" Her words broke, and she had to clear her throat. "Wes and me—we were so upset with you. Angry."

Weight sagged against him, and his shoulders sagged. "I know. I get it."

"The thing is, we don't. We don't understand why you're bringing in that franchise."

Clenching his jaw, Lance shook his head, ready to tell her that he hadn't gone through with it.

"But we should have asked. Should have talked to you, instead of being mad and silent and cold. You must have your reasons, right?"

*I did. I thought I did.* All of it tangled in his mind—the reasons he'd had, the frustration he carried concerning his brother, the loneliness that filled him about all of it, and now...now this loss that would likely ruin him. Them. The mess of everything swirled and tangled, making him painfully confused.

Jaycee's hand covered his arm, bringing a solid warmth into his cold chaos. "I'm listening now, Lance. Really listening—as your neighbor, your father's friend. And yours too."

"I didn't go through with it." The words felt harsh from his swollen throat.

Her hand stayed with him while a fresh space of silence washed over them. In it, a bulge of frustration grew.

Maybe if he had signed the contracts, there would be something left to cling to in the middle of this devastation. Something solid, promising even.

*Cling to Me.*

The impression of the words branded themselves in his heart and in his mind as sure as the table beneath his hands. Lance shut his eyes and wondered over it. Back in Kansas City, he'd wondered if he was crazy, *hearing* that voice. Now...

Now he hoped desperately that it would stay.

"Even still," Jaycee said softly, "I'd like to know. Tell me why, Lance. Help me understand."

"Because I inherited. Lane got nothing—and he resents it." Explaining suddenly became easy, knowing that she sat there without condemnation. More, with compassion. The anger fizzled, and Lance looked at her as a friend, not an enemy. "Me and Dad—Lane is so angry with both of us. I hoped that if I could establish a stable alternative income, I could sign the ranch over to him, and then he'd come home. He'd stop living a life of dangerous wandering and embrace the man he's capable of being."

With a sheen glazing her eyes, Jaycee processed quietly and then nodded. Her brow furrowed, as if she felt his desperation and heartache. "So much to shoulder for such a young man."

Lance looked at his hands, his fingers rolling into his palms. Her touch slid over his arm and covered one of his clenched fists.

"I am sorry, Lance."

The simplicity of her apology, drenched with sincerity, moved to a deep place in his heart. With so much exhaustion and emotion piling up from the months before, and the day they'd passed through, Lance felt as if his heart was that failing dam. Terrified he would break in front of her, but at the same time, too wrung out to stop it, he leaned forward until his head rested on those fists.

Jaycee remained in silence, her grip still firm on his hand. Clinging to him. And in her touch, her grip, it seemed he could feel Another's.

One whose hold would not let him go.

# Chapter Twenty-Four

More than a foot of sand covered the vineyard, leaving the vines poking out as if half-mast, entombed and suffocating beneath the flood's debris.

Even from the dirt road into the River's Edge Vineyard—which was heavily rutted with thick mud on the edges—Sophie could see the profound marks of the flood. Much of the river's bank had been eaten away, leaving downed trees as an added testimony to the power of water. Atop earth that had been peeking with spring green only five days before, lay a thick layer of pale sand.

She parked in her usual spot—near the kitchen door, beside Lance's truck. With a fragile thread of hope, she noted that Lane's vehicle was also there, sitting on the other side of the drive.

"Lance?" She called from beside her car into the cool afternoon air. The sun smiled down as if nothing in the world had ever been wrong—a contradiction to everything her eyes beheld. She stepped toward the house but changed her direction midway when she saw the layers of sand reaching all the way to the front of the Carson dwelling. The lodge was a winding walk from the home—nearly a football field length's distance closer to the river.

Sophie's heart plummeted as she shifted her path. There would be damage—more so than Lance had predicted. More than he had told.

Lance and Lane had come back home three days before—as soon as the roads were passable. Sophie had classes to teach, though she found it difficult to put her whole heart into her work. Prayers for Lance were ever scrawling through her mind and lifting from her heart. Especially when and after she talked to Lance on the phone.

"There's a lot of damage." That was what he'd said when she'd asked for reports. "So much damage."

What he didn't say in words had made her worry so much more. He'd sounded distant and defeated.

Now she knew he'd not been telling her the vast depth of it. *Damage* was a benign word for the destruction she was taking in.

Lance had been more than shielding her. To Sophie, it had felt like he'd been pushing her away. More so now, as she walked through the mess Lance had been wading through without her.

"Lance?" She called for him again as she stepped up the stairs to the lodge's deck. A coating of silty sand crunched under her boots.

"Lance? Lane?" She pushed through the back door to the main gathering area, then sucked in a hard breath.

The river had washed through the lodge. Streaks of mud, piles of sand, and pockets of standing water were scattered across the now-ruined pine-planked floor. Tables and chairs were littered across the scene helter skelter. Some lay tipped and skewed, others outright broken, as if a fighting mob had ripped through with angry destruction.

"Oh no," Sophie whispered.

Lance hadn't told her the waters had reached all the way to his lodge. She hadn't imagined *a lot of damage* meant this.

No ranch. No farm. No vineyard. No tourism. The flood had swept through with rage, cutting damage where it could and leaving what remained in its engorged path buried beneath hopeless mess.

*Lord, what will we do?*

Answers didn't whisper through her heart. A whine at her back alerted her to Mutt's presence, and before she could turn, Lance's dog was at her feet, her sad eyes lifted toward her.

"Where is he, girl?" Sophie knelt to love on the loyal pup and then stepped toward an overturned table. She scooped away the eight-inch pile of dirty debris deposited against the tabletop and then tugged the furniture back to its feet.

"Such a mess, isn't it?" The low rumble of Lane's voice dropped to her from the loft above.

Startled, Sophie turned and looked up. On the top step, she found a clean-shaven version of Lance's brother.

"Where's Lance?"

"Digging in the sand."

"Where?"

He motioned toward the vineyard and then started down the stairway. "We've looked for cows since the moment we got back. Sunup to sundown. Recovered about a dozen. But passing bloated carcasses got to be too much, so we quit after lunch today. Came back and showered." He ran a hand over his bare chin. "I had phone calls to make—people were expecting me by the end of the month." He grunted a deprecating laugh. "I know—that's shocking. But they were. Lance, though—" Lane stepped onto the mud- and sand-littered floor and met Sophie where she stood. "Been out there since we got back this afternoon. Digging like he's possessed."

Sophie reached for Lane's arm and squeezed. "He didn't tell me—" Emotion provoked by the reality around her cut her off.

Lane nodded. Brow furrowed with thought, he tipped his head to the side. "He doesn't know, I think."

"Know what?"

"That his way of dealing with things—with the hard things— that he cuts people away. Leaves them feeling abandoned or rejected."

Blinking, she looked toward the large windows that gave view to what had only days before been a vineyard on the verge of a new spring promise.

"No, he doesn't realize that. Lane, he never meant to cut you off," Sophie said softly. "Never wanted you to leave."

Lane remained mute at her side, his attention settled on a spot near his right boot.

She ran a hand over the table she'd righted. The granules of sand were rough under her palm, as were the scratches and water damage. The wood would need to be refinished.

With time and attention, the damage was reparable.

"He wanted you to come home." Clearing her clogged throat, she looked into Lane's caramel eyes, waiting until he met her gaze. "If only you knew how much."

\*\*\*

His back ached with a tight, burning pain that in other circumstances might have made him quit for the day. But not now, not on this.

If he could get to the root crown on every vine, maybe they could breathe. Maybe he'd buy enough time to get the skid steer in between the rows. Maybe there would be something salvageable.

"Hey, cowboy." Sophie's gentle voice washed over him as he reached for another armload of packed wet sand. Mutt stayed at her heels, his dog walking as if she too felt the despair of everything around them.

He froze, his heart lurching at the simple idea of Sophie showing up here in the middle of his latest nightmare. After several nights of fuzzy, exhausted consideration, he hadn't been able to think his way around the facts. He had nothing left to offer her—nothing stable, anyway. He couldn't hold her to a promise she'd made before the flood had ruined him.

But the thought of letting her go... He looked at the ground, blinking.

*Give me strength.*

Her yellow Muk boot landed softly near his bent knee, and then his hat was gently tugged from his head. Squatting next to him, she danced her fingertips into his hair, sending his mind into an anesthetized fog from which he didn't want to leave. *God, I love this woman. Her tender touch. Her ready smile...*

Love wasn't selfish though. Love, in fact, was the reason he needed to give her the out she deserved.

"Sophie..." Her name on his breath was a sigh and a lament. A dirge of lost joy and fresh mourning.

Rather than giving him whispers of hoped-for brighter days, promises of *everything's going to be okay*, or speeches about how strong he was to bear this—things that experience had shown him were typical from people in times of crisis—Sophie Shultz lowered herself into the silt-blackened sand next to him, tugged on his shoulders until he gave, and held him.

And that was why he broke. If she had given him the prescribed speeches, he would have been able to restrain the buildup of defeat and grief and even anger at the unfairness of it all. Instead, she stepped into his pain, sat with him in the dirt, and cried—her tears now mingled with his.

Suddenly desperate for something to cling to, he pulled her tighter into his arms. Though they were caked with gritty wet sand and muck, Lance curled his fingers into her shirt and hair. Sophie didn't protest but leaned her head against his.

"It's gone, Soph." His whisper was jagged and harsh. "There's almost nothing left."

"I know," she said gently.

Another shudder of emotion shook through him. "How can I begin again when the fields are buried, the cattle are dead, and the lodge is ruined?"

"I don't know." She pulled back enough to find his eyes and frame his heavily whiskered face.

Ah, those eyes. Deep brown, so big they could swallow him, and so beautiful she could bewitch him into anything. They held him with such gentle love, piercing his heart with a fresh sense of unworthiness. How could she sit there, tangled arms and legs with him, knowing that the future looked like...*this*—and stare at him with only eyes filled with love?

Oh, he wanted to take it. Clench her loyalty with both fists and never let go.

But as he studied her, savoring each detail—those eyes, the fullness of her lips so easily given to smiles, high cheekbones, silky mocha skin, glossy black curls—his vision blurred again.

He fingered a ringlet that had drifted to her cheek. *Do it. Because you love her.*

"Sophie." He moved, setting her back.

Her brows rumpled, and she gripped his hand, bringing it to her cheek.

Lance shook his head. "Don't make this harder," he whispered.

"What harder?"

"To—" He clenched his teeth, dug for resolve. "To let you go."

With a small turn of her head, she eyed him in uncertainty. "Let me go?"

"Yes." The word was broken from his lips.

"Where do you think I'm going to go?"

"I don't know. But I can't ask this of you."

"What are you asking of me?"

"This life—it's too uncertain. My world, it breaks. It falls apart. When I think I've got it put back together, something else comes unraveled. I can't ask you to be a part of that."

She stared at him, blinking, as giant, heartbreaking tears rolled down her face. "Lance..."

He couldn't do it anymore. Couldn't watch her normally positive, ready-to-smile expression drown into this weeping. After a moment behind shut eyes, in which he inhaled and gathered the last tendrils of courage the storm hadn't taken, Lance pushed his way off the sand and stood slowly. The ache in his back screamed, sending fissures of pain down his legs and up to his shoulders. He welcomed the distraction.

"I'm sorry I dragged you into this."

Sophie scrambled up and tugged on his hand. "Do you really think that little of me, Lance Carson?"

He whipped his look back to her. "Little? I think everything of you."

"You think I said yes because of all of this?" She held up his ring, still secure on her left hand, and then stepped back, opening her arms as a grand gesture to all that surrounded them.

"Sophie, that's not—"

"That's exactly what this is. But let me make something clear to you, Lance Carson." She stepped close enough that he could feel the heat of her body soaking through his damp clothes. With a firm hand against his jaw, she held his face steady as if she was afraid he'd look away. "Are you listening?"

He couldn't answer.

"I said yes because of this." Her other palm covered the spot on his chest beneath which his heart throbbed.

Tears blurred his vision again, and he rolled his lips together, trying to find the strength to maintain that resolve he'd found before. Shaking his head, he tried to step back, but she curled her fingers around his neck and gripped his shirtfront.

"Sophie, this life is hard." He inhaled a shaky breath. "*My* life is hard."

"Don't make it harder."

He winced. "I'll hate myself if I make you miserable."

"Ah, my love." That hand that had clutched his shirt released, and her palm slid up his chest, to his shoulder, and then his neck. She reached up on her toes, a magnetic move that demanded his body respond. As he leaned into her, their foreheads touched. "I will go with you. Your home will be mine. Your trials will be mine as well. I will cry with you when life is hard, and I will laugh with you when there is joy. I will not miss any of your moments, and I will never regret giving you all of mine. I will go with you through this life. Because I love you, Lance. I will always love you."

Lance trembled as he closed her in tight. Where did such a love come from?

He sighed, his face tucked into the beautiful mess of her hair. "I wish I had something to give you, Sophie. Something that wasn't broken and a mess."

"How about your name? I'd very much like that."

# *Chapter Twenty-Five*

"You and Sophie okay?" Lane filled his coffee mug at the counter, his back turned toward Lance, who sat at the kitchen table.

The brothers hadn't seen each other throughout the rest of the afternoon the day before—Lance had sought refuge from the anger and disappointment by working to unbury his vines. He had no idea what Lane had done with the rest of his day, besides obviously showered and shaved. He'd mentioned phone calls, but Lance hadn't asked about them. After Sophie had come, and they'd both reached new stability together, she'd found a pair of leather work gloves, shoved her arms through the sleeves of an old flannel she'd snatched from Lance's room, and spent the rest of daylight digging at Lance's side.

He couldn't believe such a woman loved him.

"Why me?" he'd asked her softly while holding her before she'd headed back to town later that night. "Why would you want to spend your life with someone like me?"

She'd breathed a soft chuckle. "Someone like you? Kind and determined, strong and gentle? Not to mention handsome." She'd looked up at him, that wonderful smile lighting her face. "Oh so handsome. Why wouldn't I want to marry you?"

"Because I feel lost, or like a misfit, most of the time, Soph."

Cupping his face, she held him in a strong, tender gaze. "I know, Lance. And I know how that feels—the sense that you're in the fog, unseen. Or maybe unaccepted."

His heart had shivered when she'd said that, because he knew for her how true that had been most of her life. A life, it seemed, lived between two worlds that still didn't always find a way to meet. But somehow, even through that experience of never quite fitting in, never quite being known and accepted for the beautiful person she was, she'd found a constancy. Sophie lived in a steadiness that flowed with a sense of peace that wrote joy all over her person. Both reasons he loved her so very much.

"But, Lance, we're never lost to *Him*, you know?" Conviction strengthened Sophie's whispered words. "God doesn't lose sight of us. In our wanderings, our heartaches, our trials, and our joys... He's always there. *He* is the constant."

It was as if she'd read his thoughts. Perhaps because she truly understood his heart. In that place of vulnerability birthed from being so deeply known, he found the freedom to ask what had been needling him for weeks. Or maybe, for his whole life.

"What if I can't see Him in this?"

Her hands slid from his face to his chest. For a moment, she was silent, and then she nodded. "I don't see Him in it either, Lance. Not yet."

"But you believe God is still here. With you?"

"With us. With you. And with me."

"How do you know?"

"He promised. Several times throughout the Bible, actually. He said He would never leave us or forsake us, because He's the Good Shepherd."

Lance had studied her, wishing for her simple, extraordinary faith. Long after he'd kissed her good night and sent her back toward town with a *drive careful, and text me when you get there,* he'd considered that faith of hers. It seemed her foundation, her backbone, and her endurance. And the times he'd questioned her about it, she had a similar answer that pointed him back to the

Bible. She knew God through His Word every bit as much as she knew Him through her experience.

Late into the night, driven by her example, Lance had dug through his own copy of the Bible, looking for those promises Sophie had spoken of. Using the concordance at the back, he'd found several. Joshua 1:9, Psalm 139:7–12, Isaiah 41:10, Hebrews 13:5, and then Romans 8:38–39. There he'd stayed for a quite a while, rereading the words, pondering the vastness of that great possibility.

*For I am sure that neither death nor life, nor angels nor rulers, nor things present nor things to come, nor powers, nor height nor depth, nor anything else in all creation, will be able to separate us from the love of God in Christ Jesus our Lord.*

Lance had woken with a new sort of awe he wasn't sure he could explain.

"Hey," Lane barked from the other side of the kitchen. "Are you ignoring me?"

"No, sorry." Lance jerked his attention from the depths of his coffee. "Sophie? Is she what you wanted to know about?"

Lane wandered to the table and lowered into a chair opposite Lance. "I asked if you two were okay."

"Oh. Yes, we're okay."

"Kind of seemed like you were thinking about cutting things off."

How on earth had Lane discerned that?

Lane must have read his mild scowl with precision. "Glad she wasn't having it. She's good for you."

"Since when did you pay attention?"

"Since always, my uppity brother. I'm not entirely engulfed in myself. At least, not always." He sipped his coffee.

"How did you know I was thinking—" Lance didn't finish it. Thank God Sophie was not having it, even though Lane was exactly right. Yesterday, he'd had every good intention of letting Sophie go.

Across the table, Lane leaned on both forearms and narrowed a penetrating look on him. "For so long I thought you were selfish.

Did you know that? I thought you didn't want to deal with my tears. My pain. So you pushed me away."

"What?"

"It occurred to me yesterday that that's how you deal with *your* pain."

Lance stared at him, blinking. "I never intended to push you away."

Nodding, Lane lowered his gaze. "That's what Sophie said."

"I had no idea that—" Lance stumbled on the words as in rapid succession, the darkest moments of grief that they'd been through flashed through his mind. In those memories, he found himself alone, drowning in the heartaches of loss. Now, hearing his brother say he'd felt abandoned by him...

He hadn't known. Truly, he hadn't. But how could he have failed his brother like that?

"Lane, I'm so sorry..."

A hard sniff from his brother brought his eyes back to focus on him. Lance reached across the distance, gripping Lane's arm. "I'm so sorry."

Lane glanced up, a wince contorting his face, and he nodded. "Don't let her go, Lance. Just—" His features eased, and he pulled away from Lance's hold, the more familiar, held-off brother resurfacing. "Just don't be an idiot and let her go."

"She wouldn't let me, so..."

He nodded. With a look toward the window at their side, Lane let the subject die into a silence that felt distant. Keenly, freshly aware of his own failures, Lance leaned heavily against his chair, absently sipping his coffee.

"There's a dozen cows left." Lance spoke almost timidly, afraid this would be yet another blunder.

Lane's attention slowly drifted back. He nodded.

"They're yours, if you want them."

His eyes pinched as he cocked his head oddly. "Say again?"

"The cattle—and all the pastureland. They're yours. I'd hoped to offer you this house, but the best I can do now is to say that we can share it."

"You'd hoped..."

Lance nodded, the weariness of defeat sagging through his body. "Yeah, well, I'd had a plan—one where you could have the ranching operation, because I thought you had liked that part of our life at one point, and maybe even the farming part too."

"Could you have lived on the vineyard?"

Apparently, Lane understood more about Lance's business than he'd thought. Lance shook his head, looking at the table. "No. Not yet."

"Then—"

"Like I said, I'd had a plan. But it didn't work out, even before the flood."

"And now?"

"I still want you to have the ranch—what's left of it. If you want it."

Steel surfaced in Lane's incredulous stare. "Dad left it to you. It's *your* inheritance."

A fight sparked in his chest. "And you'll always hate him for it. Always resent me for it. Won't you?"

Lane returned the question with a hard, lock-jawed glare.

"You never understood Dad, though." He shook his head. "To you he was all rules and discipline."

"And to you, he was a best pal."

"He was hardly here enough to be a best pal, Lane, and you know that. Not sure why you fault him for it. Trucking was sure income. The ranch—it was never stable. After Mom died he—"

"After Mom died, he used it as an escape. That's the fault, Lance. The ranch did fine—you've done fine without being on the road six days a week." Bitterness seethed from his brother. "It was Dad's choice to be gone. Maybe that didn't bother you since when he was here, you were the favorite. For me? It was either he was gone or he was yelling. Both options sucked."

"He wanted you safe, Lane. Why was that so hard to understand? You did stupid things all the time, and you didn't seem to care that he'd already lost more than he could handle when Mom died."

The air in the house seemed to have turned to ice, and the brothers held each other in a stubborn silence bearing the weight of years' worth of anger.

This wasn't how he'd wanted it. Lance had imagined giving his brother a share in their inheritance, and having a fight unleash hadn't been in the script. Why couldn't they ever find common ground?

Lance exhaled, searching his heart for something stable and calm. "He wanted you taken care of," he said quietly. "That's why he did what he did with his will. He left it to me to make sure you were taken care of."

"By cutting me out? That doesn't make sense."

"He wasn't cutting you out, Lane. Why do you refuse—"

"So I'm to depend on you for the rest of my life?"

Lance shut his eyes. This was impossible. Had been a setup for failure from the beginning. All he wanted now was to move forward. "No. No you're not. Like I said, the cattle and pastureland are yours." Feeling old and exhausted, and once again entirely misunderstood, Lance rose from the table. "Do with it what you will."

\*\*\*

*Help me to see You in this.*

Lance prayed silently in the darkness of his room. He thought back to the verses Sophie's dad had texted him earlier that day—the whole passage from Psalm 23.

*It said You're with me in the valley. Can you show me that You're with me? I hate feeling alone...*

He breathed in deeply, the unshed tears seaming his closed eyes. After a long exhale, his body relaxed.

Lance slept. For the first time in over a week, he slept hard.

# Chapter Twenty-Six

Daddy had agreed. Had a few questions first, but he'd agreed, and if she knew her father at all by his voice, he'd agreed with a smile.

Sophie texted an update to Brenna and then to Miss Jane. Her friends would spread the news from there, as this plan had been hatched between the three of them over Miss Jane's French Vanilla Hot Chocolate and a comment about Sophie loving yellow tulips.

Was it crazy? Yes. Perfectly crazy. Emphasis on the *perfect*. Even Daddy agreed.

*Forces are being mobilized as we speak.* This return text came from Miss Jane. *Daisy has talked to Lane. Wes will have a crew out at the lodge within forty minutes. I have the other details in hand. Daisy will help Brenna and me. You see only to your business, young lady. That's also an order.* 😊

Pure, unfiltered joy bubbled up from deep within Sophie, and she laughed out loud to her empty house.

*Miss Jane, you are the bossy one today!* Brenna punctuated that text with a laughing face. *Heaven bless you for that! Craig and the boys said they're heading out with some of the other guys. Craig's mom will be with me. Hopefully she'll make it the whole day, but she said if not, be sure to video it. This is thrilling!*

It was happening. Tears suddenly welled in her eyes. This town...this community. It was everything she'd longed for during those lonely years of never feeling like she fit in anywhere. Big Prairie was quite literally the answer to her many prayers all those years ago.

There were flawed people here. Some who had even said some not very thoughtful things when they didn't know she was listening. But there were others—so many others—who loved like Jesus. Maybe that was what she'd found in the midst of this small town—she found the Church. Not *a* church, because Wes and Jaycee were Baptists, and she attended the Community Bible Church. She happened to know that many of the people heading out to the lodge even as she was still at her home belonged to the Free Church, and still others were Methodist, Episcopalian, and Lutheran.

No, what she'd found in Big Prairie wasn't simply a nice small town in which to belong, and it wasn't a single denomination or building. She'd discovered *the* Church, flawed though it may be, practicing love to one another in the best ways frail humans could figure. In beautiful ways that made her want to sing and cry and laugh all at once.

"Jesus, You are *with* us," she said once again to her empty house. With a joyful, shouting sort of laugh, she twirled, arms splayed wide, head tipped back. "Oh, show him, will You? Show Lance too."

The beep of another text drew her out of her undignified joy. Brenna had sent her another one.

*What time does the preacher cometh?*

Sophie's smile could have gone on for days as she sent a quick reply.

*Daddy said they'd make it by five.*

\*\*\*

Lance felt a peace he'd never experienced before as he drank his morning coffee. That sleep last night, best of his life, bar none. Could be the result of pure exhaustion.

No. No, Lance knew that it certainly was not.

Seated at his kitchen table, he flipped through the pages of his Bible. *Day one*, he thought. Habits took what, seven days to anchor? He had a feeling this habit was one worth the time, and he'd never regret it.

His fingers found Psalm 121 on the thin page, and he reread the words Derrick Shultz had texted him last night. This time, though, in his own Bible.

*I lift up my eyes to the hills—where does my help come from?*
*My help comes from the LORD, the Maker of heaven and earth.*
*He will not let your foot slip—he who watches over you will not slumber*

An overwhelming sense rushed through him as Lance read through the psalm slowly, carefully taking in every word, as if a promise given to *him* personally. The rush was one of being seen and known. Of being loved, not merely as one of many in a group, but individually.

*The LORD will keep you from all harm—He will watch over your life;*
*The LORD will watch over your coming and your going both now and forevermore.*

Bowing, Lance surrendered to the current stirring within. The irony of it didn't escape him—the fact that he was sitting there in his kitchen, a good stone's throw away from the destruction of nature's rage wrought only days before, in the middle of a life that appeared ruined, and yet the flood within him had turned to one of peace. Of love.

Of hope.

How could such a thing be?

*Trust in the Lord and do good.*

For the second time in less than a handful of months, those words—also from Psalms—whispered through his heart. This time he didn't question his sanity as he had back in that high-rise office in Kansas City. This time he knew for certain.

The Spirit of God was moving.

So then. Today, what good thing could he do while he trusted the Lord with his life? His attention drifted from the open pages of his Bible on the table to the window that gave an angled view of both the lodge and the vineyard.

It was time to get back to work. Not with a heart of resentment, not with a spirit buried in defeat. But with one open to whatever God provided for the day.

A shuffling noise interrupted his mental planning. Lane meandered into the kitchen, his long hair a wild, lion's mane about his head.

"Morning," Lance said.

Lane lifted an eyebrow, as if hearing Lance speak had been unexpected. Perhaps it was—Lance typically kept himself to himself.

"Morning yourself." Lane's look paused on the book open on the table. "That's new."

"My Bible isn't new."

"Not what I meant."

Lance grinned. "True enough then. I thought reading a psalm would be a better way to start my day than to stare at nothing while swimming in a foul mood."

With a grunt, Lane reached for a mug. "Who should I thank for that? Sophie?"

"Yes—and her dad, actually."

Lane didn't respond. Simply filled his mug, grabbed a muffin Sophie had left for the brothers, and trudged to the table.

Today, the silence between them still felt chilly, but far less combative. Lance turned his attention back to Psalm 121 and reread the passage while Lane ate the blueberry pastry in silence.

"What does it say?"

Lane's sudden question took Lance by surprise. "The psalm?"

"Yeah."

Clearing his throat, Lance felt a rising heat climb his chest. Always happened when someone asked him something direct. Maybe he needed more practice at sharing himself with others? He brushed away the straying thoughts and focused on the Bible, reading the short passage out loud.

Lane responded with a grunt. When Lance looked up at him, he found his brother's attention latched on to the window—or the view beyond. "Thinking I'll take it, if you're still offering."

Trying to follow his brother's derailment of thought, Lance squinted.

"The cattle and the ranch?" Lane scowled. "Of course, you probably changed your mind..."

Lance felt his brow smooth. "I haven't. I told you—it's yours."

Lane looked back out the window, whatever he was thinking screwing his expression into something that resembled pain.

"I'm glad," Lance said. He swallowed the last of his coffee, waiting for Lane to look back at him.

"You think I'm gonna screw it up."

"I don't. Besides, it can't get much worse than it is at this moment, can it?"

A hint of a laugh pushed from Lane's mouth. "Let it be known that was not my fault."

"Noted." Lance pressed his palms to the tabletop, wondering what the future would look like. At the moment, he couldn't imagine, but even with the full uncertainty ahead, the sense of foreboding and failure had been lifted from his shoulders.

*Trust in the Lord and do good.*

That would be his new life goal, no matter how that life twisted and turned.

He stood, taking his mug and plate to the sink, and then turned back to Lane. "And for the record, I am glad. I'm glad you'll be home."

When he expected his brother to say something snarky—his typical effort to remove the discomfort of real emotion—Lane's focus dipped to his hands on the table, and he remained silent.

Yeah, things between them would still be strained. Couldn't rebuild burned bridges in a day. But this was a start.

With that, Lance turned his mind back to the lodge. Another restoration project on which he'd start. Today.

\*\*\*

Lance stood with a flathead shovel in hand, staring.

He'd been at it for only thirty minutes, pushing the three-inch layer of sand off the wood flooring with the shovel, like it was a coating of snow on a deck rather than dirt in his lodge. The job was a big one—just clearing out the sand and figuring out what to do with it all would take days.

Scratch that now. Not with the crew who followed Wes into his building, all brandishing shovels, brooms, garbage cans, and a whole litany of other materials that might or might not be useful.

"I don't understand..." Lance continued watching while the people spread out in front of him.

"We're here to help." Wes jabbed his shovel into the pile of sand Lance had started near the door. "Set us on a job."

"But—"

"Burning daylight, son. We clearing the floor? Seems as good a place to start as any." Wes nodded toward Craig and Jeremiah Colts, and the pair started in on the project, each taking several high school kids with him, hatching a plan for the removal as they went.

"I'll get these tables and chairs out into the sun." Jaycee went into motion before she even finished. "What do you think, Grant? Some of the youngers could help us with the chairs, right?"

"Sure can." Grant Hillman assembled a company of five elementary kids—two of whom were Craig Erikson's boys. Trent, in his tamed ten-year-old sass, flung a salute at Grant after he'd been given instructions.

And then there was controlled chaos all around Lance. Mutt darted from one new friend to another, her yip the happy sort and the bounce in her movements like hope rebounding. Dumbstruck, Lance stood in the middle of the room, turning a slow circle and wondering if he'd ever actually woken up that morning. How was this possible?

"We are Nebraska strong, my friend, and sure ain't having you work through this alone." Wes's thick hand clamped over Lance's shoulder, causing him a small startle.

"But...but Wes. What I was doing...what I almost did..."

"Doesn't mean we stopped being neighbors."

Lance looked at him, eyes wide as something overwhelming creased his heart. "I don't deserve this."

Wes met Lance's humble whisper with another squeeze of his arm. "There is a lot of good in this life that, if we were honest, we'd have to admit we didn't deserve. But I want you to know, Lance, that I am sorry for the silent daggers I sent at you all these months. I think if I'd have asked you the simple question of *why*, you might have told me. And I might have understood. Even if I still didn't agree."

Would that have changed things? Lance couldn't know for sure, and it didn't matter now. Even still, he didn't deserve all of this.

*This is grace.*

As Wes moved away, clearing sand with the others faster than Lance could have imagined, a moment crept back into Lance's mind. A conversation he'd had with Sophie, when she'd told him that God had a way of making His presence known.

At the time he'd believed that for her, but not for himself.

But there he stood, right in the middle of the presence of grace, delivered by humble people who chose to do good.

# Chapter Twenty-Seven

"You're here!" Sophie squealed as she opened her front door.

Mom stood on the other side with a beaming smile, tears sheening her eyes. "Your dad refused to speed. If I'd been driving, we'd have been here an hour ago."

Daddy's deep chuckle sent a thrill through Sophie's heart.

"I am here to maintain order," he said.

"You are here to make sure this is done properly." Mom looked up at him.

"Both of you get in here!" Sophie grabbed an arm of both parents and tugged. "Meet my little party." She turned to the living room, which had been turned into bride headquarters in record time. Tulips in tin vases, candles, various colors of scraps of fabrics, homemade mints stacked carefully in plastic containers—all of it had been sorted, repacked, and was now waiting to be loaded in cars. Among the loot stood her three conspirators. "This is Brenna—but you met her when we came to shop."

Mom wrapped Brenna in a warm hug. "I hear you need some congratulating too." She pulled away and grinned.

Brenna also smiled. "Thank you."

Sophie grabbed Daisy's hand. "This is my newest friend, Daisy. She started working at the ranch last October."

"A ranch hand?" Dad raised his brows in surprise.

"Don't you doubt it, Daddy. Lance says she's the best hand he's had in years."

Dad laughed, and Daisy said a quiet hello.

"And this"—Sophie wrapped Miss Jane in a side hug—"this is the one and only Miss Jane."

"Ah, the famous Miss Jane." Mom held out her hand. "At last we meet. I've heard so much about you."

"Well…" Miss Jane seemed flustered. "I have no idea why Sophie would want to tell you about me. So many fine people in her life."

Sophie and Brenna exchanged a glance and laughed. It wasn't an act Miss Jane was putting on—the woman was as humble as anyone they'd ever met, which made the irony funny. She was also one of the most extraordinary people a person could ever know.

"Enough of this formal business now." Miss Jane clapped her hands. "We have a bride to deliver."

"I can't help feeling like that young man is gonna feel like he's caught in a shotgun wedding," Dad said, amusement in his tone.

Sophie looked at her father, and her smile faded. "Do you really think that?"

"Oh stop it." Mom swatted at him. "You'll give her doubts."

Too late. Now there were definitely doubts popping all her excitement bubbles. "But maybe…"

Miss Jane stepped beside Mom. "Exactly right—do stop. That boy has been lamenting that you didn't elope since Christmas. He'd marry you in pajamas and mud boots in the middle of a rainstorm, and he'd do it with his whole heart."

Daddy's eyes met Sophie's, and something tender warmed them. "I am teasing you, Sophie." He untangled his arm from Mom's and stepped closer. The other occupants of the room set themselves to work, grabbing boxes and going toward the door. Daddy, however, placed his hands on her shoulders. "I need to know if you're sure, princess?"

"I am, Daddy."

"Then I will make sure Lance is too."

"Promise?"

"You have my word, as your father and as your pastor." He leaned in and kissed her forehead.

Sophie shut her eyes and soaked in the warmth of her dad's reassurance. Once more, she sent a prayer up for God's guidance.

Once again, she knew the peace of His smile.

\*\*\*

"Just go shower it off." Lane pushed against Lance's back with both hands.

Looking over his shoulder at his brother—the all-smiles-and-jokes version of the man having returned somewhere about the same time half the town had shown up to work—and scowled. "You really think I'm going to go in and take a shower while all these people do *my* work?"

"You might better," Jaycee said. "That sudsy water was half soap, I think. You'll be itching something fierce if you don't go rinse it off."

Lance looked over at Jaycee. Wes nodded, standing beside his wife. "Won't take but ten minutes anyway. We could all use a ten-minute break."

*How do you argue with that?* Lance nodded, then sent a pointed scowl to his brother. "Try not to dump anymore buckets of wash water."

Lane grinned, flung a mocking salute, and pushed against his back again. "Get going. You stink anyhow."

And this was how it was gonna be forever now that Lane was staying around. Lane could claim the *spill* from the stairs onto Lance's head had been an accident all he wanted. Lance wasn't buying it.

He strode from the lodge, onto the deck, and then toward the house, and as the early evening sun filled his view, he released a sigh. Honestly, he'd rather have Lane there, his antics and all, than to never know where his brother was exactly, or imagining the kind of life Lane was out there living. Besides, how could he possible stay cross on such a day? There was so much to be thankful for.

Lance showered, selfishly enjoying the warm spray of water and maybe even lingering in it longer than he should have. When he emerged from his room with dry jeans and a fresh button-down work shirt, he found Lane in the kitchen at the table. Cleaning his boots.

"What are you doing?"

Lane didn't look up but kept the polish brush moving.

"Lane, what on earth are you doing?"

"Giving these a polish. They're a mess."

"You're polishing my boots? The boots I'm going to put on in about thirty seconds to go out and work in muddy sand again?"

"Yep."

"Have you lost your mind?"

"Nope."

Lance stared at him for another moment and then moved to snatch his boots back.

Lane smiled. "Think Sophie's here."

With a quick bend back, Lance looked out the window. Yep, there was her orange Renegade. He'd texted her a few times that day—first to tell her how shocked he was that half the town was helping him clean up the lodge. She seemed thrilled for him, then had said she was tied up helping Miss Jane with a project, and would he be upset if she didn't come out until later?

No, he wasn't upset. Maybe a little bummed, because he really wanted to share the wonder of this day with the woman he couldn't wait to call his wife. But he'd not been mad.

Now she was there. With more motivation, Lance stomped into his boots and sent one more squinted look at his brother.

"Nut," he said.

"You'll thank me."

Lance shook his head and pushed through the back door. No more than two steps out, and Lane had caught up with him.

"You two set a date?"

"End of May. After school's out." His mood sank a bit. "But might have to move that back. We were going to use the lodge." Even with all the work that had been done today, the lodge might not be ready by then. Not to mention, the location of the venue looked like a natural disaster had hit—because it had. He couldn't have the grounds cleared by then.

"I don't think Sophie would care about that."

Lance glanced at him. "For being such a lady's man, you're clueless. Women care about those kinds of details when it comes to their wedding."

"Says the guy who couldn't talk to a girl until he was twenty-six years old."

As he took the steps to the deck, Lance ignored his brother.

"Hey."

With a sigh, he turned. "What?"

"Might want to put this on." Lane extended Lance's suit coat.

"What?"

"Sophie's request."

"What are you up to?"

Lane shoved the coat against Lance's chest and then held out a cut tulip with a long pin running through its stem. "And this."

"Where did you get that?"

"Just put it on, Lance." Jaycee spoke from behind him, and Lance turned to find her striding toward him. Behind her, Derrick Shultz emerged from the lodge.

"Mr. Shultz..." Lance froze, feeling like he had the first time he'd met Sophie's dad. They'd come a long way in a short time, but for some reason, this unexpected visit felt...big.

"Derrick, right?" Mr. Shultz extended his hand. "We agreed on Derrick."

Lance caught the handshake, and Sophie's dad pulled him into a strong hug. "I'm so sorry about the flood, son."

*Son...*

Lance fought against the emotion that endearment provoked.

Derrick stepped back and addressed Lane and Jaycee. "Would you give me a moment with Lance?"

Both nodded and moved back toward the lodge.

Lance steeled himself, sensing that whatever Derrick had to say was serious. Maybe, given the circumstances, the man had concerns about the wedding being so soon? Lance could agree to wait—

"You still want to marry my daughter?"

"Yes, sir."

His low chuckle came as a reassurance. "She sure wants to marry you."

Lance looked to his feet—to his freshly polished boots. "Sometimes I'm not sure why."

"Something about love."

Lance looked back up, finding Derrick's dark-brown eyes steady on him. "I need to know a couple of things before we go on in that room, all filled up with people who care a lot about you and my princess."

"Okay..."

"Who are you trusting with your life, Lance Carson?"

Lance stepped back and leaned against the deck rail. He thought for a moment and then nodded. "You know, if you'd have asked me that question six months ago, I would have given you the answer I knew you wanted—that I'm trusting God with my life. But I wouldn't have been truly honest. These past months have shown me how much control I *don't* have. But the crazy thing is, in all the chaos, I've seen not only that I'm not in charge, but also that God is."

"You've seen that in this mess?"

Looking at the buried vineyard, the sand-loaded fields beyond, the marks of life spun out of control all around him, Lance nodded. "Yeah, incredibly, I have. I've seen God's power in the storm that did all this, but also, I've seen His faithfulness in your daughter's stubborn love, and His kindness in the people that have shown up to help me. And in the things that I've really wrestled with, even before the flood, I've known His presence like I've never experienced before. A presence that kept me from following through with a decision that would have been a mistake."

Derrick looked out toward the western horizon, and Lance followed the direction of his gaze. The lowering sun was setting off a sky full of warm color.

"I think," Lance said, almost in a whisper, "I think Sophie—and maybe you and Abi—were praying for me. Praying that I would know His presence."

"You're right."

For several beats, they both simply soaked in the deepening colors of the sunset.

"I hope you'll never forget this moment," Derrick said. "Standing here watching this display of glory out there, and your feet still in the mess here. If we were looking only at the mess, we'd miss the glory. And maybe we wouldn't fully appreciate the glory if we didn't experience the mess."

A simple truth. Lance prayed it would imprint on his heart for keeps.

"And now, about marrying my daughter..."

"I still can, right?"

Derrick chuckled. "This moment, if you choose."

"What?"

He pointed toward the open door to the lodge. When Lance turned and found her there, his heart nearly stopped. The world around faded as he gazed upon the woman in white.

Derrick pushed off the rail and strode back toward the lodge without another word. He stopped to kiss his daughter's temple and then disappeared.

Lance was afraid to breathe as he held her gaze. If he blinked, would she disappear? A shy, heart-melting smile formed on Sophie's lips, and then she lifted her lovely white dress and stepped toward him.

And he chuckled. A flash of yellow peeked from the hem of her perfect dress—the toes of the Muk boots he'd bought her.

"I think, since we started in mud, we should simply continue on." Sophie closed the space between them. "We seem to navigate it well."

He laughed, cupping her face with one hand. "Are you modeling your wedding dress for the whole town?"

"No, I'm wearing it for you. For our wedding day."

His heart skipped and then squeezed as he lowered his head to touch hers. "This can't possibly be what you've dreamed of."

Her hand rested on his chest. "Dreams are fickle things, you know? But love? This love I have for you? Lance Carson, it is more than I ever hoped."

As her whisper fanned across his lips, he could not resist a taste. She returned his kiss and then stepped back. "So. Will you marry me?"

"Right now?"

"Right now."

"In this mess?"

"In this mess."

He smiled, the fullness and beauty of the moment making his heart nearly burst with joy. "I think that would be the perfect way to begin."

Her hand in his, they walked into the surprisingly beautiful gathering room of the lodge. The fringes of his mind caught the colorful splashes of tulips and the dancing light of candles flickering on the tables that must have been returned to the room while he'd been in the shower. He was vaguely aware of Brenna handing Sophie a bouquet of yellow tulips, and mildly conscious of the many people who circled them as they reached the center of the room, where Derrick waited.

"I told you you'd thank me." Lane nudged Lance's shoulder.

Lance sent him a smile and nodded to the spot beside him, indicating his hope for Lane to stand with him as best man. His brother straightened his shoulders and grinned his cocky grin, as if that had already been the plan.

Of all the wonders of that day—and wow, there had been some *wonders!*—Lance would later close them out with the memory of Sophie pledging her heart, her faithfulness, and her life to him.

If, in the future, he ever questioned the goodness of God to him—if he ever lost his way again—he would only need to look back on that moment.

The day Sophie Joyanne Shultz became Sophie Joyanne Carson. His wife.

Proof indeed. God was good.

# *Epilogue*

Sophie watched the sky in wonder as the firework display continued. Blues, reds, oranges, yellows, and white filled the canvas of semidarkness framed by the branches of trees. Disney sure knew how to put on a show.

The hand that swallowed hers squeezed, and she shifted her view to the tall man at her side. Weird to see him outdoors without his cowboy hat. Stranger still, that even in the vast crowd surrounding them, he stood there relaxed, a smile of wonder lifting his jaw.

She hadn't believed it when he'd suggested he purchase a ticket and come along as well.

"It'll be sort of like the honeymoon we didn't take," he'd said.

Oh, they'd had a honeymoon, all right. Granted, they hadn't gone anywhere farther than her rented house in town, but they'd stayed within that little bungalow, just the two of them, for three days straight. Honeymooning. What girl needed extravagant trips, expensive hotels, and heaps of entertainment after she'd married the likes of Lance Carson? Not Sophie.

She did not have one single regret. Not even after they'd stepped back into real life as a married couple after that weekend of honeymooning and Lance doubled down on work at the ranch and vineyard. Sophie had had the rest of the semester to finish, and the band's Disney trip was a part of that. Being a newlywed, she'd felt a twinge of disappointment as she prepared for that event. One Lance had noticed and wasn't okay with. Thus, the offer to go with her.

"It will be nothing like a honeymoon, Lance," she'd replied. "We'll be chaperoning thirty-eight high schoolers through one of the biggest tourist locations in the world."

He'd shrugged.

"Do you understand how many people will be there?"

A lazy grin had moved on those kissable lips. "Only one I care about."

"You hate crowds."

"I love my wife."

At that memory, Sophie's smile bloomed full. Another round of gunpowder magic lit up the sky above Cinderella's castle, but she continued to watch the man at her side. His attention slowly moved to her, and he aimed on her that smile that made her heart do a happy dance.

"You're missing the show," he murmured.

"Nope. I'm seeing exactly what I want to see."

"What's that?"

"My husband."

"Hmm...I do like that."

"What?"

"Hearing you call me that. Like you like it."

She chuckled and shifted to her toes to kiss his cheek. "How do you think Lane's holding up at the ranch?"

Lance snorted. "Lane will be fine. It's Daisy I'm worried about."

"Daisy? The girl could work circles around your brother."

Lance's jaw tensed. "That's not the concern."

Drawing a nervous breath, Sophie leaned in to him. She knew exactly her husband's concern. Still, she felt like she should try to reassure him—or maybe both of them. "Daisy's no fool. And Lane's a better person than he pretends to be."

Squeezing her fingers again, Lance nodded. "True on both counts. Let's just hope they both act like the people we know they're capable of being."

"How about we do better than that?"

One brow lifted as he looked at her.

"We'll pray, Lance."

His smile returned, admiring and humble, making her feel like their hearts beat as one. "Yes, my beautiful, smart wife. That's a much better plan." He leaned down to swipe a kiss. "We'll pray."

*The End*

# Note From the Author

Dear reader,

It's been a little more than a year since I sat in horrified amazement as I watched raw footage of the 2019 flooding in Nebraska. I couldn't stop crying as I witnessed, via social media, my neighbors to the north lose the lands and livelihoods that for so many had been a way of life for multiple generations.

We had never seen a flood like that. Dams that had held fast for decades broke under the trifecta of a very wet spring, rapidly thawing ground, and the breakage of ice blocks—many of which were the size of a small pickup. I remember driving to a track meet several weeks after the disaster and being stunned by the damage that remained. Highways had been eaten away. Fields that had never seen the crest of the river had been swallowed up by water and then left under a residual pile of sand. Even now, at the memory of it, tears burn my eyes.

My friends, we cannot mitigate every disaster. Now, in the spring of 2020, we are all living with an uncertainty that we've never been pressed with before. And so many of us are asking hard questions. What happens now? What do we do?

Why didn't or doesn't God intervene?

I can't give you a why, and that isn't the point. But God has given us the means to press on—and to do it well.

He has given us prayer. Not *just* prayer—but the ear of the King of heaven Himself. Prayer is the weapon of a warrior—it's about time you and I learn to use it.

And He has given us his presence. Even in the hard places. Even when we're standing ankle deep in the mess. He is with us. Always. Sometimes, though, we *have to look*.

Can I leave you with this moment from the story?

"I HOPE YOU'LL NEVER FORGET THIS MOMENT," DERRICK SAID. "STANDING HERE WATCHING THIS DISPLAY OF GLORY OUT THERE, AND YOUR FEET STILL IN THE MESS HERE. IF WE WERE LOOKING ONLY AT THE MESS, WE'D MISS THE GLORY. AND MAYBE WE WOULDN'T FULLY APPRECIATE THE GLORY IF WE DIDN'T EXPERIENCE THE MESS."

Look for His glory, my friend. In the uncertainty and the chaos, keep watch.

He is still good.

Jen

# *More Big Prairie Romance!*

First, my friend, can I ask a big favor? Would you leave a review for *When I Lost My Way*? I'd be so grateful!

Next! I'm excited to tell you that there's more Big Prairie in store. If you've jumped into the series with Lance and Sophie, I'd love for you to go back to book 1, *When I Come Home Again*, where you will witness the power of forgiveness in Craig and Brenna's story. Also, book 3, *When I'm With You*, is well underway and will (Lord willing!) be released in the fall of 2020. Be watching for news on Lane and Daisy's tale.

If you want to keep up to date on my work, book deals that I'm aware of, and the thoughts that pass through my mind every now and then, I invite you to join my newsletter.

Thank you so much for spending the time with me in this book! I'm so looking forward to sharing more stories of romance and redemption with you.

Made in United States
Troutdale, OR
10/14/2023

13696542R00170